At Sunwich Port by W. W. Jacobs

William Wymark Jacobs was born on September 8th, 1863 in the Wapping district of London, England. Jacobs grew up near the docks, where his father was a wharf manager.   The docks and river side would be a constant theme of his writing in years to come.

Although surrounded by poverty, he received a formal education in London, first at a private prep school and later at the Birkbeck Literary and Scientific Institute.

His working life began with a less than exciting clerical position at the Post Office Savings Bank. Jacobs put his imagination to good use writing short stories, sketches and articles, many for the Post Office house publication "Blackfriars Magazine."

In 1896 Jacobs published Many Cargoes, a selection of sea-faring yarns, which established him as a popular writer with a knack for authentic dialogue and trick endings.

A year later he published a novelette, The Skipper's Wooing, and in 1898 another collection of short stories; Sea Urchins. These works painted vivid pictures of dockland and seafaring London full of colourful characters.

By 1899, Jacobs was able to quit the post office and write full-time.

He married the noted suffragist Agnes Eleanor Williams (who had been jailed for her protest activities) in 1900. They set up households both in Loughton, Essex and in central London.

The publication in 1902 of At Sunwich Port and Dialstone Lane, in 1904, cemented Jacobs' reputation as one of the leading British authors of the new century.

There followed a string of further successful publications, including Captain's All (1905), Night Watches (1914), The Castaways (1916), and Sea Whispers (1926).

Though Jacobs would create little in the way of new work after 1911, he still wrote and was recognized as a leading humorist, ranked alongside such writers as P. G. Wodehouse.

William Wymark Jacobs died in a North London nursing home in Hornsey Lane, Islington on September 1st, 1943.

Index of Contents

CHAPTER I

The ancient port of Sunwich was basking in the sunshine of a July afternoon. A rattle of cranes and winches sounded from the shipping in the harbour, but the town itself was half asleep. Somnolent shopkeepers in dim back parlours coyly veiled their faces in red handkerchiefs from the too ardent flies, while small boys left in charge noticed listlessly the slow passing of time as recorded by the church clock.

It is a fine church, and Sunwich is proud of it. The tall grey tower is a landmark at sea, but from the narrow streets of the little town itself it has a disquieting appearance of rising suddenly above the roofs huddled beneath it for the purpose of displaying a black-faced clock with gilt numerals whose mellow chimes have recorded the passing hours for many generations of Sunwich men.

Regardless of the heat, which indeed was mild compared with that which raged in his own bosom, Captain Nugent, fresh from the inquiry of the collision of his ship *Conqueror* with the German barque *Hans Muller*, strode rapidly up the High Street in the direction of home. An honest seafaring smell, compounded of tar, rope, and fish, known to the educated of Sunwich as ozone, set his thoughts upon the sea. He longed to be aboard ship again, with the Court of Inquiry to form part of his crew. In all his fifty years of life he had never met such a collection of fools. His hard blue eyes blazed as he thought of them, and the mouth hidden by his well-kept beard was set with anger.

Mr. Samson Wilks, his steward, who had been with him to London to give evidence, had had a time upon which he looked back in later years with much satisfaction at his powers of endurance. He was with the captain, and yet not with him. When they got out of the train at Sunwich he hesitated as to whether he should follow the captain or leave him. His excuse for following was the bag, his reason for leaving the volcanic condition of its owner's temper, coupled with the fact that he appeared to be sublimely ignorant that the most devoted steward in the world was tagging faithfully along a yard or two in the rear.

The few passers-by glanced at the couple with interest. Mr. Wilks had what is called an expressive face, and he had worked his sandy eyebrows, his weak blue eyes, and large, tremulous mouth into such an expression of surprise at the finding of the Court, that he had all the appearance of a beholder of visions. He changed the bag to his other hand as they left the town behind them, and regarded with gratitude the approaching end of his labours.

At the garden-gate of a fair-sized house some half-mile along the road the captain stopped, and after an impatient fumbling at the latch strode up the path, followed by Mr. Wilks, and knocked at the door. As he paused on the step he half turned, and for the first time noticed the facial expression of his faithful follower.

"What the dickens are you looking like that for?" he demanded.

"I've been surprised, sir," conceded Mr. Wilks; "surprised and astonished."

Wrath blazed again in the captain's eyes and set lines in his forehead. He was being pitied by a steward!

"You've been drinking," he said, crisply; "put that bag down."

"Arsking your pardon, sir," said the steward, twisting his unusually dry lips into a smile, "but I've 'ad no opportunity, sir—I've been follerin' you all day, sir."

A servant opened the door. "You've been soaking in it for a month," declared the captain as he entered the hall. "Why the blazes don't you bring that bag in? Are you so drunk you don't know what you are doing?"

Mr. Wilks picked the bag up and followed humbly into the house. Then he lost his head altogether, and gave some colour to his superior officer's charges by first cannoning into the servant and then wedging the captain firmly in the doorway of the sitting-room with the bag.

"Steward!" rasped the captain.

"Yessir," said the unhappy Mr. Wilks.

"Go and sit down in the kitchen, and don't leave this house till you're sober."

Mr. Wilks disappeared. He was not in his first lustre, but he was an ardent admirer of the sex, and in an absent-minded way he passed his arm round the handmaiden's waist, and sustained a buffet which made his head ring.

"A man o' your age, and drunk, too," explained the damsel.

Mr. Wilks denied both charges. It appeared that he was much younger than he looked, while, as for drink, he had forgotten the taste of it. A question as to the reception Ann would have accorded a boyish teetotaler remained unanswered.

In the sitting-room Mrs. Kingdom, the captain's widowed sister, put down her crochet-work as her brother entered, and turned to him expectantly. There was an expression of loving sympathy on her mild and rather foolish face, and the captain stiffened at once.

"I was in the wrong," he said, harshly, as he dropped into a chair; "my certificate has been suspended for six months, and my first officer has been commended."

"Suspended?" gasped Mrs. Kingdom, pushing back the white streamer to the cap which she wore in memory of the late Mr. Kingdom, and sitting upright. You?"

"I think that's what I said," replied her brother.

Mrs. Kingdom gazed at him mournfully, and, putting her hand behind her, began a wriggling search in her pocket for a handkerchief, with the idea of paying a wholesome tribute of tears. She was a past-master in the art of grief, and, pending its extraction, a docile tear hung on her eyelid and waited. The captain eyed her preparations with silent anger.

"I am not surprised," said Mrs. Kingdom, dabbing her eyes; "I expected it somehow. I seemed to have a warning of it. Something seemed to tell me; I couldn't explain, but I seemed to know."

She sniffed gently, and, wiping one eye at a time, kept the disengaged one charged with sisterly solicitude upon her brother. The captain, with steadily rising anger, endured this game of one-eyed bo-peep for five minutes; then he rose and, muttering strange things in his beard, stalked upstairs to his room.

Mrs. Kingdom, thus forsaken, dried her eyes and resumed her work. The remainder of the family were in the kitchen ministering to the wants of a misunderstood steward, and, in return, extracting information which should render them independent of the captain's version.

"Was it very solemn, Sam?" inquired Miss Nugent, aged nine, who was sitting on the kitchen table.

Mr. Wilks used his hands and eyebrows to indicate the solemnity of the occasion.

"They even made the cap'n leave off speaking," he said, in an awed voice.

"I should have liked to have been there," said Master Nugent, dutifully.

"Ann," said Miss Nugent, "go and draw Sam a jug of beer."

"Beer, Miss?" said Ann.

"A jug of beer," repeated Miss Nugent, peremptorily.

Ann took a jug from the dresser, and Mr. Wilks, who was watching her, coughed helplessly. His perturbation attracted the attention of his hostess, and, looking round for the cause, she was just in time to see Ann disappearing into the larder with a cream jug.

"The big jug, Ann," she said, impatiently; "you ought to know Sam would like a big one."

Ann changed the jugs, and, ignoring a mild triumph in Mr. Wilks's eye, returned to the larder, whence ensued a musical trickling. Then Miss Nugent, raising the jug with some difficulty, poured out a tumbler for the steward with her own fair hands.

"Sam likes beer," she said, speaking generally.

"I knew that the first time I see him, Miss," re-marked the vindictive Ann.

Mr. Wilks drained his glass and set it down on the table again, making a feeble gesture of repulse as Miss Nugent refilled it.

"Go on, Sam," she said, with kindly encouragement; "how much does this jug hold, Jack?"

"Quart," replied her brother.

"How many quarts are there in a gallon?"

"Four."

Miss Nugent looked troubled. "I heard father say he drinks gallons a day," she remarked; "you'd better fill all the jugs, Ann."

"It was only 'is way o' speaking," said Mr. Wilks, hurriedly; "the cap'n is like that sometimes."

"I knew a man once, Miss," said Ann, "as used to prefer to 'ave it in a wash-hand basin. Odd, ugly-looking man 'e was; like Mr. Wilks in the face, only better-looking."

Mr. Wilks sat upright and, in the mental struggle involved in taking in this insult in all its ramifications, did not notice until too late that Miss Nugent had filled his glass again.

"It must ha' been nice for the captain to 'ave you with 'im to-day," remarked Ann, carelessly.

"It was," said Mr. Wilks, pausing with the glass at his lips and eyeing her sternly. "Eighteen years I've bin with 'im—ever since 'e 'ad a ship. 'E took a fancy to me the fust time 'e set eyes on me."

"Were you better-looking then, Sam?" inquired Miss Nugent, shuffling closer to him on the table and regarding him affectionately.

"Much as I am now, Miss," replied Mr. Wilks, setting down his glass and regarding Ann's giggles with a cold eye.

Miss Nugent sighed. "I love you, Sam," she said, simply. "Will you have some more beer?"

Mr. Wilks declined gracefully. "Eighteen years I've bin with the cap'n," he remarked, softly; "through calms and storms, fair weather and foul, Samson Wilks 'as been by 'is side, always ready in a quiet and 'umble way to do 'is best for 'im, and now—now that 'e is on his beam-ends and lost 'is ship, Samson

Wilks'll sit down and starve ashore till he gets another."

At these touching words Miss Nugent was undisguisedly affected, and wiping her bright eyes with her pinafore, gave her small, well-shaped nose a slight touch *en passant* with the same useful garment, and squeezed his arm affectionately.

"It's a lively look-out for me if father is going to be at home for long," remarked Master Nugent. Who'll get his ship, Sam?"

"Shouldn't wonder if the fust officer, Mr. Hardy, got it," replied the steward. "He was going dead-slow in the fog afore he sent down to rouse your father, and as soon as your father came on deck 'e went at 'arfspeed. Mr. Hardy was commended, and your father's certifikit was suspended for six months."

Master Nugent whistled thoughtfully, and quitting the kitchen proceeded upstairs to his room, and first washing himself with unusual care for a boy of thirteen, put on a clean collar and brushed his hair. He was not going to provide a suspended master-mariner with any obvious reasons for fault-finding. While he was thus occupied the sitting-room bell rang, and Ann, answering it, left Mr. Wilks in the kitchen listening with some trepidation to the conversation.

"Is that steward of mine still in the kitchen?" demanded the captain, gruffly.

"Yessir," said Ann.

"What's he doing?"

Mr. Wilks's ears quivered anxiously, and he eyed with unwonted disfavour the evidences of his late debauch.

"Sitting down, sir," replied Ann.

"Give him a glass of ale and send him off," commanded the captain; "and if that was Miss Kate I heard talking, send her in to me."

Ann took the message back to the kitchen and, with the air of a martyr engaged upon an unpleasant task, drew Mr. Wilks another glass of ale and stood over him with well-affected wonder while he drank it. Miss Nugent walked into the sitting-room, and listening in a perfunctory fashion to a shipmaster's platitude on kitchen-company, took a seat on his knee and kissed his ear.

CHAPTER II

The downfall of Captain Nugent was for some time a welcome subject of conversation in marine circles at Sunwich. At The Goblets, a rambling old inn with paved courtyard and wooden galleries, which almost backed on to the churchyard, brother-captains attributed it to an error of judgment; at the Two Schooners on the quay the profanest of sailormen readily attributed it to an all-seeing Providence with a dislike of over-bearing ship-masters.

The captain's cup was filled to the brim by the promotion of his first officer to the command of the *Conqueror*. It was by far the largest craft which sailed from the port of Sunwich, and its master held a corresponding dignity amongst the captains of lesser vessels. Their allegiance was now transferred to Captain Hardy, and the master of a brig which was in the last stages of senile decay, meeting Nugent in The Goblets, actually showed him by means of two lucifer matches how the collision might have been avoided.

A touching feature in the business, and a source of much gratification to Mr. Wilks by the sentimental applause evoked by it, was his renunciation of the post of steward on the ss. *Conqueror*. Sunwich buzzed with the tidings that after eighteen years' service with Captain Nugent he preferred starvation ashore to serving under another master. Although comfortable in pocket and known to be living with his mother, who kept a small general shop, he was regarded as a man on the brink of starvation. Pints were thrust upon him, and the tale of his nobility increased with much narration. It was considered that the whole race of stewards had acquired fresh lustre from his action.

His only unfavourable critic was the erring captain himself. He sent a peremptory summons to Mr. Wilks to attend at Equator Lodge, and the moment he set eyes upon that piece of probity embarked upon such a vilification of his personal defects and character as Mr. Wilks had never even dreamt of. He wound up by ordering him to rejoin the ship forthwith.

"Arsking your pardon, sir," said Mr. Wilks, with tender reproach, "but I couldn't."

"Are you going to live on your mother, you hulking rascal?" quoth the incensed captain.

"No, sir," said Mr. Wilks. "I've got a little money, sir; enough for my few wants till we sail again."

"When I sail again you won't come with me," said the captain, grimly. "I suppose you want an excuse for a soak ashore for six months!"

Mr. Wilks twiddled his cap in his hands and smiled weakly.

"I thought p'r'aps as you'd like me to come round and wait at table, and help with the knives and boots and such-like," he said, softly. "Ann is agreeable."

"Get out of the house," said the captain in quiet, measured tones.

Mr. Wilks went, but on his way to the gate he picked up three pieces of paper which had blown into the garden, weeded two pieces of grass from the path, and carefully removed a dead branch from a laurel facing the window. He would have done more but for an imperative knocking on the glass, and he left the premises sadly, putting his collection of rubbish over the next garden fence as he passed it.

But the next day the captain's boots bore such a polish that he was able to view his own startled face in them, and at dinner-time the brightness of the knives was so conspicuous that Mrs. Kingdom called Ann in for the purpose of asking her why she didn't always do them like that. Her brother ate his meal in silence, and going to his room afterwards discovered every pair of boots he possessed, headed by the tall sea-boots, standing in a nicely graduated line by the wall, and all shining their hardest.

For two days did Mr. Wilks do good by stealth, leaving Ann to blush to find it fame; but on the third day at dinner, as the captain took up his knife and fork to carve, he became aware of a shadow standing behind his chair. A shadow in a blue coat with metal buttons, which, whipping up the first plate carved, carried it to Mrs. Kingdom, and then leaned against her with the vegetable dishes.

The dishes clattered a little on his arm as he helped the captain, but the latter, after an impressive pause and a vain attempt to catch the eye of Mr. Wilks, which was intent upon things afar off, took up the spoon and helped himself. From the unwonted silence of Miss Nugent in the presence of anything unusual it was clear to him that the whole thing had been carefully arranged. He ate in silence, and a resolution to kick Mr. Wilks off the premises vanished before the comfort, to say nothing of the dignity, afforded by his presence. Mr. Wilks, somewhat reassured, favoured Miss Nugent with a wink to which, although she had devoted much time in trying to acquire the art, she endeavoured in vain to respond.

It was on the day following this that Jack Nugent, at his sister's instigation, made an attempt to avenge the family honour. Miss Nugent, although she treated him with scant courtesy herself, had a touching faith in his prowess, a faith partly due to her brother occasionally showing her his bicep muscles in moments of exaltation.

"There's that horrid Jem Hardy," she said, suddenly, as they walked along the road.

"So it is," said Master Nugent, but without any display of enthusiasm.

"Halloa, Jack," shouted Master Hardy across the road.

"The suspense became painful."

"Halloa," responded the other.

"He's going to fight you," shrilled Miss Nugent, who thought these amenities ill-timed; "he said so."

Master Hardy crossed the road. "What for?" he demanded, with surprise.

"Because you're a nasty, horrid boy," replied Miss Nugent, drawing herself up.

"Oh," said Master Hardy, blankly.

The two gentlemen stood regarding each other with uneasy grins; the lady stood by in breathless expectation. The suspense became painful.

"Who are you staring at?" demanded Master Nugent, at last.

"You," replied the other; "who are you staring at?"

"You," said Master Nugent, defiantly.

There was a long interval, both gentlemen experiencing some difficulty in working up sufficient heat for the engagement.

"You hit me and see what you'll get," said Master Hardy, at length.

"You hit me," said the other.

"Cowardy, cowardy custard," chanted the well-bred Miss Nugent, "ate his mother's mustard. Cowardy, cowardy cus—"

"Why don't you send that kid home?" demanded Master Hardy, eyeing the fair songstress with strong disfavour.

"You leave my sister alone," said the other, giving him a light tap on the shoulder. "There's your coward's blow."

Master Hardy made a ceremonious return. "There's yours," he said. "Let's go behind the church."

His foe assented, and they proceeded in grave silence to a piece of grass screened by trees, which stood between the church and the beach. Here they removed their coats and rolled up their shirt-sleeves. Things look different out of doors, and to Miss Nugent the arms of both gentlemen seemed somewhat stick-like in their proportions.

The preliminaries were awful, both combatants prancing round each other with their faces just peering above their bent right arms, while their trusty lefts dealt vicious blows at the air. Miss Nugent turned pale and caught her breath at each blow, then she suddenly reddened with wrath as James Philip Hardy, having paid his tribute to science, began to hammer John Augustus Nugent about the face in a most painful and workmanlike fashion.

She hid her face for a moment, and when she looked again Jack was on the ground, and Master Hardy just rising from his prostrate body. Then Jack rose slowly and, crossing over to her, borrowed her handkerchief and applied it with great tenderness to his nose.

"Does it hurt, Jack?" she inquired, anxiously. "No," growled her brother.

He threw down the handkerchief and turned to his opponent again; Miss Nugent, who was careful about her property, stooped to recover it, and immediately found herself involved in a twisting tangle of legs, from which she escaped by a miracle to see Master Hardy cuddling her brother round the neck with one hand and punching him as hard and as fast as he could with the other. The unfairness of it maddened her, and the next moment Master Hardy's head was drawn forcibly backwards by the hair. The pain was so excruciating that he released his victim at once, and Miss Nugent, emitting a series of terrified yelps, dashed off in the direction of home, her hair bobbing up and down on her shoulders, and her small black legs in an ecstasy of motion.

Master Hardy, with no very well-defined ideas of what he was going to do if he caught her, started in pursuit. His scalp was still smarting and his eyes watering with the pain as he pounded behind her. Panting wildly she heard him coming closer and closer, and she was just about to give up when, to her joy, she saw her father coming towards them.

Master Hardy, intent on his quarry, saw him just in time, and, swerving into the road, passed in safety as Miss Nugent flung herself with some violence at her father's waistcoat and, clinging to him convulsively, fought for breath. It was some time before she could furnish the astonished captain with full details, and she was pleased to find that his indignation led him to ignore the hair-grabbing episode, on which, to do her justice, she touched but lightly.

That evening, for the first time in his life, Captain Nugent, after some deliberation, called upon his late mate. The old servant who, since Mrs. Hardy's death the year before, had looked after the house, was out, and Hardy, unaware of the honour intended him, was scandalized by the manner in which his son received the visitor. The door opened, there was an involuntary grunt from Master Hardy, and the next moment he sped along the narrow passage and darted upstairs. His father, after waiting in vain for his return, went to the door himself.

"Good evening, cap'n," he said, in surprise.

Nugent responded gruffly, and followed him into the sitting-room. To an invitation to sit, he responded more gruffly still that he preferred to stand. He then demanded instant and sufficient punishment of Master Hardy for frightening his daughter.

Even as he spoke he noticed with strong disfavour the change which had taken place in his late first officer. The change which takes place when a man is promoted from that rank to that of master is subtle, but unmistakable—sometimes, as in the present instance, more unmistakable than subtle. Captain Hardy coiled his long, sinewy form in an arm-chair and, eyeing him calmly, lit his pipe before replying.

"Boys will fight," he said, briefly.

"I'm speaking of his running after my daughter," said Nugent, sternly.

Hardy's eyes twinkled. "Young dog," he said, genially; "at his age, too."

Captain Nugent's face was suffused with wrath at the pleasantry, and he regarded him with a fixed stare. On board the *Conqueror* there was a witchery in that glance more potent than the spoken word, but in his own parlour the new captain met it calmly.

"I didn't come here to listen to your foolery," said Nugent; "I came to tell you to punish that boy of yours."

"And I sha'n't do it," replied the other. "I have got something better to do than interfere in children's quarrels. I haven't got your spare time, you know."

Captain Nugent turned purple. Such language from his late first officer was a revelation to him.

"I also came to warn you," he said, furiously, "that I shall take the law into my own hands if you refuse."

"Aye, aye," said Hardy, with careless contempt; "I'll tell him to keep out of your way. But I should advise you to wait until I have sailed."

Captain Nugent, who was moving towards the door, swung round and confronted him savagely.

"What do you mean?" he demanded.

"What I say," retorted Captain Hardy. "I don't want to indulge Sunwich with the spectacle of two middle-aged ship-masters at fisticuffs, but that's what'll happen if you touch my boy. It would probably please the spectators more than it would us."

"I'll cane him the first time I lay hands on him," roared Captain Nugent.

Captain Hardy's stock of patience was at an end, and there was, moreover, a long and undischarged account between himself and his late skipper. He rose and crossed to the door.

"Jem," he cried, "come downstairs and show Captain Nugent out."

There was a breathless pause. Captain Nugent ground his teeth with fury as he saw the challenge, and realized the ridiculous position into which his temper had led him; and the other, who was also careful of appearances, repented the order the moment he had given it. Matters had now, however, passed out of their hands, and both men cast appraising glances at each other's form. The only one who kept his head was Master Hardy, and it was a source of considerable relief to both of them when, from the top of the stairs, the voice of that youthful Solomon was heard declining in the most positive terms to do anything of the kind.

Captain Hardy repeated his command. The only reply was the violent closing of a door at the top of the house, and after waiting a short time he led the way to the front door himself.

"You will regret your insolence before I have done with you," said his visitor, as he paused on the step. "It's the old story of a beggar on horseback."

"It's a good story," said Captain Hardy, "but to my mind it doesn't come up to the one about Humpty-Dumpty. Good-night."

CHAPTER III

If anything was wanted to convince Captain Nugent that his action had been foolish and his language intemperate it was borne in upon him by the subsequent behaviour of Master Hardy. Generosity is seldom an attribute of youth, while egotism, on the other hand, is seldom absent. So far from realizing that the captain would have scorned such lowly game, Master Hardy believed that he lived for little else, and his Jack-in-the-box ubiquity was a constant marvel and discomfort to that irritable mariner. Did he approach a seat on the beach, it was Master Hardy who rose (at the last moment) to make room for him. Did he stroll down to the harbour, it was in the wake of a small boy looking coyly at him over his shoulder. Every small alley as he passed seemed to contain a Jem Hardy, who whizzed out like a human firework in front of him, and then followed dancing on his toes a pace or two in his rear.

This was on week-days; on the Sabbath Master Hardy's daring ingenuity led him to still further flights. All the seats at the parish church were free, but Captain Nugent, whose admirable practice it was to take his entire family to church, never thoroughly realized how free they were until Master Hardy squeezed his way in and, taking a seat next to him, prayed with unwonted fervour into the interior of a new hat, and then sitting back watched with polite composure the efforts of Miss Nugent's family to re-strain her growing excitement.

Charmed with the experiment, he repeated it the following Sunday. This time he boarded the seat from the other end, and seeing no place by the captain, took one, or more correctly speaking made one, between Miss Nugent and Jack, and despite the former's elbow began to feel almost like one of the family. Hostile feelings vanished, and with an amiable smile at the half-frantic Miss Nugent he placed a "bull's-eye" of great strength in his cheek, and leaning forward for a hymn-book left one on the ledge in front of jack. A double-distilled perfume at once assailed the atmosphere.

Miss Nugent sat dazed at his impudence, and for the first time in her life doubts as to her father's capacity stirred within her. She attempted the poor consolation of an "acid tablet," and it was at once impounded by the watchful Mrs. Kingdom. Mean-time the reek of "bull's-eyes" was insufferable.

The service seemed interminable, and all that time the indignant damsel, wedged in between her aunt and the openly exultant enemy of her House, was compelled to endure in silence. She did indeed attempt one remark, and Master Hardy, with a horrified expression of outraged piety, said "H'sh," and shook his head at her. It was almost more than flesh and blood could bear, and when the unobservant Mrs. Kingdom asked her for the text on the way home her reply nearly cost her the loss of her dinner.

The Conqueror, under its new commander, sailed on the day following. Mr. Wilks watched it from the quay, and the new steward observing him came to the side, and holding aloft an old pantry-cloth between his finger and thumb until he had attracted his attention, dropped it overboard with every circumstance of exaggerated horror. By the time a suitable retort had occurred to the ex-steward the steamer was half a mile distant, and the extraordinary and unnatural pantomime in which he indulged on the edge of the quay was grievously misinterpreted by a nervous man in a sailing boat.

Master Hardy had also seen the ship out, and, perched on the extreme end of the breakwater, he remained watching until she was hull down on the horizon. Then he made his way back to the town and the nearest confectioner, and started for home just as Miss Nugent, who was about to pay a call with her aunt, waited, beautifully dressed, in the front garden while that lady completed her preparations.

Feeling very spic and span, and still a trifle uncomfortable from the vigorous attentions of Ann, who cleansed her as though she had been a doorstep, she paced slowly up and down the path. Upon these occasions of high dress a spirit of Sabbath calm was wont to descend upon her and save her from escapades to which in a less severe garb she was somewhat prone.

She stopped at the gate and looked up the road. Then her face flushed, and she cast her eyes behind her to make sure that the hall-door stood open. The hated scion of the house of Hardy was coming down the road, and, in view of that fact, she forgot all else—even her manners.

The boy, still fresh from the loss of his natural protector, kept a wary eye on the house as he approached. Then all expression died out of his face, and he passed the gate, blankly ignoring the small girl who was leaning over it and apparently suffering from elephantiasis of the tongue. He went by quietly, and Miss Nugent, raging inwardly that she had misbehaved to no purpose, withdrew her tongue for more legitimate uses.

"Boo," she cried; "who had his hair pulled?"

Master Hardy pursued the even tenor of his way.

"Who's afraid to answer me for fear my father will thrash him?" cried the disappointed lady, raising her voice.

This was too much. The enemy retraced his steps and came up to the gate.

"You're a rude little girl," he said, with an insufferably grown-up air.

"Who had his hair pulled?" demanded Miss Nugent, capering wildly; "who had his hair pulled?"

"Don't be silly," said Master Hardy. "Here." He put his hand in his pocket, and producing some nuts offered them over the gate. At this Miss Nugent ceased her capering, and wrath possessed her that the enemy should thus misunderstand the gravity of the situation.

"Well, give 'em to Jack, then," pursued the boy; "he won't say no."

This was a distinct reflection on Jack's loyalty, and her indignation was not lessened by the fact that she knew it was true.

"Go away from our gate," she stormed. "If my father catches you, you'll suffer."

"Pooh!" said the dare-devil. He looked up at the house and then, opening the gate, strode boldly into the front garden. Before this intrusion Miss Nugent retreated in alarm, and gaining the door-step gazed at him in dismay. Then her face cleared suddenly, and Master Hardy looking over his shoulder saw that his retreat was cut off by Mr. Wilks.

"Don't let him hurt me, Sam," entreated Miss Nugent, piteously.

Mr. Wilks came into the garden and closed the gate behind him.

"I wasn't going to hurt her," cried Master Hardy, anxiously; "as if I should hurt a girl!

"Wot are you doing in our front garden, then?" demanded Mr. Wilks.

He sprang forward suddenly and, catching the boy by the collar with one huge hand, dragged him, struggling violently, down the side-entrance into the back garden. Miss Nugent, following close behind, sought to improve the occasion.

"See what you get by coming into our garden," she said.

The victim made no reply. He was writhing strenuously in order to frustrate Mr. Wilks's evident desire to arrange him comfortably for the administration of the stick he was carrying. Satisfied at last, the ex-steward raised his weapon, and for some seconds plied it briskly. Miss Nugent trembled, but sternly repressing sympathy for the sufferer, was pleased that the long arm of justice had at last over-taken him.

"Let him go now, Sam," she said; "he's crying."

"I'm not," yelled Master Hardy, frantically.

"I can see the tears," declared Miss Nugent, bending.

Mr. Wilks plied the rod again until his victim, with a sudden turn, fetched him a violent kick on the shin and broke loose. The ex-steward set off in pursuit, somewhat handicapped by the fact that he dare not go over flower-beds, whilst Master Hardy was singularly free from such prejudices. Miss Nugent ran to the side-entrance to cut off his retreat. She was willing for him to be released, but not to escape, and so it fell out that the boy, dodging beneath Mr. Wilks's outspread arms, charged blindly up the side-entrance and bowled the young lady over.

There was a shrill squeal, a flutter of white, and a neat pair of button boots waving in the air. Then Miss Nugent, sobbing piteously, rose from the puddle into which she had fallen and surveyed her garments. Mr. Wilks surveyed them, too, and a very cursory glance was sufficient to show him that the case was beyond his powers. He took the outraged damsel by the hand, and led her, howling lustily, in to the horrified Ann.

"My word," said she, gasping. "Look at your gloves! Look at your frock!"

But Miss Nugent was looking at her knees. There was only a slight redness about the left, but from the right a piece of skin was indubitably missing. This knee she gave Ann instructions to foment with fair water of a comfortable temperature, indulging in satisfied prognostications as to the fate of Master Hardy when her father should see the damage.

The news, when the captain came home, was broken to him by degrees. He was first shown the flower-beds by Ann, then Mrs. Kingdom brought in various soiled garments, and at the psychological moment his daughter bared her knees.

"What will you do to him, father?" she inquired.

The captain ignored the question in favour of a few remarks on the subject of his daughter's behaviour, coupled with stern inquiries as to where she learnt such tricks. In reply Miss Nugent sheltered herself behind a list which contained the names of all the young gentlemen who attended her kindergarten class and many of the young ladies, and again inquired as to the fate of her assailant.

Jack came in soon after, and the indefatigable Miss Nugent produced her knees again. She had to describe the injury to the left, but the right spoke for itself. Jack gazed at it with indignation, and then, without waiting for his tea, put on his cap and sallied out again.

He returned an hour later, and instead of entering the sitting-room went straight upstairs to bed, from whence he sent down word by the sympathetic Ann that he was suffering from a bad headache, which he proposed to treat with raw meat applied to the left eye. His nose, which was apparently suffering from sympathetic inflammation, he left to take care of itself, that organ bitterly resenting any treatment whatsoever.

He described the battle to Kate and Ann the next day, darkly ascribing his defeat to a mysterious compound which Jem Hardy was believed to rub into his arms; to a foolish error of judgment at the beginning of the fray, and to the sun which shone persistently in his eyes all the time. His audience received the explanations in chilly silence.

"And he said it was an accident he knocked you down," he concluded; "he said he hoped you weren't hurt, and he gave me some toffee for you."

"What did you do with it?" demanded Miss Nugent.

"I knew you wouldn't have it," replied her brother, inconsequently, "and there wasn't much of it."

His sister regarded him sharply.

"You don't mean to say you ate it?" she screamed.

"Why not?" demanded her brother. "I wanted comforting, I can tell you."

"I wonder you were not too—too proud," said Miss Nugent, bitterly.

"I'm never too proud to eat toffee," retorted Jack, simply.

He stalked off in dudgeon at the lack of sympathy displayed by his audience, and being still in need of comforting sought it amid the raspberry-canes.

His father noted his son's honourable scars, but made no comment. As to any action on his own part, he realized to the full the impotence of a law-abiding and dignified citizen when confronted by lawless youth. But Master Hardy came to church no more. Indeed, the following Sunday he was fully occupied on the beach, enacting the part of David, after first impressing the raving Mr. Wilks into that of Goliath.

CHAPTER IV

For the next month or two Master Hardy's existence was brightened by the efforts of an elderly steward who made no secret of his intentions of putting an end to it. Mr. Wilks at first placed great reliance on the saw that "it is the early bird that catches the worm," but lost faith in it when he found that it made no provision for cases in which the worm leaning from its bedroom window addressed spirited remonstrances to the bird on the subject of its personal appearance.

To the anxious inquiries of Miss Nugent, Mr. Wilks replied that he was biding his time. Every delay, he hinted, made it worse for Master Hardy when the day of retribution should dawn, and although she pleaded earnestly for a little on account he was unable to meet her wishes. Before that day came, however, Captain Nugent heard of the proceedings, and after a painful interview with the steward, during which the latter's failings by no means escaped attention, confined him to the house.

An excellent reason for absenting himself from school was thus denied to Master Hardy; but it has been well said that when one door closes another opens, and to his great satisfaction the old servant, who had been in poor health for some time, suddenly took to her bed and required his undivided attention.

He treated her at first with patent medicines purchased at the chemist's, a doctor being regarded by both of them as a piece of unnecessary extravagance; but in spite of four infallible remedies she got steadily worse. Then a doctor was called in, and by the time Captain Hardy returned home she had made a partial recovery, but was clearly incapable of further work. She left in a cab to accept a home with a niece, leaving the captain confronted with a problem which he had seen growing for some time past.

"I can't make up my mind what to do with you," he observed, regarding his son.

"I'm very comfortable," was the reply.

"You're too comfortable," said his father.

You're running wild. It's just as well poor old Martha has gone; it has brought things to a head."

"We could have somebody else," suggested his son.

The captain shook his head. "I'll give up the house and send you to London to your Aunt Mary," he said, slowly; "she doesn't know you, and once I'm at sea and the house given up, she won't be able to send you back."

Master Hardy, who was much averse to leaving Sunwich and had heard accounts of the lady in question which referred principally to her strength of mind, made tender inquiries concerning his father's comfort while ashore.

"I'll take rooms," was the reply, "and I shall spend as much time as I can with you in London. You want looking after, my son; I've heard all about you."

His son, without inquiring as to the nature of the information, denied it at once upon principle; he also alluded darkly to his education, and shook his head over the effects of a change at such a critical period of his existence.

"And you talk too much for your age," was his father's comment when he had finished. "A year or two with your aunt ought to make a nice boy of you; there's plenty of room for improvement."

He put his plans in hand at once, and a week before he sailed again had disposed of the house. Some of the furniture he kept for himself; but the bulk of it went to his sister as conscience-money.

Master Hardy, in very low spirits, watched it taken away. Big men in hob-nailed boots ran noisily up the bare stairs, and came down slowly, steering large pieces of furniture through narrow passages, and using much vain repetition when they found their hands acting as fenders. The wardrobe, a piece of furniture which had been built for larger premises, was a particularly hard nut to crack, but they succeeded at last—in three places.

A few of his intimates came down to see the last of him, and Miss Nugent, who in some feminine fashion regarded the move as a triumph for her family, passed by several times. It might have been chance, it might have been design, but the boy could not help noticing that when the piano, the wardrobe, and other fine pieces were being placed in the van, she was at the other end of the road a position from which such curios as a broken washstand or a two-legged chair never failed to entice her.

It was over at last. The second van had disappeared, and nothing was left but a litter of straw and paper. The front door stood open and revealed desolation. Miss Nugent came to the gate and stared in superciliously.

"I'm glad you're going," she said, frankly.

Master Hardy scarcely noticed her. One of his friends who concealed strong business instincts beneath a sentimental exterior had suggested souvenirs and given him a spectacle-glass said to have belonged to Henry VIII., and he was busy searching his pockets for an adequate return. Then Captain Hardy came up, and first going over the empty house, came out and bade his son accompany him to the station. A minute or two later and they were out of sight; the sentimentalist stood on the curb gloating over a newly acquired penknife, and Miss Nugent, after being strongly reproved by him for curiosity, paced slowly home with her head in the air.

Sunwich made no stir over the departure of one of its youthful citizens. Indeed, it lacked not those who would have cheerfully parted with two or three hundred more. The boy was quite chilled by the tameness of his exit, and for years afterwards the desolate appearance of the platform as the train steamed out occurred to him with an odd sense of discomfort. In all Sunwich there was only one person who grieved over his departure, and he, after keeping his memory green for two years, wrote off fivepence as a bad debt and dismissed him from his thoughts.

Two months after the *Conqueror* had sailed again Captain Nugent obtained command of a steamer sailing between London and the Chinese ports. From the gratified lips of Mr. Wilks, Sunwich heard of this new craft, the particular glory of which appeared to be the luxurious appointments of the steward's quarters. Language indeed failed Mr. Wilks in describing it, and, pressed for details, he could only murmur disjointedly of satin-wood, polished brass, and crimson velvet.

Jack Nugent hailed his father's departure with joy. They had seen a great deal of each other during the latter's prolonged stay ashore, and neither had risen in the other's estimation in consequence. He became enthusiastic over the sea as a profession for fathers, and gave himself some airs over acquaintances less fortunately placed. In the first flush of liberty he took to staying away from school, the education thus lost being only partially atoned for by a grown-up style of composition engendered by dictating excuses to the easy-going Mrs. Kingdom.

At seventeen he learnt, somewhat to his surprise, that his education was finished. His father provided the information and, simply as a matter of form, consulted him as to his views for the future. It was an important thing to decide upon at short notice, but he was equal to it, and, having suggested gold-digging as the only profession he cared for, was promptly provided by the incensed captain with a stool in the local bank.

He occupied it for three weeks, a period of time which coincided to a day with his father's leave ashore. He left behind him his initials cut deeply in the lid of his desk, a miscellaneous collection of cheap fiction, and a few experiments in book-keeping which the manager ultimately solved with red ink and a ruler.

A slight uneasiness as to the wisdom of his proceedings occurred to him just before his father's return, but he comforted himself and Kate with the undeniable truth that after all the captain couldn't eat him.

He was afraid, however, that the latter would be displeased, and, with a constitutional objection to unpleasantness, he contrived to be out when he returned, leaving to Mrs. Kingdom the task of breaking the news.

The captain's reply was brief and to the point. He asked his son whether he would like to go to sea, and upon receiving a decided answer in the negative, at once took steps to send him there. In two days he had procured him an outfit, and within a week Jack Nugent, greatly to his own surprise, was on the way to Melbourne as apprentice on the barque *Silver Stream*.

He liked it even less than the bank. The monotony of the sea was appalling to a youth of his tastes, and the fact that the skipper, a man who never spoke except to find fault, was almost loquacious with him failed to afford him any satisfaction. He liked the mates no better than the skipper, and having said as much one day to the second officer, had no reason afterwards to modify his opinions. He lived a life apart, and except for the cook, another martyr to fault-finding, had no society.

In these uncongenial circumstances the new apprentice worked for four months as he had never believed it possible he could work. He was annoyed both at the extent and the variety of his tasks, the work of an A.B. being gratuitously included in his curriculum. The end of the voyage found him desperate, and after a hasty consultation with the cook they deserted together and went up-country.

Letters, dealing mainly with the ideas and adventures of the cook, reached Sunwich at irregular intervals, and were eagerly perused by Mrs. Kingdom and Kate, but the captain forbade all mention of him. Then they ceased altogether, and after a year or two of unbroken silence Mrs. Kingdom asserted herself, and a photograph in her possession, the only one extant, exposing the missing Jack in petticoats and sash, suddenly appeared on the drawing-room mantelpiece.

The captain stared, but made no comment. Disappointed in his son, he turned for consolation to his daughter, noting with some concern the unaccountable changes which that young lady underwent during his absences. He noticed a difference after every voyage. He left behind him on one occasion a nice trim little girl, and returned to find a creature all legs and arms. He returned again and found the arms less obnoxious and the legs hidden by a long skirt; and as he complained in secret astonishment to his sister, she had developed a motherly manner in her dealings with him which was almost unbearable.

"She'll grow out of it soon," said Mrs. Kingdom; "you wait and see."

The captain growled and waited, and found his sister's prognostications partly fulfilled. The exuberance of Miss Nugent's manner was certainly modified by time, but she developed instead a quiet, unassuming habit of authority which he liked as little.

"She gets made such a fuss of, it's no wonder," said Mrs. Kingdom, with a satisfied smile. "I never heard of a girl getting as much attention as she does; it's a wonder her head isn't turned."

"Eh!" said the startled captain; "she'd better not let me see anything of it."

"Just so," said Mrs. Kingdom.

The captain dwelt on these words and kept his eyes open, and, owing to his daughter's benevolent efforts on his behalf, had them fully occupied. He went to sea firmly convinced that she would do something foolish in the matrimonial line, the glowing terms in which he had overheard her describing the charms of the new postman to Mrs. Kingdom filling him with the direst forebodings.

It was his last voyage. An unexpected windfall from an almost forgotten uncle and his own investments had placed him in a position of modest comfort, and just before Miss Nugent reached her twentieth birthday he resolved to spend his declining days ashore and give her those advantages of parental attention from which she had been so long debarred.

Mr. Wilks, to the inconsolable grief of his ship-mates, left with him. He had been for nearly a couple of years in receipt of an annuity purchased for him under the will of his mother, and his defection left a gap never to be filled among comrades who had for some time regarded him in the light of an improved drinking fountain.

CHAPTER V

On a fine afternoon, some two months after his release from the toils of the sea, Captain Nugent sat in the special parlour of The Goblets. The old inn offers hospitality to all, but one parlour has by ancient tradition and the exercise of self-restraint and proper feeling been from time immemorial reserved for the elite of the town.

The captain, confident in the security of these unwritten regulations, conversed freely with his peers. He had been moved to speech by the utter absence of discipline ashore, and from that had wandered to the growing evil of revolutionary ideas at sea. His remarks were much applauded, and two brother-captains listened with grave respect to a disquisition on the wrongs of shipmasters ensuing on the fancied rights of sailor men, the only discordant note being struck by the harbour-master, a man whose ideas had probably been insidiously sapped by a long residence ashore.

"A man before the mast," said the latter, fortifying his moral courage with whisky, "is a human being."

"Nobody denies it," said Captain Nugent, looking round.

One captain agreed with him.

"Why don't they act like it, then?" demanded the other.

Nugent and the first captain, struck by the re-mark, thought they had perhaps been too hasty in their admission, and waited for number two to continue. They eyed him with silent encouragement.

"Why don't they act like it, then?" repeated number two, who, being a man of few ideas, was not disposed to waste them.

Captain Nugent and his friend turned to the harbour-master to see how he would meet this poser.

"They mostly do," he replied, sturdily. "Treat a seaman well, and he'll treat you well."

This was rank heresy, and moreover seemed to imply something. Captain Nugent wondered dismally whether life ashore would infect him with the same opinions.

"What about that man of mine who threw a belaying-pin at me?"

The harbour-master quailed at the challenge. The obvious retort was offensive.

"I shall carry the mark with me to my grave," added the captain, as a further inducement to him to reply.

"I hope that you'll carry it a long time," said the harbour-master, gracefully.

"Here, look here, Hall!" expostulated captain number two, starting up.

"It's all right, Cooper," said Nugent.

"It's all right," said captain number one, and in a rash moment undertook to explain. In five minutes he had clouded Captain Cooper's intellect for the afternoon.

He was still busy with his self-imposed task when a diversion was created by the entrance of a new arrival. A short, stout man stood for a moment with the handle of the door in his hand, and then came in, carefully bearing before him a glass of gin and water. It was the first time that he had set foot there, and all understood that by this intrusion Mr. Daniel Kybird sought to place sea-captains and other dignitaries on a footing with the keepers of slop-shops and dealers in old clothes. In the midst of an impressive silence he set his glass upon the table and, taking a chair, drew a small clay pipe from his pocket.

Aghast at the intrusion, the quartette conferred with their eyes, a language which is perhaps only successful in love. Captain Cooper, who was usually moved to speech by externals, was the first to speak.

"You've got a sty coming on your eye, Hall," he remarked.

"I daresay."

"If anybody's got a needle," said the captain, who loved minor operations.

Nobody heeded him except the harbour-master, and he muttered something about beams and motes, which the captain failed to understand. The others were glaring darkly at Mr. Kybird, who had taken up a newspaper and was busy perusing it.

"Are you looking for anybody?" demanded Captain Nugent, at last.

"No," said Mr. Kybird, looking at him over the top of his paper.

"What have you come here for, then?" inquired the captain.

"I come 'ere to drink two o' gin cold," returned Mr. Kybird, with a dignity befitting the occasion.

"Well, suppose you drink it somewhere else," suggested the captain.

Mr. Kybird had another supposition to offer. "Suppose I don't?" he remarked. "I'm a respect-able British tradesman, and my money is as good as yours. I've as much right to be here as you 'ave. I've never done anything I'm ashamed of!"

"And you never will," said Captain Cooper's friend, grimly, "not if you live to be a hundred."

Mr. Kybird looked surprised at the tribute. "Thankee," he said, gratefully.

"Well, we don't want you here," said Captain Nugent. "We prefer your room to your company."

Mr. Kybird leaned back in his chair and twisted his blunt features into an expression of withering contempt. Then he took up a glass and drank, and discovered too late that in the excitement of the moment he had made free with the speaker's whisky.

"Don't apologize," interrupted the captain; "it's soon remedied."

He took the glass up gingerly and flung it with a crash into the fireplace. Then he rang the bell.

"I've smashed a dirty glass," he said, as the bar-man entered. "How much?"

The man told him, and the captain, after a few stern remarks about privacy and harpies, left the room with his friends, leaving the speechless Mr. Kybird gazing at the broken glass and returning evasive replies to the inquiries of the curious Charles.

He finished his gin and water slowly. For months he had been screwing up his courage to carry that room by assault, and this was the result. He had been insulted almost in the very face of Charles, a youth whose reputation as a gossip was second to none in Sunwich.

"Do you know what I should do if I was you?" said that worthy, as he entered the room again and swept up the broken glass.

"I do not," said Mr. Kybird, with lofty indifference.

"I shouldn't come 'ere again, that's what I should do," said Charles, frankly. "Next time he'll throw you in the fireplace."

"Ho," said the heated Mr. Kybird. "Ho, will he? I'd like to see 'im. I'll make 'im sorry for this afore I've done with 'im. I'll learn 'im to insult a respectable British tradesman. I'll show him who's who."

"What'll you do?" inquired the other.

"Never you mind," said Mr. Kybird, who was not in a position to satisfy his curiosity—"never you mind. You go and get on with your work, Charles, and p'r'aps by the time your moustache 'as grown big enough to be seen, you'll 'ear something."

"I 'eard something the other day," said the bar-man, musingly; "about you it was, but I wouldn't believe it."

"Wot was it?" demanded the other.

"Nothing much," replied Charles, standing with his hand on the door-knob, "but I wouldn't believe it of you; I said I couldn't."

"Wot—was—it?" insisted Mr. Kybird.

"Why, they said you once gave a man a fair price for a pair of trousers," said the barman, indignantly.

He closed the door behind him softly, and Mr. Kybird, after a brief pause, opened it again and, more softly still, quitted the precincts of The Goblets, and stepped across the road to his emporium.

Captain Nugent, in happy ignorance of the dark designs of the wardrobe dealer, had also gone home. He was only just beginning to realize the comparative unimportance of a retired shipmaster, and the knowledge was a source of considerable annoyance to him. No deferential mates listened respectfully to his instructions, no sturdy seaman ran to execute his commands or trembled mutinously at his wrath. The only person in the wide world who stood in awe of him was the general servant Bella, and she made no attempt to conceal her satisfaction at the attention excited by her shortcomings.

He paused a moment at the gate and then, walking slowly up to the door, gave it the knock of a master. A full minute passing, he knocked again, remembering with some misgivings his stern instructions of the day before that the door was to be attended by the servant and by nobody else. He had seen Miss Nugent sitting at the window as he passed it, but in the circumstances the fact gave him no comfort. A third knock was followed by a fourth, and then a distressed voice upstairs was heard calling wildly upon the name of Bella.

At the fifth knock the house shook, and a red-faced maid with her shoulders veiled in a large damp towel passed hastily down the staircase and, slipping the catch, passed more hastily still upstairs again, affording the indignant captain a glimpse of a short striped skirt as it turned the landing.

"Is there any management at all in this house?" he inquired, as he entered the room.

"Bella was dressing," said Miss Nugent, calmly, "and you gave orders yesterday that nobody else was to open the door."

"Nobody else when she's available," qualified her father, eyeing her sharply. "When I give orders I expect people to use their common sense. Why isn't my tea ready? It's five o'clock."

"The clock's twenty minutes fast," said Kate. "Who's been meddling with it?" demanded her father, verifying the fact by his watch.

Miss Nugent shook her head. "It's gained that since you regulated it last night," she said, with a smile.

The captain threw himself into an easy-chair, and with one eye on the clock, waited until, at five minutes to the hour by the right time, a clatter of crockery sounded from the kitchen, and Bella, still damp, came in with the tray. Her eye was also on the clock, and she smirked weakly in the captain's direction as she saw that she was at least two minutes ahead of time. At a minute to the hour the teapot itself was on the tray, and the heavy breathing of the handmaiden in the kitchen was audible to all.

"Punctual to the minute, John," said Mrs. Kingdom, as she took her seat at the tray. "It's wonderful how that girl has improved since you've been at home. She isn't like the same girl."

She raised the teapot and, after pouring out a little of the contents, put it down again and gave it another two minutes. At the end of that time, the colour being of the same unsatisfactory paleness, she set the pot down and was about to raise the lid when an avalanche burst into the room and, emptying some tea into the pot from a canister-lid, beat a hasty re-treat.

"Good tea and well-trained servants," muttered the captain to his plate. "What more can a man want?"

Mrs. Kingdom coughed and passed his cup; Miss Nugent, who possessed a healthy appetite, serenely attacked her bread and butter; conversation languished.

"I suppose you've heard the news, John?" said his sister.

"I daresay I have," was the reply.

"Strange he should come back after all these years," said Mrs. Kingdom; "though, to be sure, I don't know why he shouldn't. It's his native place, and his father lives here."

"Who are you talking about?" inquired the captain.

"Why, James Hardy," replied his sister. "I thought you said you had heard. He's coming back to Sunwich and going into partnership with old Swann, the shipbroker. A very good thing for him, I should think."

"I'm not interested in the doings of the Hardys," said the captain, gruffly.

"I'm sure I'm not," said his sister, defensively.

Captain Nugent proceeded with his meal in silence. His hatred of Hardy had not been lessened by the success which had attended that gentleman's career, and was not likely to be improved by the well-being of Hardy junior. He passed his cup for some more tea, and, with a furtive glance at the photograph on the mantelpiece, wondered what had happened to his own son.

"I don't suppose I should know him if I saw him," continued Mrs. Kingdom, addressing a respectable old arm-chair; "London is sure to have changed him."

"Is this water-cress?" inquired the captain, looking up from his plate.

"Yes. Why?" said Mrs. Kingdom.

"I only wanted information," said her brother, as he deposited the salad in question in the slop-basin.

Mrs. Kingdom, with a resigned expression, tried to catch her niece's eye and caught the captain's instead. Miss Nugent happening to glance up saw her fascinated by the basilisk glare of the master of the house.

"Some more tea, please," she said.

Her aunt took her cup, and in gratitude for the diversion picked out the largest lumps of sugar in the basin.

"London changes so many people," mused the persevering lady, stirring her tea. "I've noticed it before. Why it is I can't say, but the fact remains. It seems to improve them altogether. I dare say that young Hardy—"

"Will you understand that I won't have the Hardys mentiond in my house?" said the captain, looking up. "I'm not interested in their business, and I will not have it discussed here."

"As you please, John," said his sister, drawing herself up. "It's your house and you are master here. I'm sure I don't want to discuss them. Nothing was farther from my thoughts. You understand what your father says, Kate?"

"Perfectly," said Miss Nugent. "When the desire to talk about the Hardys becomes irresistible we must go for a walk."

The captain turned in his chair and regarded his daughter steadily. She met his gaze with calm affection.

"I wish you were a boy," he growled.

"You're the only man in Sunwich who wishes that," said Miss Nugent, complacently, "and I don't believe you mean it. If you'll come a little closer I'll put my head on your shoulder and convert you."

"Kate!" said Mrs. Kingdom, reprovingly.

"And, talking about heads," said Miss Nugent, briskly, "reminds me that I want a new hat. You needn't look like that; good-looking daughters always come expensive."

She moved her chair a couple of inches in his direction and smiled alluringly. The captain shifted uneasily; prudence counselled flight, but dignity forbade it. He stared hard at Mrs. Kingdom, and a smile of rare appreciation on that lady's face endeavoured to fade slowly and naturally into another expression. The chair came nearer.

"Don't be foolish," said the captain, gruffly.

The chair came still nearer until at last it touched his, and then Miss Nugent, with a sigh of exaggerated content, allowed her head to sink gracefully on his shoulder.

"Most comfortable shoulder in Sunwich," she murmured; "come and try the other, aunt, and perhaps you'll get a new bonnet."

Mrs. Kingdom hastened to reassure her brother. She would almost as soon have thought of putting her head on the block. At the same time it was quite evident that she was taking a mild joy in his discomfiture and eagerly awaiting further developments.

"When you are tired of this childish behaviour, miss," said the captain, stiffly——

There was a pause. "Kate!" said Mrs. Kingdom, in tones of mild reproof, how can you?"

"Very good," said the captain, we'll see who gets tired of it first. "I'm in no hurry."

A delicate but unmistakable snore rose from his shoulder in reply.

CHAPTER VI

For the first few days after his return Sunwich was full of surprises to Jem Hardy. The town itself had changed but little, and the older inhabitants were for the most part easily recognisable, but time had wrought wonders among the younger members of the population: small boys had attained to whiskered manhood, and small girls passing into well-grown young women had in some cases even changed their names.

The most astounding and gratifying instance of the wonders effected by time was that of Miss Nugent. He saw her first at the window, and with a ready recognition of the enchantment lent by distance took the first possible opportunity of a closer observation. He then realized the enchantment afforded by proximity. The second opportunity led him impetuously into a draper's shop, where a magnificent shop-walker, after first ceremoniously handing him a high cane chair, passed on his order for pins in a deep and thrilling baritone, and retired in good order.

By the end of a week his observations were completed, and Kate Nugent, securely enthroned in his mind as the incarnation of feminine grace and beauty, left but little room for other matters. On his second Sunday at home, to his father's great surprise, he attended church, and after contemplating Miss Nugent's back hair for an hour and a half came home and spoke eloquently and nobly on "burying hatchets," "healing old sores," "letting bygones be bygones," and kindred topics.

"I never take much notice of sermons myself," said the captain, misunderstanding.

"Sermon?" said his son. "I wasn't thinking of the sermon, but I saw Captain Nugent there, and I remembered the stupid quarrel between you. It's absurd that it should go on indefinitely."

"Why, what does it matter?" inquired the other, staring. "Why shouldn't it? Perhaps it's the music that's affected you; some of those old hymns—"

"It wasn't the sermon and it wasn't the hymns," said his son, disdainfully; "it's just common sense. It seems to me that the enmity between you has lasted long enough."

"I don't see that it matters," said the captain; "it doesn't hurt me. Nugent goes his way and I go mine, but if I ever get a chance at the old man, he'd better look out. He wants a little of the starch taken out of him."

"Mere mannerism," said his son.

"He's as proud as Lucifer, and his girl takes after him," said the innocent captain. "By the way, she's grown up a very good-looking girl. You take a look at her the next time you see her."

His son stared at him.

"She'll get married soon, I should think," continued the other. "Young Murchison, the new doctor here, seems to be the favourite. Nugent is backing him, so they say; I wish him joy of his father-in-law."

Jem Hardy took his pipe into the garden, and, pacing slowly up and down the narrow paths, determined, at any costs, to save Dr. Murchison from such a father-in-law and Kate Nugent from any husband except of his choosing. He took a seat under an old apple tree, and, musing in the twilight, tried in vain to think of ways and means of making her acquaintance.

Meantime they passed each other as strangers, and the difficulty of approaching her only made the task more alluring. In the second week he reckoned up that he had seen her nine times. It was a satisfactory total, but at the same time he could not shut his eyes to the fact that five times out of that number he had seen Dr. Murchison as well, and neither of them appeared to have seen him.

He sat thinking it over in the office one hot afternoon. Mr. Adolphus Swann, his partner, had just returned from lunch, and for about the fifth time that day was arranging his white hair and short, neatly pointed beard in a small looking-glass. Over the top of it he glanced at Hardy, who, leaning back in his chair, bit his pen and stared hard at a paper before him.

"Is that the manifest of the North Star?" he inquired.

"No," was the reply.

Mr. Swann put his looking-glass away and watched the other as he crossed over to the window and gazed through the small, dirty panes at the bustling life of the harbour below. For a short time Hardy stood gazing in silence, and then, suddenly crossing the room, took his hat from a peg and went out.

"Restless," said the senior partner, wiping his folders with great care and putting them on. "Wonder where he's put that manifest."

He went over to the other's desk and opened a drawer to search for it. Just inside was a sheet of foolscap, and Mr. Swann with growing astonishment slowly mastered the contents.

"See her as often as possible."

"Get to know some of her friends."

"Try and get hold of the old lady."

"Find out her tastes and ideas."

"Show my hand before Murchison has it all his own way."

"It seems to me," said the bewildered shipbroker, carefully replacing the paper, "that my young friend is looking out for another partner. He hasn't lost much time."

He went back to his seat and resumed his work. It occurred to him that he ought to let his partner know what he had seen, and when Hardy returned he had barely seated himself before Mr. Swann with a mysterious smile crossed over to him, bearing a sheet of foolscap.

"Try and dress as well as my partner," read the astonished Hardy. "What's the matter with my clothes? What do you mean?"

Mr. Swann, in place of answering, returned to his desk and, taking up another sheet of foolscap, began to write again, holding up his hand for silence as Hardy repeated his question. When he had finished his task he brought it over and placed it in the other's hand.

"Take her little brother out for walks."

Hardy crumpled the paper up and flung it aside. Then, with his face crimson, he stared wrathfully at the benevolent Swann.

"It's the safest card in the pack," said the latter. "You please everybody; especially the little brother. You should always hold his hand—it looks well for one thing, and if you shut your eyes—"

"I don't want any of your nonsense," said the maddened Jem. "What do you mean by reading my private papers?"

"I came over to look for the manifest," said Mr. Swann, "and I read it before I could make out what it was. You must admit it's a bit cryptic. I thought it was a new game at first. Getting hold of the old lady sounds like a sort of blind-man's buff. But why not get hold of the young one? Why waste time over—"

"Go to the devil," said the junior partner.

"Any more suggestions I can give you, you are heartily welcome to," said Mr. Swann, going back to his seat. "All my vast experience is at your service, and the best and sweetest and prettiest girls in Sunwich regard me as a sort of second father."

"What's a second father?" inquired Jim, looking up—"a grandfather?"

"Go your own way," said the other; "I wash my hands of you. You're not in earnest, or you'd clutch at any straw. But let me give you one word of advice. Be careful how you get hold of the old lady; let her understand from the commencement that it isn't her."

Mr. Hardy went on with his work. There was a pile of it in front of him and an accumulation in his drawers. For some time he wrote assiduously, but work was dry after the subject they had been discussing. He looked over at his partner and, seeing that that gentleman was gravely busy, reopened the matter with a jeer.

"Old maids always know most about rearing children," he remarked; "so I suppose old bachelors, looking down on life from the top shelf, think they know most about marriage."

"I wash my hands of you," repeated the senior, placidly. "I am not to be taunted into rendering first aid to the wounded."

The conscience-stricken junior lost his presence of mind. "Who's trying to taunt you?" he demanded, hotly. "Why, you'd do more harm than good."

"Put a bandage round the head instead of the heart, I expect," assented the chuckling Swann. "Top shelf, I think you said; well, I climbed there for safety."

"You must have been much run after," said his partner.

"I was," said the other. "I suppose that's why it is I am always so interested in these affairs. I have helped to marry so many people in this place, that I'm almost afraid to stir out after dark."

Hardy's reply was interrupted by the entrance of Mr. Edward Silk, a young man of forlorn aspect, who combined in his person the offices of messenger, cleaner, and office-boy to the firm. He brought in some letters, and placing them on Mr. Swann's desk retired.

"There's another," said the latter, as the door closed. "His complaint is Amelia Kybird, and he's got it badly. She's big enough to eat him, but I believe that they are engaged. Perseverance has done it in his case. He used to go about like a blighted flower—"

"I am rather busy," his partner reminded him.

Mr. Swann sighed and resumed his own labours. For some time both men wrote in silence. Then the elder suddenly put his pen down and hit his desk a noisy thump with his fist.

"I've got it," he said, briskly; "apologize humbly for all your candour, and I will give you a piece of information which shall brighten your dull eyes, raise the corners of your drooping mouth, and renew once more the pink and cream in your youthful cheeks."

"Look here—" said the overwrought Hardy.

"Samson Wilks," interrupted Mr. Swann, "number three, Fullalove Alley, at home Fridays, seven to nine, to the daughter of his late skipper, who always visits him on that day. Don't thank me, Hardy, in case you break down. She's a very nice girl, and if she had been born twenty years earlier, or I had been born twenty years later, or you hadn't been born at all, there's no saying what might not have happened."

"When I want you to interfere in my business," said Hardy, working sedulously, "I'll let you know."

"Very good," replied Swann; "still, remember Thursdays, seven to nine."

"Thursdays," said Hardy, incautiously; "why, you said Fridays just now."

Mr. Swann made no reply. His nose was immersed in the folds of a large handkerchief, and his eyes watered profusely behind his glasses. It was some minutes before he had regained his normal composure, and even then the sensitive nerves of his partner were offended by an occasional belated chuckle.

Although by dint of casual and cautious inquiries Mr. Hardy found that his partner's information was correct, he was by no means guilty of any feelings of gratitude towards him; and he only glared scornfully when that excellent but frivolous man mounted a chair on Friday afternoon, and putting the clock on a couple of hours or so, urged him to be in time.

The evening, however, found him starting slowly in the direction of Fullalove Alley. His father had gone to sea again, and the house was very dull; moreover, he felt a mild curiosity to see the changes wrought by time in Mr. Wilks. He walked along by the sea, and as the church clock struck the three-quarters turned into the alley and looked eagerly round for the old steward.

The labours of the day were over, and the inhabitants were for the most part out of doors taking the air. Shirt-sleeved householders, leaning against their door-posts smoking, exchanged ideas across the narrow space paved with cobble-stones which separated their small and ancient houses, while the matrons, more gregariously inclined, bunched in little groups and discussed subjects which in higher circles would have inundated the land with libel actions. Up and down the alley a tiny boy all ready for bed, with the exception of his nightgown, mechanically avoided friendly palms as he sought anxiously for his mother.

The object of Mr. Hardy's search sat at the door of his front room, which opened on to the alley, smoking an evening pipe, and noting with an interested eye the doings of his neighbours. He was just preparing to draw himself up in his chair as the intruder passed, when to his utter astonishment that gentleman stopped in front of him, and taking possession of his hand shook it fervently.

"How do you do?" he said, smiling.

Mr. Wilks eyed him stupidly and, releasing his hand, coyly placed it in his trouser-pocket and breathed hard.

"I meant to come before," said Hardy, "but I've been so busy. How are you?"

Mr. Wilks, still dazed, muttered that he was very well. Then he sat bolt upright in his chair and eyed his visitor suspiciously.

"I've been longing for a chat with you about old times," said Hardy; "of all my old friends you seem to have changed the least. You don't look a day older."

"I'm getting on," said Mr. Wilks, trying to speak coldly, but observing with some gratification the effect produced upon his neighbours by the appearance of this well-dressed acquaintance.

"I wanted to ask your advice," said the unscrupulous Hardy, speaking in low tones. "I daresay you know I've just gone into partnership in Sunwich, and I'm told there's no man knows more about the business and the ins and outs of this town than you do."

Mr. Wilks thawed despite himself. His face glistened and his huge mouth broke into tremulous smiles. For a moment he hesitated, and then noticing that a little group near them had suspended their conversation to listen to his he drew his chair back and, in a kind voice, invited the searcher after wisdom to step inside.

Hardy thanked him, and, following him in, took a chair behind the door, and with an air of youthful deference bent his ear to catch the pearls which fell from the lips of his host. Since he was a babe on his mother's knee sixty years before Mr. Wilks had never had such an attentive and admiring listener. Hardy sat as though glued to his chair, one eye on Mr. Wilks and the other on the clock, and it was not until that ancient timepiece struck the hour that the ex-steward suddenly realized the awkward state of affairs.

"Any more 'elp I can give you I shall always be pleased to," he said, looking at the clock.

Hardy thanked him at great length, wondering, as he spoke, whether Miss Nugent was of punctual habits. He leaned back in his chair and, folding his arms, gazed thoughtfully at the perturbed Mr. Wilks.

"You must come round and smoke a pipe with me sometimes," he said, casually.

Mr. Wilks flushed with gratified pride. He had a vision of himself walking up to the front door of the Hardys, smoking a pipe in a well-appointed room, and telling an incredulous and envious Fullalove Alley about it afterwards.

"I shall be very pleased, sir," he said, impressively.

"Come round on Tuesday," said his visitor. "I shall be at home then."

Mr. Wilks thanked him and, spurred on to hospitality, murmured something about a glass of ale, and retired to the back to draw it. He came back with a jug and a couple of glasses, and draining his own at a draught, hoped that the example would not be lost upon his visitor. That astute person, however, after a modest draught, sat still, anchored to the half-empty glass.

"I'm expecting somebody to-night," said the ex-steward, at last.

"No doubt you have a lot of visitors," said the other, admiringly.

Mr. Wilks did not deny it. He eyed his guest's glass and fidgeted.

"Miss Nugent is coming," he said.

Instead of any signs of disorder and preparations for rapid flight, Mr. Wilks saw that the other was quite composed. He began to entertain a poor idea of Mr. Hardy's memory.

"She generally comes for a little quiet chat," he said.

"Indeed!"

"Just between the two of us," said the other.

His visitor said "Indeed," and, as though some chord of memory had been touched, sat gazing dreamily at Mr. Wilks's horticultural collection in the window. Then he changed colour a little as a smart hat and a pretty face crossed the tiny panes. Mr. Wilks changed colour too, and in an awkward fashion rose to receive Miss Nugent.

"Late as usual, Sam," said the girl, sinking into a chair. Then she caught sight of Hardy, who was standing by the door.

"It's a long time since you and I met, Miss Nugent," he said, bowing.

"Mr. Hardy?" said the girl, doubtfully.

"Yes, miss," interposed Mr. Wilks, anxious to explain his position. "He called in to see me; quite a surprise to me it was. I 'ardly knowed him."

"The last time we three met," said Hardy, who to his host's discomfort had resumed his chair, "Wilks was thrashing me and you were urging him on."

Kate Nugent eyed him carefully. It was preposterous that this young man should take advantage of a boy and girl acquaintance of eleven years before—and such an acquaintance!—in this manner. Her eyes expressed a little surprise, not unmixed with hauteur, but Hardy was too pleased to have them turned in his direction at all to quarrel with their expression.

"You were a bit of a trial in them days," said Mr. Wilks, shaking his head. "If I live to be ninety I shall never forget seeing Miss Kate capsized the way she was. The way she——"

"How is your cold?" inquired Miss Nugent, hastily.

"Better, miss, thankee," said Mr. Wilks.

"Miss Nugent has forgotten and forgiven all that long ago," said Hardy.

"Quite," assented the girl, coldly; "one cannot remember all the boys and girls one knew as a child."

"Certainly not," said Hardy. "I find that many have slipped from my own memory, but I have a most vivid recollection of you."

Miss Nugent looked at him again, and an idea, strange and incredible, dawned slowly upon her. Childish impressions are lasting, and Jem Hardy had remained in her mind as a sort of youthful ogre. He sat before her now a frank, determined-looking young Englishman, in whose honest eyes admiration of herself could not be concealed. Indignation and surprise struggled for supremacy.

"It's odd," remarked Mr. Wilks, who had a happy knack at times of saying the wrong thing, "it's odd you should 'ave 'appened to come just at the same time as Miss Kate did."

"It's my good fortune," said Hardy, with a slight bow. Then he cocked a malignant eye at the innocent Mr. Wilks, and wondered at what age men discarded the useless habit of blushing. Opposite him sat Miss Nugent, calmly observant, the slightest suggestion of disdain in her expression. Framed in the queer, high-backed old chair which had belonged to Mr. Wilks's grandfather, she made a picture at which Jem Hardy continued to gaze with respectful ardour. A hopeless sense of self-depreciation possessed him, but the idea that Murchison should aspire to so much goodness and beauty made him almost despair of his sex. His reverie was broken by the voice of Mr. Wilks.

"A quarter to eight?" said that gentleman in-credulously; "it can't be."

"I thought it was later than that," said Hardy, simply.

Mr. Wilks gasped, and with a faint shake of his head at the floor abandoned the thankless task of giving hints to a young man who was too obtuse to see them; and it was not until some time later that Mr. Hardy, sorely against his inclinations, gave his host a hearty handshake and, with a respectful bow to Miss Nugent, took his departure.

"Fine young man he's growed," said Mr. Wilks, deferentially, turning to his remaining visitor; "greatly improved, I think."

Miss Nugent looked him over critically before replying. "He seems to have taken a great fancy to you," she remarked.

Mr. Wilks smiled a satisfied smile. "He came to ask my advice about business," he said, softly. "He's 'eard two or three speak o' me as knowing a thing or two, and being young, and just starting, 'e came to talk it over with me. I never see a young man so pleased and ready to take advice as wot he is."

"He is coming again for more, I suppose?" said Miss Nugent, carelessly.

Mr. Wilks acquiesced. "And he asked me to go over to his 'ouse to smoke a pipe with 'im on Tuesday," he added, in the casual manner in which men allude to their aristocratic connections. "He's a bit lonely, all by himself."

Miss Nugent said, "Indeed," and then, lapsing into silence, gave little occasional side-glances at Mr. Wilks, as though in search of any hidden charms about him which might hitherto have escaped her.

At the same time Mr. James Hardy, walking slowly home by the edge of the sea, pondered on further ways and means of ensnaring the affection of the ex-steward.

CHAPTER VII

The anticipations of Mr. Wilks were more than realized on the following Tuesday. From the time a trim maid showed him into the smoking-room until late at night, when he left, a feted and honoured guest, with one of his host's best cigars between his teeth, nothing that could yield him any comfort was left undone. In the easiest of easy chairs he sat in the garden beneath the leafy branches of apple trees, and undiluted wisdom and advice flowed from his lips in a stream as he beamed delightedly upon his entertainer.

Their talk was mainly of Sunwich and Sunwich people, and it was an easy step from these to Equator Lodge. On that subject most people would have found the ex-steward somewhat garrulous, but Jem

Hardy listened with great content, and even brought him back to it when he showed signs of wandering. Altogether Mr. Wilks spent one of the pleasantest evenings of his life, and, returning home in a slight state of mental exhilaration, severely exercised the tongues of Fullalove Alley by a bearing considered incompatible with his station.

Jem Hardy paid a return call on the following Friday, and had no cause to complain of any lack of warmth in his reception. The ex-steward was delighted to see him, and after showing him various curios picked up during his voyages, took him to the small yard in the rear festooned with scarlet-runner beans, and gave him a chair in full view of the neighbours.

"I'm the only visitor to-night?" said Hardy, after an hour's patient listening and waiting.

Mr. Wilks nodded casually. "Miss Kate came last night," he said. "Friday is her night, but she came yesterday instead."

Mr. Hardy said, "Oh, indeed," and fell straight-way into a dismal reverie from which the most spirited efforts of his host only partially aroused him.

Without giving way to undue egotism it was pretty clear that Miss Nugent had changed her plans on his account, and a long vista of pleasant Friday evenings suddenly vanished. He, too, resolved to vary his visits, and, starting with a basis of two a week, sat trying to solve the mathematical chances of selecting the same as Kate Nugent; calculations which were not facilitated by a long-winded account from Mr. Wilks of certain interesting amours of his youthful prime.

Before he saw Kate Nugent again, however, another old acquaintance turned up safe and sound in Sunwich. Captain Nugent walking into the town saw him first: a tall, well-knit young man in shabby clothing, whose bearing even in the distance was oddly familiar. As he came closer the captain's misgivings were confirmed, and in the sunburnt fellow in tattered clothes who advanced upon him with out-stretched hand he reluctantly recognized his son.

"What have you come home for?" he inquired, ignoring the hand and eyeing him from head to foot.

"Change," said Jack Nugent, laconically, as the smile left his face.

The captain shrugged his shoulders and stood silent. His son looked first up the road and then down.

"All well at home?" he inquired.

"Yes."

Jack Nugent looked up the road again.

"Not much change in the town," he said, at length.

"No," said his father.

"Well, I'm glad to have seen you," said his son. "Good-bye."

"Good-bye," said the captain.

His son nodded and, turning on his heel, walked back towards the town. Despite his forlorn appearance his step was jaunty and he carried his head high. The captain watched him until he was hidden by a bend in the road, and then, ashamed of himself for displaying so much emotion, turned his own steps in the direction of home.

"Well, he didn't whine," he said, slowly. "He's got a bit of pride left."

Meantime the prodigal had reached the town again, and stood ruefully considering his position.

He looked up the street, and then, the well-known shop of Mr. Kybird catching his eye, walked over and inspected the contents of the window. Sheath-knives, belts, tobacco-boxes, and watches were displayed alluringly behind the glass, sheltered from the sun by a row of cheap clothing dangling from short poles over the shop front. All the goods were marked in plain figures in reduced circumstances, Mr. Kybird giving a soaring imagination play in the first marking, and a good business faculty in the second.

At these valuables Jack Nugent, with a view of obtaining some idea of prices, gazed for some time. Then passing between two suits of oilskins which stood as sentinels in the doorway, he entered the shop and smiled affably at Miss Kybird, who was in charge. At his entrance she put down a piece of fancy-work, which Mr. Kybird called his sock, and with a casual glance at his clothes regarded him with a prejudiced eye.

"Beautiful day," said the customer; "makes one feel quite young again."

"What do you want?" inquired Miss Kybird.

Mr. Nugent turned to a broken cane-chair which stood by the counter, and, after applying severe tests, regardless of the lady's feelings, sat down upon it and gave a sigh of relief.

"I've walked from London," he said, in explanation. "I could sit here for hours."

"Look here——" began the indignant Miss Kybird.

"Only people would be sure to couple our names together," continued Mr. Nugent, mournfully.

"When a handsome young man and a good-looking girl——"

"Do you want to buy anything or not?" demanded Miss Kybird, with an impatient toss of her head.

"No," said Jack, "I want to sell."

"You've come to the wrong shop, then," said Miss Kybird; "the warehouse is full of rubbish now."

The other turned in his chair and looked hard at the window. "So it is," he assented. "It's a good job I've brought you something decent to put there."

He felt in his pockets and, producing a silver-mounted briar-pipe, a battered watch, a knife, and a few other small articles, deposited them with reverent care upon the counter.

"No use to us," declared Miss Kybird, anxious to hit back; "we burn coal here."

"These'll burn better than the coal you buy," said the unmoved customer.

"Well, we don't want them," retorted Miss Kybird, raising her voice, "and I don't want any of your impudence. Get up out of our chair."

Her heightened tones penetrated to the small and untidy room behind the shop. The door opened, and Mr. Kybird in his shirt-sleeves appeared at the opening.

"Wot's the row?" he demanded, his little black eyes glancing from one to the other.

"Only a lovers' quarrel," replied Jack. "You go away; we don't want you."

"Look 'ere, we don't want none o' your nonsense," said the shopkeeper, sharply; "and, wot's more, we won't 'ave it. Who put that rubbish on my counter?"

He bustled forward, and taking the articles in his hands examined them closely.

"Three shillings for the lot—cash," he remarked. "Done," said the other.

"Did I say three?" inquired Mr. Kybird, startled at this ready acceptance.

"Five you said," replied Mr. Nugent, "but I'll take three, if you throw in a smile."

Mr. Kybird, much against his inclinations, threw in a faint grin, and opening a drawer produced three shillings and flung them separately on the counter. Miss Kybird thawed somewhat, and glancing from the customer's clothes to his face saw that he had a pleasant eye and a good moustache, together with a general air of recklessness much appreciated by the sex.

"Don't spend it on drink," she remarked, not unkindly.

"I won't," said the other, solemnly; "I'm going to buy house property with it."

"Why, darn my eyes," said Mr. Kybird, who had been regarding him closely; "darn my old eyes, if it ain't young Nugent. Well, well!"

"That's me," said young Nugent, cheerfully; "I should have known you anywhere, Kybird: same old face, same old voice, same old shirt-sleeves."

"'Ere, come now," objected the shopkeeper, shortening his arm and squinting along it.

"I should have known you anywhere," continued the other, mournfully; "and here I've thrown up a splendid berth and come all the way from Australia just for one glimpse of Miss Kybird, and she doesn't know me. When I die, Kybird, you will find the word 'Calais' engraven upon my heart."

Mr. Kybird said, "Oh, indeed." His daughter tossed her head and bade Mr. Nugent take his nonsense to people who might like it.

"Last time I see you," said Mr. Kybird, pursing up his lips and gazing at the counter in an effort of memory; "last time I see you was one fifth o' November when you an' another bright young party was going about in two suits o' oilskins wot I'd been 'unting for 'igh and low all day long."

Jack Nugent sighed. "They were happy times, Kybird."

"Might ha' been for you," retorted the other, his temper rising a little at the remembrance of his wrongs.

"Have you come home for good? inquired Miss Kybird, curiously. Have you seen your father? He passed here a little while ago."

"I saw him," said Jack, with a brevity which was not lost upon the astute Mr. Kybird. "I may stay in Sunwich, and I may not—it all depends."

"You're not going 'ome?" said Mr. Kybird.

"No."

The shopkeeper stood considering. He had a small room to let at the top of his house, and he stood divided between the fear of not getting his rent and the joy to a man fond of simple pleasures, to be obtained by dunning the arrogant Captain Nugent for his son's debts. Before he could arrive at a decision his meditations were interrupted by the entrance of a stout, sandy-haired lady from the back parlour, who, having conquered his scruples against matrimony some thirty years before, had kept a particularly wide-awake eye upon him ever since.

"Your tea's a-gettin' cold," she remarked, severely.

Her husband received the news with calmness. He was by no means an enthusiast where that liquid was concerned, the admiration evoked by its non-inebriating qualities having been always something in the nature of a mystery to him.

"I'm coming," he retorted; "I'm just 'aving a word with Mr. Nugent 'ere."

"Well, I never did," said the stout lady, coming farther into the shop and regarding the visitor. "I shouldn't 'ave knowed 'im. If you'd asked me who 'e was I couldn't ha' told you—I shouldn't 'ave knowed 'im from Adam."

Jack shook his head. "It's hard to be forgotten like this," he said, sadly. "Even Miss Kybird had forgotten me, after all that had passed between us."

"Eh?" said Mr. Kybird.

"Oh, don't take any notice of him," said his daughter. "I'd like to see myself."

Mr. Kybird paid no heed. He was still thinking of the son of Captain Nugent being indebted to him for lodging, and the more he thought of the idea the better he liked it.

"Well, now you're 'ere," he said, with a great assumption of cordiality, "why not come in and 'ave a cup o' tea?"

The other hesitated a moment and then, with a light laugh, accepted the offer. He followed them into the small and untidy back parlour, and being requested by his hostess to squeeze in next to 'Melia at the small round table, complied so literally with the order that that young lady complained bitterly of his encroachments.

"And where do you think of sleeping to-night?" inquired Mr. Kybird after his daughter had, to use her own expressive phrase, shown the guest "his place."

Mr. Nugent shook his head. "I shall get a lodging somewhere," he said, airily.

"There's a room upstairs as you might 'ave if you liked," said Mr. Kybird, slowly. "It's been let to a very respectable, clean young man for half a crown a week. Really it ought to be three shillings, but if you like to 'ave it at the old price, you can."

"Done with you," said the other.

"No doubt you'll soon get something to do," continued Mr. Kybird, more in answer to his wife's inquiring glances than anything else. "Half a crown every Saturday and the room's yours."

Mr. Nugent thanked him, and after making a tea which caused Mr. Kybird to congratulate himself upon the fact that he hadn't offered to board him, sat regaling Mrs. Kybird and daughter with a recital of his adventures in Australia, receiving in return a full and true account of Sunwich and its people up to date.

"There's no pride about 'im, that's what I like," said Mrs. Kybird to her lord and master as they sat alone after closing time over a glass of gin and water. "He's a nice young feller, but bisness is bisness, and s'pose you don't get your rent?"

"I shall get it sooner or later," said Mr. Kybird. "That stuck-up father of 'is 'll be in a fine way at 'im living here. That's wot I'm thinking of."

"I don't see why," said Mrs. Kybird, bridling. "Who's Captain Nugent, I should like to know? We're as good as what 'e is, if not better. And as for the gell, if she'd got 'all Amelia's looks she'd do."

"'Melia's a fine-looking gal," assented Mr. Kybird. "I wonder——"

He laid his pipe down on the table and stared at the mantelpiece. "He seems very struck with 'er," he concluded. "I see that directly."

"Not afore I did," said his wife, sharply.

"See it afore you come into the shop," said Mr. Kybird, triumphantly. "It 'ud be a strange thing to marry into that family, Emma."

"She's keeping company with young Teddy Silk," his wife reminded him, coldly; "and if she wasn't she could do better than a young man without a penny in 'is pocket. Pride's a fine thing, Dan'l, but you can't live on it."

"I know what I'm talking about," said Mr. Kybird, impatiently. "I know she's keeping company with Teddy as well as wot you do. Still, as far as money goes, young Nugent 'll be all right."

"'Ow?" inquired his wife.

Mr. Kybird hesitated and took a sip of his gin and water. Then he regarded the wife of his bosom with a calculating glance which at once excited that lady's easily kindled wrath.

"You know I never tell secrets," she cried.

"Not often," corrected Mr. Kybird, "but then I don't often tell you any. Wot would you say to young Nugent coming into five 'undred pounds 'is mother left 'im when he's twenty-five? He don't know it, but I do."

"Five 'undred," repeated his wife, "sure?"

"No," said the other, "I'm not sure, but I know. I 'ad it from young Roberts when 'e was at Stone and Dartnell's. Five 'undred pounds! I shall get my money all right some time, and, if 'e wants a little bit to go on with, 'e can have it. He's honest enough; I can see that by his manner."

Upstairs in the tiny room under the tiles Mr. Jack Nugent, in blissful ignorance of his landlord's generous sentiments towards him, slept the sound, dreamless sleep of the man free from monetary cares. In the sanctity of her chamber Miss Kybird, gazing approvingly at the reflection of her yellow hair and fine eyes in the little cracked looking-glass, was already comparing him very favourably with the somewhat pessimistic Mr. Silk.

CHAPTER VIII

Mr. Nugent's return caused a sensation in several quarters, the feeling at Equator Lodge bordering close upon open mutiny. Even Mrs. Kingdom plucked up spirit and read the astonished captain a homily upon the first duties of a parent—a homily which she backed up by reading the story of the Prodigal Son through to the bitter end. At the conclusion she broke down entirely and was led up to bed by Kate and Bella, the sympathy of the latter taking an acute form, and consisting mainly of innuendoes which could only refer to one person in the house.

Kate Nugent, who was not prone to tears, took a different line, but with no better success. The captain declined to discuss the subject, and, after listening to a description of himself in which Nero and other celebrities figured for the purpose of having their characters whitewashed, took up his hat and went out.

Jem Hardy heard of the new arrival from his partner, and, ignoring that gentleman's urgent advice to make hay while the sun shone and take Master Nugent for a walk forthwith sat thoughtfully considering how to turn the affair to the best advantage. A slight outbreak of diphtheria at Fullalove Alley had, for a time, closed that thoroughfare to Miss Nugent, and he was inclined to regard the opportune arrival of her brother as an effort of Providence on his behalf.

For some days, however, he looked for Jack Nugent in vain, that gentleman either being out of doors engaged in an earnest search for work, or snugly seated in the back parlour of the Kybirds, indulging in the somewhat perilous pastime of paying compliments to Amelia Kybird. Remittances which had reached him from his sister and aunt had been promptly returned, and he was indebted to the amiable Mr. Kybird for the bare necessaries of life. In these circumstances a warm feeling of gratitude towards the family closed his eyes to their obvious shortcomings.

He even obtained work down at the harbour through a friend of Mr. Kybird's. It was not of a very exalted nature, and caused more strain upon the back than the intellect, but seven years of roughing it had left him singularly free from caste prejudices, a freedom which he soon discovered was not shared by his old acquaintances at Sunwich. The discovery made him somewhat bitter, and when Hardy stopped him one afternoon as he was on his way home from work he tried to ignore his outstretched hand and continued on his way.

"It is a long time since we met," said Hardy, placing himself in front of him.

"Good heavens," said Jack, regarding him closely, "it's Jemmy Hardy— grown up spick and span like the industrious little boys in the school-books. I heard you were back here."

"I came back just before you did," said Hardy. "Brass band playing you in and all that sort of thing, I suppose," said the other. "Alas, how the wicked prosper—and you were wicked. Do you remember how you used to knock me about?"

"Come round to my place and have a chat," said Hardy.

Jack shook his head. "They're expecting me in to tea," he said, with a nod in the direction of Mr. Kybird's, "and honest waterside labourers who earn their bread by the sweat of their brow—when the foreman is looking —do not frequent the society of the upper classes."

"Don't be a fool," said Hardy, politely.

"Well, I'm not very tidy," retorted Mr. Nugent, glancing at his clothes. "I don't mind it myself; I'm a philosopher, and nothing hurts me so long as I have enough to eat and drink; but I don't inflict myself on my friends, and I must say most of them meet me more than half-way."

"Imagination," said Hardy.

"All except Kate and my aunt," said Jack, firmly. "Poor Kate; I tried to cut her the other day."

"Cut her?" echoed Hardy.

Nugent nodded. "To save her feelings," he replied; "but she wouldn't be cut, bless her, and on the distinct understanding that it wasn't to form a precedent, I let her kiss me behind a waggon. Do you know, I fancy she's grown up rather good-looking, Jem?"

"You are observant," said Mr. Hardy, admiringly.

"Of course, it may be my partiality," said Mr. Nugent, with judicial fairness. "I was always a bit fond of Kate. I don't suppose anybody else would see anything in her. Where are you living now?"

"Fort Road," said Hardy; "come round any evening you can, if you won't come now."

Nugent promised, and, catching sight of Miss Kybird standing in the doorway of the shop, bade him good-bye and crossed the road. It was becoming quite a regular thing for her to wait and have her tea with him now, an arrangement which was provocative of many sly remarks on the part of Mrs. Kybird.

"Thought you were never coming," said Miss Kybird, tartly, as she led the way to the back room and took her seat at the untidy tea-tray.

"And you've been crying your eyes out, I suppose," remarked Mr. Nugent, as he groped in the depths of a tall jar for black-currant jam. "Well, you're not the first, and I don't suppose you'll be the last. How's Teddy?"

"Get your tea," retorted Miss Kybird, "and don't make that scraping noise on the bottom of the jar with your knife. It puts my teeth on edge."

"So it does mine," said Mr. Nugent, "but there's a black currant down there, and I mean to have it. 'Waste not, want not.'"

"Make him put that knife down," said Miss Kybird, as her mother entered the room. Mrs. Kybird shook her head at him. "You two are always quarrelling," she said, archly, "just like a couple of—couple of——"

"Love-birds," suggested Mr. Nugent.

Mrs. Kybird in great glee squeezed round to him and smote him playfully with her large, fat hand, and then, being somewhat out of breath with the exertion, sat down to enjoy the jest in comfort.

"That's how you encourage him," said her daughter; "no wonder he doesn't behave. No wonder he acts as if the whole place belongs to him."

The remark was certainly descriptive of Mr. Nugent's behaviour. His easy assurance and affability had already made him a prime favourite with Mrs. Kybird, and had not been without its effect upon her daughter. The constrained and severe company manners of Mr. Edward Silk showed up but poorly beside those of the paying guest, and Miss Kybird had on several occasions drawn comparisons which would have rendered both gentlemen uneasy if they had known of them.

Mr. Nugent carried the same easy good-fellowship with him the following week when, neatly attired in a second-hand suit from Mr. Kybird's extensive stock, he paid a visit to Jem Hardy to talk over old times and discuss the future.

"You ought to make friends with your father," said the latter; "it only wants a little common sense and mutual forbearance."

"That's all," said Nugent; "sounds easy enough, doesn't it? No, all he wants is for me to clear out of Sunwich, and I'm not going to—until it pleases me, at any rate. It's poison to him for me to be living at the Kybirds' and pushing a trolley down on the quay. Talk about love sweetening toil, that does."

Hardy changed the subject, and Nugent, nothing loath, discoursed on his wanderings and took him on a personally conducted tour through the continent of Australia. "And I've come back to lay my bones in Sunwich Churchyard," he concluded, pathetically; "that is, when I've done with 'em."

"A lot of things'll happen before then," said Hardy.

"I hope so," rejoined Mr. Nugent, piously; "my desire is to be buried by my weeping great-grandchildren. In fact, I've left instructions to that effect in my will—all I have left, by the way."

"You're not going to keep on at this water-side work, I suppose?" said Hardy, making another effort to give the conversation a serious turn.

"The foreman doesn't think so," replied the other, as he helped himself to some whisky; "he has made several remarks to that effect lately."

He leaned back in his chair and smoked thoughtfully, by no means insensible to the comfort of his surroundings. He had not been in such comfortable quarters since he left home seven years before. He thought of the untidy litter of the Kybirds' back parlour, with the forlorn view of the yard in the rear. Something of his reflections he confided to Hardy as he rose to leave.

"But my market value is about a pound a week," he concluded, ruefully, "so I must cut my coat to suit my cloth. Good-night."

He walked home somewhat soberly at first, but the air was cool and fresh and a glorious moon was riding in the sky. He whistled cheerfully, and his spirits rose as various chimerical plans of making money occurred to him. By the time he reached the High Street, the shops of which were all closed for the night, he was earning five hundred a year and spending a thousand. He turned the handle of the door and, walking in, discovered Miss Kybird entertaining company in the person of Mr. Edward Silk.

"Halloa," he said, airily, as he took a seat. "Don't mind me, young people. Go on just as you would if I were not here."

Mr. Edward Silk grumbled something under his breath; Miss Kybird, turning to the intruder with a smile of welcome, remarked that she had just thought of going to sleep.

"Going to sleep?" repeated Mr. Silk, thunder-struck.

"Yes," said Miss Kybird, yawning.

Mr. Silk gazed at her, open-mouthed. "What, with me 'ere?" he inquired, in trembling tones.

"You're not very lively company," said Miss Kybird, bending over her sewing. "I don't think you've spoken a word for the last quarter of an hour, and before that you were talking of death-warnings. Made my flesh creep, you did."

"Shame!" said Mr. Nugent.

"You didn't say anything to me about your flesh creeping," muttered Mr. Silk.

"You ought to have seen it creep," interposed Mr. Nugent, severely.

"I'm not talking to you," said Mr. Silk, turning on him; "when I want the favour of remarks from you I'll let you know."

"Don't you talk to my gentlemen friends like that, Teddy," said Miss Kybird, sharply, "because I won't have it. Why don't you try and be bright and cheerful like Mr. Nugent?"

Mr. Silk turned and regarded that gentleman steadfastly; Mr. Nugent meeting his gaze with a pleasant smile and a low-voiced offer to give him lessons at half a crown an hour.

"I wouldn't be like 'im for worlds," said Mr. Silk, with a scornful laugh. "I'd sooner be like anybody."

"What have you been saying to him?" inquired Nugent.

"Nothing," replied Miss Kybird; "he's often like that. He's got a nasty, miserable, jealous disposition. Not that I mind what he thinks."

Mr. Silk breathed hard and looked from one to the other.

"Perhaps he'll grow out of it," said Nugent, hopefully. "Cheer up, Teddy. You're young yet."

"Might I arsk," said the solemnly enraged Mr. Silk, "might I arsk you not to be so free with my Christian name?"

"He doesn't like his name now," said Nugent, drawing his chair closer to Miss Kybird's, "and I don't wonder at it. What shall we call him? Job? What's that work you're doing? Why don't you get on with that fancy waistcoat you are doing for me?"

Before Miss Kybird could deny all knowledge of the article in question her sorely tried swain created a diversion by rising. To that simple act he imparted an emphasis which commanded the attention of both beholders, and, drawing over to Miss Kybird, he stood over her in an attitude at once terrifying and reproachful.

"Take your choice, Amelia," he said, in a thrilling voice. "Me or 'im— which is it to be?"

"Here, steady, old man," cried the startled Nugent. "Go easy."

"Me or 'im?" repeated Mr. Silk, in stern but broken accents.

Miss Kybird giggled and, avoiding his gaze, looked pensively at the faded hearthrug.

"You're making her blush," said Mr. Nugent, sternly. "Sit down, Teddy; I'm ashamed of you. We're both ashamed of you. You're confusing us dreadfully proposing to us both in this way."

Mr. Silk regarded him with a scornful eye, but Miss Kybird, bidding him not to be foolish, punctuated her remarks with the needle, and a struggle, which Mr. Silk regarded as unseemly in the highest degree, took place between them for its possession.

Mr. Nugent secured it at last, and brandishing it fiercely extorted feminine screams from Miss Kybird by threatening her with it. Nor was her mind relieved until Mr. Nugent, remarking that he would put it back in the pincushion, placed it in the leg of Mr. Edward Silk.

Mr. Kybird and his wife, entering through the shop, were just in time to witness a spirited performance on the part of Mr. Silk, the cherished purpose of which was to deprive them of a lodger. He drew back as they entered and, raising his voice above Miss Kybird's, began to explain his action.

"Teddy, I'm ashamed of you," said Mr. Kybird, shaking his head. "A little joke like that; a little innercent joke."

"If it 'ad been a darning-needle now—" began Mrs. Kybird.

"All right," said the desperate Mr. Silk, "'ave it your own way. Let 'Melia marry 'im—I don't care—-I give 'er up."

"Teddy!" said Mr. Kybird, in a shocked voice. "Teddy!"

Mr. Silk thrust him fiercely to one side and passed raging through the shop. The sound of articles falling in all directions attested to his blind haste, and the force with which he slammed the shop-door was sufficient evidence of his state of mind.

"Well, upon my word," said the staring Mr. Kybird; "of all the outrageyous—"

"Never mind 'im," said his wife, who was sitting in the easy chair, distributing affectionate smiles between her daughter and the startled Mr. Nugent. "Make 'er happy, Jack, that's all I arsk. She's been a good gal, and she'll make a good wife. I've seen how it was between you for some time."

"So 'ave I," said Mr. Kybird. He shook hands warmly with Mr. Nugent, and, patting that perturbed man on the back, surveyed him with eyes glistening with approval.

"It's a bit rough on Teddy, isn't it?" inquired Mr. Nugent, anxiously; "besides—"

"Don't you worry about 'im," said Mr. Kybird, affectionately. "He ain't worth it."

"I wasn't," said Mr. Nugent, truthfully. The situation had developed so rapidly that it had caught him at a disadvantage. He had a dim feeling that, having been the cause of Miss Kybird's losing one young man, the most elementary notions of chivalry demanded that he should furnish her with another. And this idea was clearly uppermost in the minds of her parents. He looked over at Amelia and with characteristic philosophy accepted the position.

"We shall be the handsomest couple in Sunwich," he said, simply.

"Bar none," said Mr. Kybird, emphatically.

The stout lady in the chair gazed ax the couple fondly. "It reminds me of our wedding," she said, softly. "What was it Tom Fletcher said, father? Can you remember?"

"'Arry Smith, you mean," corrected Mr. Kybird.

"Tom Fletcher said something, I'm sure," persisted his wife.

"He did," said Mr. Kybird, grimly, "and I pretty near broke 'is 'ead for it. 'Arry Smith is the one you're thinking of."

Mrs. Kybird after a moment's reflection admitted that he was right, and, the chain of memory being touched, waxed discursive about her own wedding and the somewhat exciting details which accompanied it. After which she produced a bottle labelled "Port wine" from the cupboard, and, filling four glasses, celebrated the occasion in a befitting but sober fashion.

"This," said Mr. Nugent, as he sat on his bed that night to take his boots off, "this is what comes of trying to make everybody happy and comfortable with a little fun. I wonder what the governor'll say."

CHAPTER IX

The news of his only son's engagement took Captain Nugent's breath away, which, all things considered, was perhaps the best thing it could have done. He sat at home in silent rage, only exploding when the well-meaning Mrs. Kingdom sought to minimize his troubles by comparing them with those of Job. Her reminder that to the best of her remembrance he had never had a boil in his life put the finishing touch to his patience, and, despairing of drawing-room synonyms for the words which trembled on his lips, he beat a precipitate retreat to the garden.

His son bore his new honours bravely. To an appealing and indignant letter from his sister he wrote gravely, reminding her of the difference in their years, and also that he had never interfered in her flirtations, however sorely his brotherly heart might have been wrung by them. He urged her to forsake such diversions for the future, and to look for an alliance with some noble, open-handed man with a large banking account and a fondness for his wife's relatives.

To Jem Hardy, who ventured on a delicate re-monstrance one evening, he was less patient, and displayed a newly acquired dignity which was a source of considerable embarrassment to that well-meaning gentleman. He even got up to search for his hat, and was only induced to resume his seat by the physical exertions of his host.

"I didn't mean to be offensive," said the latter. "But you were," said the aggrieved man. Hardy apologized.

"Talk of that kind is a slight to my future wife," said Nugent, firmly. "Besides, what business is it of yours?"

Hardy regarded him thoughtfully. It was some time since he had seen Miss Nugent, and he felt that he was losing valuable time. He had hoped great things from the advent of her brother, and now his intimacy seemed worse than useless. He resolved to take him into his confidence.

"I spoke from selfish motives," he said, at last. I wanted you to make friends with your father again."

"What for?" inquired the other, staring.

"To pave the way for me," said Hardy, raising his voice as he thought of his wrongs; "and now, owing to your confounded matrimonial business, that's all knocked on the head. I wouldn't care whom you married if it didn't interfere with my affairs so."

"Do you mean," inquired the astonished Mr. Nugent, "that you want to be on friendly terms with my father?"

"Yes."

Mr. Nugent gazed at him round-eyed. "You haven't had a blow on the head or anything of that sort at any time, have you?" he inquired.

Hardy shook his head impatiently. "You don't seem to suffer from an excess of intellect yourself," he retorted. "I don't want to be offensive again, still, I should think it is pretty plain there is only one reason why I should go out of my way to seek the society of your father."

"Say what you like about my intellect," replied the dutiful son, "but I can't think of even one—not even a small one. Not—Good gracious! You don't mean—you can't mean—"

Hardy looked at him.

"Not that," said Mr. Nugent, whose intellect had suddenly become painfully acute—"not her?"

"Why not?" inquired the other.

Mr. Nugent leaned back in his chair and regarded him with an air of kindly interest. "Well, there's no need for you to worry about my father for that," he said; "he would raise no objection."

"Eh?" said Hardy, starting up from his chair.

"He would welcome it," said Mr. Nugent, positively. "There is nothing that he would like better; and I don't mind telling you a secret—she likes you."

Hardy reddened. "How do you know?" he stammered.

"I know it for a fact," said the other, impressively. "I have heard her say so. But you've been very plain-spoken about me, Jem, so that I shall say what I think."

"Do," said his bewildered friend.

"I think you'd be throwing yourself away," said Nugent; "to my mind it's a most unsuitable match in every way. She's got no money, no looks, no style. Nothing but a good kind heart rather the worse for wear. I suppose you know she's been married once?"

"*What!*" shouted the other. "*Married?*"

Mr. Nugent nodded. His face was perfectly grave, but the joke was beginning to prey upon his vitals in a manner which brooked no delay.

"I thought everybody knew it," he said. "We have never disguised the fact. Her husband died twenty years ago last——"

"Twenty" said his suddenly enlightened listener. "Who?—What?"

Mr. Nugent, incapable of reply, put his head on the table and beat the air frantically with his hand, while gasping sobs rent his tortured frame.

"Dear—aunt," he choked, "how pleas—pleased she'd be if—she knew. Don't look like that, Hardy. You'll kill me."

"You seem amused," said Hardy, between his teeth.

"And you'll be Kate's uncle," said Mr. Nugent, sitting up and wiping his eyes. "Poor little Kate."

He put his head on the table again. "And mine," he wailed. "*Uncle jemmy!*—will you tip us half-crowns, nunky?"

Mr. Hardy's expression of lofty scorn only served to retard his recovery, but he sat up at last and, giving his eyes a final wipe, beamed kindly upon his victim.

"Well, I'll do what I can for you," he observed, "but I suppose you know Kate's off for a three months' visit to London to-morrow?"

The other observed that he didn't know it, and, taught by his recent experience, eyed him suspiciously.

"It's quite true," said Nugent; "she's going to stay with some relatives of ours. She used to be very fond of one of the boys—her cousin Herbert—so you mustn't be surprised if she comes back engaged. But I daresay you'll have forgotten all about her in three months. And, anyway, I don't suppose she'd look at you if you were the last man in the world. If you'll walk part of the way home with me I'll regale you with anecdotes of her chilhood which will probably cause you to change your views altogether."

In Fullalove Alley Mr. Edward Silk, his forebodings fulfilled, received the news of Amelia Kybird's faithlessness in a spirit of' quiet despair, and turned a deaf ear to the voluble sympathy of his neighbours. Similar things had happened to young men living there before, but their behaviour had been widely different to Mr. Silk's. Bob Crump, for instance, had been jilted on the very morning he had arranged for his wedding, but instead of going about in a state of gentle melancholy he went round and fought his beloved's father—merely because it was her father—and wound up an exciting day by selling off his household goods to the highest bidders. Henry Jones in similar circumstances relieved his great grief by walking up and down the alley smashing every window within reach of his stick.

But these were men of spirit; Mr. Silk was cast in a different mould, and his fair neighbours sympathized heartily with him in his bereavement, while utterly failing to understand any man breaking his heart over Amelia Kybird.

His mother, a widow of uncertain age, shook her head over him and hinted darkly at consumption, an idea which was very pleasing to her son, and gave him an increased interest in a slight cold from which he was suffering.

"He wants taking out of 'imself," said Mr. Wilks, who had stepped across the alley to discuss the subject with his neighbour; "cheerful society and 'obbies—that's what 'e wants."

"He's got a faithful 'eart," sighed Mrs. Silk. "It's in the family; 'e can't 'elp it."

"But 'e might be lifted out of it," urged Mr. Wilks. "I 'ad several disappointments in my young days. One time I 'ad a fresh gal every v'y'ge a'most."

Mrs. Silk sniffed and looked up the alley, whereat two neighbours who happened to be at their doors glanced up and down casually, and retreated inside to continue their vigil from the windows.

"Silk courted me for fifteen years before I would say 'yes,'" she said, severely.

"Fifteen years!" responded the other. He cast his eyes upwards and his lips twitched. The most casual observer could have seen that he was engaged in calculations of an abstruse and elusive nature.

"I was on'y seven when 'e started," said Mrs. Silk, sharply.

Mr. Wilks brought his eyes to a level again. "Oh, seven," he remarked.

"And we was married two days before my nineteenth birthday," added Mrs. Silk, whose own arithmetic had always been her weak point.

"Just so," said Mr. Wilks. He glanced at the sharp white face and shapeless figure before him. "It's hard to believe you can 'ave a son Teddy's age," he added, gallantly.

"It makes you feel as if you're getting on," said the widow.

The ex-steward agreed, and after standing a minute or two in silence made a preliminary motion of withdrawal.

"Beautiful your plants are looking," said Mrs. Silk, glancing over at his window; "I can't think what you do to 'em."

The gratified Mr. Wilks began to explain. It appeared that plants wanted almost as much looking after as daughters.

"I should like to see 'em close," said Mrs. Silk. "Come in and 'ave a look at 'em," responded her neighbour.

Mrs. Silk hesitated and displayed a maidenly coyness far in excess of the needs of the situation. Then she stepped across, and five seconds later the two matrons, with consternation writ large upon their faces, appeared at their doors again and, exchanging glances across the alley, met in the centre.

They were more surprised an evening or two later to see Mr. Wilks leave his house to pay a return visit, bearing in his hand a small bunch of his cherished blooms. That they were blooms which would have paid the debt of Nature in a few hours at most in no way detracted from the widow's expressions of pleasure at receiving them, and Mr. Wilks, who had been invited over to cheer up Mr. Silk, who was in a particularly black mood, sat and smiled like a detected philanthropist as she placed them in water.

"Good evenin', Teddy," he said, breezily, with a side-glance at his hostess. "What a lovely day we've 'ad."

"So bright," said Mrs. Silk, nodding with spirit.

Mr. Wilks sat down and gave vent to such a cheerful laugh that the ornaments on the mantelpiece shook with it. "It's good to be alive," he declared.

"Ah, you enjoy your life, Mr. Wilks," said the widow.

"Enjoy it!" roared Mr. Wilks; "enjoy it! Why shouldn't I? Why shouldn't everybody enjoy their lives? It was what they was given to us for."

"So they was," affirmed Mrs. Silk; "nobody can deny that; not if they try."

"Nobody wants to deny it, ma'am," retorted Mr. Wilks, in the high voice he kept for cheering-up purposes. "I enjoy every day o' my life."

He filled his pipe, chuckling serenely, and having lit it sat and enjoyed that. Mrs. Silk retired for a space, and returning with a jug of ale poured him out a glass and set it by his elbow.

"Here's your good 'ealth, ma'am," said Mr. Wilks, raising it. "Here's yours, Teddy—a long life and a 'appy one."

Mr. Silk turned listlessly. "I don't want a long life," he remarked.

His mother and her visitor exchanged glances.

"That's 'ow 'e goes on," remarked the former, in an audible whisper. Mr. Wilks nodded, reassuringly.

"I 'ad them ideas once," he said, "but they go off. If you could only live to see Teddy at the age o' ninety-five, 'e wouldn't want to go then. 'E'd say it was crool hard, being cut off in the flower of 'is youth."

Mrs. Silk laughed gaily and Mr. Wilks bellowed a gruff accompaniment. Mr. Edward Silk eyed them pityingly.

"That's the 'ardship of it," he said, slowly, as he looked round from his seat by the fireplace; "that's where the 'ollowness of things comes in. That's where I envy Mr. Wilks."

"Envy me?" said the smiling visitor; "what for?"

"Because you're so near the grave," said Mr. Silk.

Mr. Wilks, who was taking another draught of beer, put the glass down and eyed him fixedly.

"That's why I envy you," continued the other.

"I don't want to live, and you do, and yet I dessay I shall be walking about forty and fifty years after you're dead and forgotten."

"Wot d'ye mean—near the grave?" inquired

Mr. Wilks, somewhat shortly.

"I was referring to your age," replied the other; "it's strange to see 'ow the aged 'ang on to life. You can't 'ave much pleasure at your time o' life. And you're all alone; the last withered branch left."

"Withered branch!" began Mr. Wilks; "'ere, look 'ere, Teddy——"

"All the others 'ave gone," pursued Mr. Silk, and they're beckoning to you."

"Let 'em beckon," said Mr. Wilks, coldly. "I'm not going yet."

"You're not young," said Mr. Silk, gazing meditatively at the grate, "and I envy you that. It can only be a matter of a year or two at most before you are sleeping your last long sleep."

"Teddy!" protested Mrs. Silk.

"It's true, mother," said the melancholy youth. "Mr. Wilks is old. Why should 'e mind being told of it? If 'e had 'ad the trouble I've 'ad 'e'd be glad to go. But he'll 'ave to go, whether 'e likes it or not. It might be to-night. Who can tell?"

Mr. Wilks, unasked, poured himself out another glass of ale, and drank it off with the air of a man who intended to make sure of that. It seemed a trifle more flat than the last.

"So many men o' your age and thereabouts," continued Mr. Silk, "think that they're going to live on to eighty or ninety, but there's very few of 'em do. It's only a short while, Mr. Wilks, and the little children'll be running about over your grave and picking daisies off of it."

"Ho, will they?" said the irritated Mr. Wilks; "they'd better not let me catch 'em at it, that's all."

"He's always talking like that now," said Mrs. Silk, not without a certain pride in her tones; "that's why I asked you in to cheer 'im up."

"All your troubles'll be over then," continued the warning voice, "and in a month or two even your name'll be forgotten. That's the way of the world. Think 'ow soon the last five years of your life 'ave passed; the next five'll pass ten times as fast even if you live as long, which ain't likely."

"He talks like a clergyman," said Mrs. Silk, in a stage whisper.

Mr. Wilks nodded, and despite his hostess's protests rose to go. He shook hands with her and, after a short but sharp inward struggle, shook hands with her son. It was late in the evening as he left, but the houses had not yet been lit up. Dim figures sat in doorways or stood about the alley, and there was an air of peace and rest strangely and uncomfortably in keeping with the conversation to which he had just been listening. He looked in at his own door; the furniture seemed stiffer than usual and the tick of the clock more deliberate. He closed the door again and, taking a deep breath, set off towards the life and bustle of the Two Schooners.

CHAPTER X

Time failed to soften the captain's ideas concerning his son's engagement, and all mention of the subject in the house was strictly forbidden. Occasionally he was favoured with a glimpse of his son and Miss Kybird out together, a sight which imparted such a flavour to his temper and ordinary intercourse that Mrs. Kingdom, in unconscious imitation of Mr. James Hardy, began to count the days which must elapse before her niece's return from London. His ill-temper even infected the other members of the household, and Mrs. Kingdom sat brooding in her bedroom all one afternoon, because Bella had called her an "overbearing dish-pot."

The finishing touch to his patience was supplied by a little misunderstanding between Mr. Kybird and the police. For the second time in his career the shopkeeper appeared before the magistrates to explain the circumstances in which he had purchased stolen property, and for the second time he left the court without a stain on his character, but with a significant magisterial caution not to appear there again.

Jack Nugent gave evidence in the case, and some of his replies were deemed worthy of reproduction in the Sunwich Herald, a circumstance which lost the proprietors a subscriber of many years' standing.

One by one various schemes for preventing his son's projected alliance were dismissed as impracticable. A cherished design of confining him in an asylum for the mentally afflicted until such time as he should have regained his senses was spoilt by the refusal of Dr. Murchison to arrange for the necessary certificate; a refusal which was like to have been fraught with serious consequences to that gentleman's hopes of entering the captain's family.

Brooding over his wrongs the captain, a day or two after his daughter's return, strolled slowly down towards the harbour. It was afternoon, and the short winter day was already drawing towards a close. The shipping looked cold and desolate in the greyness, but a bustle of work prevailed on the Conqueror, which was nearly ready for sea again. The captain's gaze wandered from his old craft to the small vessels dotted about the harbour and finally dwelt admiringly on the lines of the whaler Seabird, which had put in a few days before as the result of a slight collision with a fishing-boat. She was high out of the water and beautifully rigged. A dog ran up and down her decks barking, and a couple of squat figures leaned over the bulwarks gazing stolidly ashore.

There was something about the vessel which took his fancy, and he stood for some time on the edge of the quay, looking at her. In a day or two she would sail for a voyage the length of which would depend upon her success; a voyage which would for a long period keep all on board of her out of the mischief which so easily happens ashore. If only Jack——

He started and stared more intently than before. He was not an imaginative man, but he had in his mind's eye a sudden vision of his only son waving farewells from the deck of the whaler as she emerged from the harbour into the open sea, while Amelia Kybird tore her yellow locks ashore. It was a vision to cheer any self-respecting father's heart, and he brought his mind back with some regret to the reality of the anchored ship.

He walked home slowly. At the Kybirds' door the proprietor, smoking a short clay pipe, eyed him with furtive glee as he passed. Farther along the road the Hardys, father and son, stepped briskly together. Altogether a trying walk, and calculated to make him more dissatisfied than ever with the present state of affairs. When his daughter shook her head at him and accused him of going off on a solitary frolic his stock of patience gave out entirely.

A thoughtful night led to a visit to Mr. Wilks the following evening. It required a great deal of deliberation on his part before he could make up his mind to the step, but he needed his old steward's assistance in a little plan he had conceived for his son's benefit, and for the first time in his life he paid him the supreme honour of a call.

The honour was so unexpected that Mr. Wilks, coming into the parlour in response to the tapping of the captain's stick on the floor, stood for a short time eyeing him in dismay. Only two minutes before he had taken Mr. James Hardy into the kitchen to point out the interior beauties of an ancient clock, and the situation simply appalled him. The captain greeted him almost politely and bade him sit down. Mr. Wilks smiled faintly and caught his breath.

"Sit down," repeated the captain.

"I've left something in the kitchen, sir," said Mr. Wilks. "I'll be back in half a minute."

The captain nodded. In the kitchen Mr. Wilks rapidly and incoherently explained the situation to Mr. Hardy.

"I'll sit here," said the latter, drawing up a comfortable oak chair to the stove.

"You see, he don't know that we know each other," explained the apologetic steward, "but I don't like leaving you in the kitchen."

"I'm all right," said Hardy; "don't you trouble about me."

He waved him away, and Mr. Wilks, still pale, closed the door behind him and, rejoining the captain, sat down on the extreme edge of a chair and waited.

"I've come to see you on a little matter of business," said his visitor.

Mr. Wilks smiled; then, feeling that perhaps that was not quite the right thing to do, looked serious again.

"I came to see you about my—my son," continued the captain.

"Yes, sir," said Mr. Wilks. "Master Jack, you mean?"

"I've only got one son," said the other, unpleasantly, "unless you happen to know of any more."

Mr. Wilks almost fell off the edge of the chair in his haste to disclaim any such knowledge. His ideas were in a ferment, and the guilty knowledge of what he had left in the kitchen added to his confusion. And just at that moment the door opened and Miss Nugent came briskly in.

Her surprise at seeing her father ensconced in a chair by the fire led to a rapid volley of questions. The captain, in lieu of answering them, asked another.

"What do you want here?"

"I have come to see Sam," said Miss Nugent. "Fancy seeing you here! How are you, Sam?"

"Pretty well, miss, thank'ee," replied Mr. Wilks, "considering," he added, truthfully, after a moment's reflection.

Miss Nugent dropped into a chair and put her feet on the fender. Her father eyed her restlessly.

"I came here to speak to Sam about a private matter," he said, abruptly.

"Private matter," said his daughter, looking round in surprise. "What about?"

"A private matter," repeated Captain Nugent. "Suppose you come in some other time."

Kate Nugent sighed and took her feet from the fender. "I'll go and wait in the kitchen," she said, crossing to the door.

Both men protested. The captain because it ill-assorted with his dignity for his daughter to sit in the kitchen, and Mr. Wilks because of the visitor already there. The face of the steward, indeed, took on such extraordinary expressions in his endeavour to convey private information to the girl that she gazed at him in silent amazement. Then she turned the handle of the door and, passing through, closed it with a bang which was final.

Mr. Wilks stood spellbound, but nothing happened. There was no cry of surprise; no hasty reappearance of an indignant Kate Nugent. His features working nervously he resumed his seat and gazed dutifully at his superior officer.

"I suppose you've heard that my son is going to get married?" said the latter.

"I couldn't help hearing of it, sir," said the steward in self defence— "nobody could."

"He's going to marry that yellow-headed Jezebel of Kybird's," said the captain, staring at the fire.

Mr. Wilks murmured that he couldn't understand anybody liking yellow hair, and, more than that, the general opinion of the ladies in Fullalove Alley was that it was dyed.

"I'm going to ship him on the Seabird," continued the captain. "She'll probably be away for a year or two, and, in the meantime, this girl will probably marry somebody else. Especially if she doesn't know what has become of him. He can't get into mischief aboard ship."

"No, sir," said the wondering Mr. Wilks. "Is Master Jack agreeable to going, sir?"

"That's nothing to do with it," said the captain, sharply.

"No, sir," said Mr. Wilks, "o' course not. I was only a sort o' wondering how he was going to be persuaded to go if 'e ain't."

"That's what I came here about," said the other. "I want you to go and fix it up with Nathan Smith."

"Do you want 'im to be *crimped,* sir?" stammered Mr. Wilks.

"I want him shipped aboard the *Seabird,*" returned the other, "and Smith's the man to do it."

"It's a very hard thing to do in these days, sir," said Mr. Wilks, shaking his head. "What with signing on aboard the day before the ship sails, and before the Board o' Trade officers, I'm sure it's a wonder that anybody goes to sea at all."

"You leave that to Smith," said the captain, impatiently. "The Seabird sails on Friday morning's tide. Tell Smith I'll arrange to meet my son here on Thursday night, and that he must have some liquor for us and a fly waiting on the beach."

Mr. Wilks wriggled: "But what about signing on, sir?" he inquired.

"He won't sign on," said the captain, "he'll be a stowaway. Smith must get him smuggled aboard, and bribe the hands to let him lie hidden in the fo'c's'le. The Seabird won't put back to put him ashore. Here is five pounds; give Smith two or three now, and the remainder when the job is done."

The steward took the money reluctantly and, plucking up his courage, looked his old master in the face.

"It's a 'ard life afore the mast, sir," he said, slowly.

"Rubbish!" was the reply. "It'll make a man of him. Besides, what's it got to do with you?"

"I don't care about the job, sir," said Mr. Wilks, bravely.

"What's that got to do with it?" demanded the other, frowning. "You go and fix it up with Nathan Smith as soon as possible."

Mr. Wilks shuffled his feet and strove to remind himself that he was a gentleman of independent means, and could please himself.

"I've known 'im since he was a baby," he murmured, defiantly.

"I don't want to hear anything more from you, Wilks," said the captain, in a hard voice. "Those are my orders, and you had better see that they are carried out. My son will be one of the first to thank you later on for getting him out of such a mess."

Mr. Wilks's brow cleared somewhat. "I s'pose Miss Kate 'ud be pleased too," he remarked, hope-fully.

"Of course she will," said the captain. "Now I look to you, Wilks, to manage this thing properly. I wouldn't trust anybody else, and you've never disappointed me yet."

The steward gasped and, doubting whether he had heard aright, looked towards his old master, but in vain, for the confirmation of further compliments. In all his long years of service he had never been praised by him before. He leaned forward eagerly and began to discuss ways and means.

In the next room conversation was also proceeding, but fitfully. Miss Nugent's consternation when she closed the door behind her and found herself face to face with Mr. Hardy was difficult of concealment. Too late she understood the facial contortions of Mr. Wilks, and, resigning herself to the inevitable, accepted the chair placed for her by the highly pleased Jem, and sat regarding him calmly from the other side of the fender.

"I am waiting here for my father," she said, in explanation.

"In deference to Wilks's terrors I am waiting here until he has gone," said Hardy, with a half smile.

There was a pause. "I hope that he will not be long," said the girl.

"Thank you," returned Hardy, wilfully misunderstanding, "but I am in no hurry."

He gazed at her with admiration. The cold air had heightened her colour, and the brightness of her eyes shamed the solitary candle which lit up the array of burnished metal on the mantelpiece.

"I hope you enjoyed your visit to London," he said.

Before replying Miss Nugent favoured him with a glance designed to express surprise at least at his knowledge of her movements. "Very much, thank you," she said, at last.

Mr. Hardy, still looking at her with much comfort to himself, felt an insane desire to tell her how much she had been missed by one person at least in Sunwich. Saved from this suicidal folly by the little common sense which had survived the shock of her sudden appearance, he gave the information indirectly.

"Quite a long stay," he murmured; "three months and three days; no, three months and two days."

A sudden wave of colour swept over the girl's face at the ingenuity of this mode of attack. She was used to attention and took compliments as her due, but the significant audacity of this one baffled her. She sat with downcast eyes looking at the fender occasionally glancing from the corner of her eye to see whether he was preparing to renew the assault. He had certainly changed from the Jem Hardy of olden days. She had a faint idea that his taste had improved.

"Wilks keeps his house in good order," said Hardy, looking round.

"Yes," said the girl.

"Wonder why he never married," said Hardy, musingly; "for my part I can't understand a man remaining single all his life; can you?"

"I never think of such things," said Miss Nugent, coldly—and untruthfully.

"If it was only to have somebody to wait on him and keep his house clean," pursued Hardy, with malice.

Miss Nugent grew restless, and the wrongs of her sex stirred within her. "You have very lofty ideas on the subject," she said, scornfully, "but I believe they are not uncommon."

"Still, you have never thought about such things, you know," he reminded her.

"And no doubt you have devoted a great deal of time to the subject."

Hardy admitted it frankly. "But only since I returned to Sunwich," he said.

"Caused by the spectacle of Sam's forlorn condition, I suppose," said Miss Nugent.

"No, it wasn't that," he replied.

Miss Nugent, indignant at having been drawn into such a discussion, lapsed into silence. It was safer and far more dignified, but at the same time she yearned for an opportunity of teaching this presumptuous young man a lesson. So far he had had it all his own way. A way strewn with ambiguities which a modest maiden had to ignore despite herself.

"Of course, Wilks may have had a disappointment," said Hardy, with the air of one willing to make allowances.

"I believe he had about fifty," said the girl, carelessly.

Hardy shook his head in strong disapproval. "No man should have more than one," he said, firmly; "a man of any strength of will wouldn't have that."

"Strength of will?" repeated the astonished Miss Nugent.

Their eyes met; hers sparkling with indignation; his full of cold calculation. If he had had any doubts before, he was quite sure now that he had gone the right way to work to attract her attention; she was almost quivering with excitement.

"Your ideas will probably change with age—and disappointment," she said, sweetly.

"I shall not be disappointed," said Hardy, coolly. "I'll take care of that."

Miss Nugent eyed him wistfully and racked her brains for an appropriate and crushing rejoinder. In all her experience—and it was considerable considering her years—she had never met with such carefully constructed audacity, and she longed, with a great longing, to lure him into the open and destroy him. She was still considering ways and means of doing this when the door opened and revealed the surprised and angry form of her father and behind it the pallid countenance of Mr. Wilks. For a moment anger deprived the captain of utterance.

"Who—" he stammered. "What—"

"What a long time you've been, father," said Miss Nugent, in a reproving voice. "I began to be afraid you were never going."

"You come home with me," said the captain, recovering.

The command was given in his most imperious manner, and his daughter dropped her muff in some resentment as she rose, in order to let him have the pleasure of seeing Mr. Hardy pick it up. It rolled, however, in his direction, and he stooped for it just as Hardy darted forward. Their heads met with a crash, and Miss Nugent forgot her own consternation in the joy of beholding the pitiable exhibition which terror made of Mr. Wilks.

"I'm very sorry," said Hardy, as he reverently dusted the muff on his coat-sleeve before returning it. "I'm afraid it was my fault."

"It was," said the infuriated captain, as he held the door open for his daughter. "Now, Kate."

Miss Nugent passed through, followed by her father, and escorted to the front door by the steward, whose faint "Good-night" was utterly ignored by his injured commander. He stood at the door until they had turned the corner, and, returning to the kitchen, found his remaining guest holding his aching head beneath the tap.

"And now," said the captain, sternly, to his daughter, "how dare you sit and talk to that young cub? Eh? How dare you?"

"He was there when I went in," said his daughter. "Why didn't you come out, then?" demanded her father.

"I was afraid of disturbing you and Sam," said Miss Nugent. "Besides, why shouldn't I speak to him?"

"Why?" shouted the captain. "Why? Because I won't have it."

"I thought you liked him," said Miss Nugent, in affected surprise. "You patted him on the head."

The captain, hardly able to believe his ears, came to an impressive stop in the roadway, but Miss Nugent walked on. She felt instinctively that the joke was thrown away on him, and, in the absence of any other audience, wanted to enjoy it without interruption. Convulsive and half-suppressed sounds, which she ascribed to a slight cold caught while waiting in the kitchen, escaped her at intervals for the remainder of the journey home.

CHAPTER XI

Jack Nugent's first idea on seeing a letter from his father asking him to meet him at Samson Wilks's was to send as impolite a refusal as a strong sense of undutifulness and a not inapt pen could arrange, but the united remonstrances of the Kybird family made him waver.

"You go," said Mr. Kybird, solemnly; "take the advice of a man wot's seen life, and go. Who knows but wot he's a thinking of doing something for you?"

"Startin' of you in business or somethin'," said Mrs. Kybird. "But if 'e tries to break it off between you and 'Melia I hope you know what to say."

"He won't do that," said her husband.

"If he wants to see me," said Mr. Nugent, "let him come here."

"I wouldn't 'ave 'im in my house," retorted Mr. Kybird, quickly. "An Englishman's 'ouse is his castle, and I won't 'ave him in mine."

"Why not, Dan'l," asked his wife, "if the two families is to be connected?"

Mr. Kybird shook his head, and, catching her eye, winked at her with much significance.

"'Ave it your own way," said Mrs. Kybird, who was always inclined to make concessions in minor matters. "'Ave it your own way, but don't blame me, that's all I ask."

Urged on by his friends Mr. Nugent at last consented, and, in a reply to his father, agreed to meet him at the house of Mr. Wilks on Thursday evening. He was not free him-self from a slight curiosity as to the reasons which had made the captain unbend in so unusual a fashion.

Mr. Nathan Smith put in an appearance at six o'clock on the fatal evening. He was a short, slight man, with a clean-shaven face mapped with tiny wrinkles, and a pair of colourless eyes the blankness of whose expression defied research. In conversation, especially conversation of a diplomatic nature, Mr. Smith seemed to be looking through his opponent at something beyond, an uncomfortable habit which was a source of much discomfort to his victims.

"Here we are, then, Mr. Wilks," he said, putting his head in the door and smiling at the agitated steward.

"Come in," said Mr. Wilks, shortly.

Mr. Smith obliged. "Nice night outside," he said, taking a chair; "clear over'ead. Wot a morning it 'ud be for a sail if we was only young enough. Is that terbacker in that canister there?"

The other pushed it towards him.

"If I was only young enough—and silly enough," said the boarding-house master, producing a pipe with an unusually large bowl and slowly filling it, "there's nothing I should enjoy more than a three years' cruise. Nothing to do and everything of the best."

"'Ave you made all the arrangements?" inquired Mr. Wilks, in a tone of cold superiority.

Mr. Smith glanced affectionately at a fish-bag of bulky appearance which stood on the floor between his feet. "All ready," he said, cheerfully, an' if you'd like a v'y'ge yourself I can manage it for you in two twos. You've on'y got to say the word."

"I don't want one," said the steward, fiercely; "don't you try none o' your larks on me, Nathan Smith, cos I won't have it."

"Lord love your 'art," said the boarding-master, "I wouldn't 'urt you. I'm on'y acting under your orders now; yours and the captin's. It ain't in my reg'lar way o' business at all, but I'm so good-natured I can't say 'no.'"

"Can't say 'no' to five pounds, you mean," retorted Mr. Wilks, who by no means relished these remarks.

"If I was getting as much out of it as you are I'd be a 'appy man," sighed Mr. Smith.

"Me!" cried the other; do you think I'd take money for this—why, I'd sooner starve, I'd sooner. Wot are you a-tapping your nose for?"

"Was I tapping it?" demanded Mr. Smith, in surprise. "Well, I didn't know it. I'm glad you told me."

"You're quite welcome," said the steward, sharply. "Crimping ain't in my line; I'd sooner sweep the roads."

"'Ear, 'ear," exclaimed Mr. Smith, approvingly. "Ah! wot a thing it is to come acrost an honest man. Wot a good thing it is for the eyesight."

He stared stonily somewhere in the direction of Mr. Wilks, and then blinking rapidly shielded his eyes with his hand as though overcome by the sight of so much goodness. The steward's wrath rose at the performance, and he glowered back at him until his eyes watered.

"Twenty past six," said Mr. Smith, suddenly, as he fumbled in his waistcoat-pocket and drew out a small folded paper. "It's time I made a start. I s'pose you've got some salt in the house?"

"Plenty," said Mr. Wilks.

"And beer?" inquired the other.

"Yes, there is some beer," said the steward.

"Bring me a quart of it," said the boarding-master, slowly and impressively. "I want it drawed in a china mug, with a nice foaming 'ead on it."

"Wot do you want it for?" inquired Mr. Wilks, eyeing him very closely.

"Bisness purposes," said Mr. Smith. "If you're very good you shall see 'ow I do it."

Still the steward made no move. "I thought you brought the stuff with you," he remarked.

Mr. Smith looked at him with mild reproach. "Are you managing this affair or am I?" he inquired.

The steward went out reluctantly, and drawing a quart mug of beer set it down on the table and stood watching his visitor.

"And now I want a spoonful o' sugar, a spoonful o' salt, and a spoonful o' vinegar," said Mr. Smith. "Make haste afore the 'ead goes off of it."

Mr. Wilks withdrew grumbling, and came back in a wonderfully short space of time considering, with the articles required.

"Thankee," said the other; "you 'ave been quick. I wish I could move as quick as you do. But you can take 'em back now, I find I can do without 'em."

"Where's the beer?" demanded the incensed Mr. Wilks; where's the beer, you underhanded swab?"

"I altered my mind," said Mr. Smith, "and not liking waste, and seeing by your manner that you've 'ad more than enough already to-night, I drunk it. There isn't another man in Sunwich I could ha' played that trick on, no, nor a boy neither."

Mr. Wilks was about to speak, but, thinking better of it, threw the three spoons in the kitchen, and resuming his seat by the fire sat with his back half turned to his visitor.

"Bright, cheerful young chap, 'e is," said Mr. Smith; "you've knowed 'im ever since he was a baby, haven't you?"

Mr. Wilks made no reply.

"The Conqueror's sailing to-morrow morning, too," continued his tormentor; "his father's old ship. 'Ow strange it'll seem to 'im following it out aboard a whaler. Life is full o' surprises, Mr. Wilks, and wot a big surprise it would be to you if you could 'ear wot he says about you when he comes to 'is senses."

"I'm obeying orders," growled the other.

"Quite right," said Mr. Smith, approvingly, as he drew a bottle of whisky from his bag and placed it on the table. "Two glasses and there we are. We don't want any salt and vinegar this time."

Mr. Wilks turned a deaf ear. "But 'ow are you going to manage so as to make one silly and not the other?" he inquired.

"It's a trade secret," said the other; "but I don't mind telling you I sent the cap'n something to take afore he comes, and I shall be in your kitchen looking arter things."

"I s'pose you know wot you're about?" said Mr. Wilks, doubtfully.

"I s'pose so," rejoined the other. "Young Nu-gent trusts you, and, of course, he'll take anything from your 'ouse. That's the beauty of 'aving a character, Mr. Wilks; a good character and a face like a baby with grey whiskers."

Mr. Wilks bent down and, taking up a small brush, carefully tidied up the hearth.

"Like as not, if my part in it gets to be known," pursued Mr. Smith, mournfully, "I'll 'ave that gal of Kybird's scratching my eyes out or p'r'aps sticking a hat-pin into me. I had that once; the longest hat-pin that ever was made, I should think."

He shook his head over the perils of his calling, and then, after another glance at the clock, withdrew to the kitchen with his bag, leaving Mr. Wilks waiting in a state of intense nervousness for the arrival of the others.

Captain Nugent was the first to put in an appearance, and by way of setting a good example poured a little of the whisky in his glass and sat there waiting. Then Jack Nugent came in, fresh and glowing, and Mr. Wilks, after standing about helplessly for a few moments, obeyed the captain's significant nod and joined Mr. Smith in the kitchen.

"You'd better go for a walk," said that gentle-man, regarding him kindly; "that's wot the cap'n thought."

Mr. Wilks acquiesced eagerly, and tapping at the door passed through the room again into the street. A glance as he went through showed him that Jack Nugent was drinking, and he set off in a panic to get away from the scene which he had contrived.

He slackened after a time and began to pace the streets at a rate which was less noticeable. As he passed the Kybirds' he shivered, and it was not until he had consumed a pint or two of the strongest brew procurable at the *Two Schooners* that he began to regain some of his old self-esteem. He felt almost maudlin at the sacrifice of character he was enduring for the sake of his old master, and the fact that he could not narrate it to sympathetic friends was not the least of his troubles.

The shops had closed by the time he got into the street again, and he walked down and watched with much solemnity the reflection of the quay lamps in the dark water of the harbour. The air was keen and the various craft distinct in the starlight. Perfect quiet reigned aboard the Seabird, and after a vain attempt to screw up his courage to see the victim taken aboard he gave it up and walked back along the beach.

By the time he turned his steps homewards it was nearly eleven o'clock. Fullalove Alley was quiet, and after listening for some time at his window he turned the handle of the door and passed in. The nearly empty bottle stood on the table, and an over-turned tumbler accounted for a large, dark patch on the table-cloth. As he entered the room the kitchen door opened and Mr. Nathan Smith, with a broad smile on his face, stepped briskly in.

"All over," he said, rubbing his hands; "he went off like a lamb, no trouble nor fighting. He was a example to all of us."

"Did the cap'n see 'im aboard?" inquired Mr. Wilks.

"Certainly not," said the other. "As a matter o' fact the cap'n took a little more than I told 'im to take, and I 'ad to help 'im up to your bed. Accidents will 'appen, but he'll be all right in the morning if nobody goes near 'im. Leave 'im perfectly quiet, and when 'e comes downstairs give 'im a strong cup o' tea."

"In my bed?" repeated the staring Mr. Wilks.

"He's as right as rain," said the boarding master. "I brought down a pillow and blankets for you and put 'em in the kitchen. And now I'll take the other two pound ten and be getting off 'ome. It ought to be ten pounds really with the trouble I've 'ad."

Mr. Wilks laid the desired amount on the table, and Mr. Nathan Smith placing it in his pocket rose to go.

"Don't disturb 'im till he's 'ad 'is sleep out, mind," he said, pausing at the door, "else I can't answer for the consequences. If 'e should get up in the night and come down raving mad, try and soothe 'im. Good-night and pleasant dreams."

He closed the door after him quietly, and the horrified steward, after fetching the bed-clothes on tiptoe from the kitchen, locked the door which led to the staircase, and after making up a bed on the floor lay down in his clothes and tried to get to sleep.

He dozed off at last, but woke up several times during the night with the cold. The lamp burnt itself out, and in the dark he listened intently for any sounds of life in the room above. Then he fell asleep again, until at about half-past seven in the morning a loud crash overhead awoke him with a start.

In a moment he was sitting up with every faculty on the alert. Footsteps blundered about in the room above, and a large and rapidly widening patch of damp showed on the ceiling. It was evident that the sleeper, in his haste to quench an abnormal thirst, had broken the water jug.

Mr. Wilks, shivering with dread, sprang to his feet and stood irresolute. Judging by the noise, the captain was evidently in a fine temper, and Mr. Smith's remarks about insanity occurred to him with redoubled interest. Then he heard a hoarse shout, the latch of the bedroom door clicked, and the prisoner stumbled heavily downstairs and began to fumble at the handle of the door at the bottom. Trembling with excitement Mr. Wilks dashed forward and turned the key, and then retreating to the street door prepared for instant flight.

He opened the door so suddenly that the man on the other side, with a sudden cry, fell on all fours into the room, and raising his face stared stupidly at the steward. Mr. Wilks's hands dropped to his sides and his tongue refused its office, for in some strange fashion, quite in keeping with the lawless proceedings of the previous night, Captain Nugent had changed into a most excellent likeness of his own son.

CHAPTER XII

For some time Mr. Wilks stood gazing at this unexpected apparition and trying to collect his scattered senses. Its face was pale and flabby, while its glassy eyes, set in rims of red eyelids, were beginning to express unmistakable signs of suspicion and wrath. The shock was so sudden that the steward could not even think coherently. Was the captain upstairs? And if so, what was his condition? Where was Nathan Smith? And where was the five pounds?

A voice, a husky and discordant voice, broke in upon his meditations; Jack Nugent was also curious.

"What does all this mean?" he demanded, angrily. "How did I get here?"

"You—you came downstairs," stammered Mr. Wilks, still racking his brains in the vain effort to discover how matters stood.

Mr. Nugent was about to speak, but, thinking better of it, turned and blundered into the kitchen. Sounds of splashing and puffing ensued, and the steward going to the door saw him with his head under the tap. He followed him in and at the right time handed him a towel. Despite the disordered appearance of his hair the improvement in Mr. Nugent's condition was so manifest that the steward, hoping for similar results, turned the tap on again and followed his example.

"Your head wants cooling, I should think," said the young man, returning him the towel. "What's it all about?"

Mr. Wilks hesitated; a bright thought occurred to him, and murmuring something about a dry towel he sped up the narrow stairs to his bedroom. The captain was not there. He pushed open the small lattice window and peered out into the alley; no sign of either the captain or the ingenious Mr. Nathan Smith. With a heavy heart he descended the stairs again.

"Now," said Mr. Nugent, who was sitting down with his hands in his pockets, "perhaps you'll be good enough to explain what all this means."

"You were 'ere last night," said Mr. Wilks, "you and the cap'n."

"I know that," said Nugent. "How is it I didn't go home? I didn't understand that it was an all-night invitation. Where is my father?"

The steward shook his head helplessly. "He was 'ere when I went out last night," he said, slowly. "When I came back the room was empty and I was told as 'e was upstairs in my bed."

"Told he was in your bed?" repeated the other. "Who told you?"

He pushed open the small lattice window and peered out into the alley.

Mr. Wilks caught his breath. "I mean I told myself 'e was in my bed," he stammered, "because when I came in I see these bed-clothes on the floor, an' I thought as the cap'n 'ad put them there for me and taken my bed 'imself."

Mr. Nugent regarded the litter of bed-clothes as though hoping that they would throw a little light on the affair, and then shot a puzzled glance at Mr. Wilks.

"Why should you think my father wanted your bed?" he inquired.

"I don't know," was the reply. "I thought p'r'aps 'e'd maybe taken a little more than 'e ought to have taken. But it's all a myst'ry to me. I'm more astonished than wot you are."

"Well, I can't make head or tail of it," said Nugent, rising and pacing the room. "I came here to meet my father. So far as I remember I had one drink of whisky—your whisky—and then I woke up in your bedroom with a splitting headache and a tongue like a piece of leather. Can you account for it?"

Mr. Wilks shook his head again. "I wasn't here," he said, plucking up courage. "Why not go an' see your father? Seems to me 'e is the one that would know most about it."

Mr. Nugent stood for a minute considering, and then raising the latch of the door opened it slowly and inhaled the cold morning air. A subtle and delicate aroma of coffee and herrings which had escaped from neighbouring breakfast-tables invaded the room and reminded him of an appetite. He turned to go, but had barely quitted the step before he saw Mrs. Kingdom and his sister enter the alley.

Mr. Wilks saw them too, and, turning if anything a shade paler, supported himself by the door-pest. Kate Nugent quickened her pace as she saw them, and, after a surprised greeting to her brother, breathlessly informed him that the captain was missing.

"Hasn't been home all night," panted Mrs. Kingdom, joining them. "I don't know what to think."

They formed an excited little group round the steward's door, and Mr. Wilks, with an instinctive feeling that the matter was one to be discussed in private, led the way indoors. He began to apologize for the disordered condition of the room, but Jack Nugent, interrupting him brusquely, began to relate his own adventures of the past few hours.

Mrs. Kingdom listened to the narrative with unexpected calmness. She knew the cause of her nephew's discomfiture. It was the glass of whisky acting on a system unaccustomed to alcohol, and she gave a vivid and moving account of the effects of a stiff glass of hot rum which she had once taken for a cold. It was quite clear to her that the captain had put his son to bed; the thing to discover now was where he had put himself.

"Sam knows something about it," said her nephew, darkly; "there's something wrong."

"I know no more than a babe unborn," declared Mr. Wilks. "The last I see of the cap'n 'e was a-sitting at this table opposite you."

"Sam wouldn't hurt a fly," said Miss Nugent, with a kind glance at her favourite.

"Well, where is the governor, then?" inquired her brother. "Why didn't he go home last night? He has never stayed out before."

"Yes, he has," said Mrs. Kingdom, folding her hands in her lap. "When you were children. He came home at half-past eleven next morning, and when I asked him where he'd been he nearly bit my head off. I'd been walking the floor all night, and I shall never forget his remarks when he opened the door to the police, who'd come to say they couldn't find him. Never."

A ghostly grin flitted across the features of Mr. Wilks, but he passed the back of his hand across his mouth and became serious again as he thought of his position. He was almost dancing with anxiety to get away to Mr. Nathan Smith and ask for an explanation of the proceedings of the night before.

"I'll go and have a look round for the cap'n," he said, eagerly; "he can't be far."

"I'll come with you," said Nugent. "I should like to see him too. There are one or two little things that want explaining. You take aunt home, Kate, and I'll follow on as soon as there is any news."

As he spoke the door opened a little way and a head appeared, only to be instantly withdrawn at the sight of so many people. Mr. Wilks stepped forward hastily, and throwing the door wide open revealed the interesting features of Mr. Nathan Smith.

"How do you do, Mr. Wilks?" said that gentleman, softly. "I just walked round to see whether you was in. I've got a message for you. I didn't know you'd got company."

He stepped into the room and, tapping the steward on the chest with a confidential finger, backed him into a corner, and having got him there gave an expressive wink with one eye and gazed into space with the other.

"I thought you'd be alone," he said, looking round, "but p'r'aps it's just as well as it is. They've got to know, so they may as well know now as later on."

"Know what?" inquired Jack Nugent, abruptly. "What are you making that face for, Sam?"

Mr. Wilks mumbled something about a decayed tooth, and to give colour to the statement continued a series of contortions which made his face ache.

"You should take something for that tooth," said the boarding-master, with great solicitude. "Wot do you say to a glass o' whisky?"

He motioned to the fatal bottle, which still stood on the table; the steward caught his breath, and then, rising to the occasion, said that he had already had a couple of glasses, and they had done no good.

"What's your message?" inquired Jack Nugent, impatiently.

"I'm just going to tell you," said Mr. Smith. "I was out early this morning, strolling down by the harbour to get a little appetite for breakfast, when who should I see coming along, looking as though 'e 'ad just come from a funeral, but Cap'n Nugent! I was going to pass 'im, but he stopped me and asked me to take a message from 'im to 'is old and faithful steward, Mr. Wilks."

"Why, has he gone away?" exclaimed Mrs. Kingdom.

"His old and faithful steward," repeated Mr. Smith, motioning her to silence. "'Tell 'im,' he says, 'that I am heartily ashamed of myself for wot took place last night—and him, too. Tell 'im that, after my father's 'art proved too much for me, I walked the streets all night, and now I can't face may injured son and family yet awhile, and I'm off to London till it has blown over.'"

"But what's it all about?" demanded Nugent. Why don't you get to the point?"

"So far as I could make out," replied Mr. Smith, with the studious care of one who desires to give exact information, "Cap'n Nugent and Mr. Wilks 'ad a little plan for giving you a sea blow."

"Me?" interrupted the unfortunate steward. "Now, look 'ere, Nathan Smith——"

"Them was the cap'n's words," said the boarding-master, giving him a glance of great significance; "are you going to take away or add to wot the cap'n says?"

Mr. Wilks collapsed, and avoiding the indignant eyes of the Nugent family tried to think out his position.

"It seems from wot the cap'n told me," continued Mr. Smith, "that there was some objection to your marrying old—Mr. Kybird's gal, so 'e and Mr. Wilks, after putting their 'eads together, decided to get you 'ere and after giving you a little whisky that Mr. Wilks knows the trick of—"

"Me?" interrupted the unfortunate steward, again.

"Them was the cap'n's words," said Mr. Smith, coldly. "After you'd 'ad it they was going to stow you away in the Seabird, which sailed this morning. However, when the cap'n see you overcome, his 'art melted, and instead o' putting you aboard the whaler he took your feet and Mr. Wilks your 'ead, and after a great deal o' trouble got you upstairs and put you to bed."

"You miserable scoundrel," said the astonished Mr. Nugent, addressing the shrinking steward; "you infernal old reprobate—you—you—I didn't think you'd got it in you."

"So far as I could make out," said Mr. Smith, kindly, "Mr. Wilks was only obeying orders. It was the cap'n's plan, and Mr. Wilks was aboard ship with 'im for a very long time. O' course, he oughtn't to ha' done it, but the cap'n's a masterful man, an' I can quite understand Mr. Wilks givin' way; I dessay I should myself if I'd been in 'is place—he's all 'art, is Mr. Wilks—no 'ead."

"It's a good job for you you're an old man, Sam," said Mr. Nugent.

"I can hardly believe it of you, Sam," said Miss Nugent. "I can hardly think you could have been so deceitful. Why, we've trusted you all our lives."

The unfortunate steward quailed beneath the severity of her glance. Even if he gave a full account of the affair it would not make his position better. It was he who had made all the arrangements with Mr. Smith, and after an indignant glance at that gentleman he lowered his gaze and remained silent.

"It is rather odd that my father should take you into his confidence," said Miss Nugent, turning to the boarding-master.

"Just wot I thought, miss," said the complaisant Mr. Smith; "but I s'pose there was nobody else, and he wanted 'is message to go for fear you should get worrying the police about 'im or something. He wants it kep' quiet, and 'is last words to me as 'e left me was, 'If this affair gets known I shall never come back. Tell 'em to keep it quiet.'"

"I don't think anybody will want to go bragging about it," said Jack Nugent, rising, "unless it is Sam Wilks. Come along, Kate."

Miss Nugent followed him obediently, only pausing at the door to give a last glance of mingled surprise and reproach at Mr. Wilks. Then they were outside and the door closed behind them.

"Well, that's all right," said Mr. Smith, easily.

"All right!" vociferated the steward. "Wot did you put it all on to me for? Why didn't you tell 'em your part in it?"

"Wouldn't ha' done any good," said Mr. Smith; "wouldn't ha' done you any good. Besides, I did just wot the cap'n told me."

"When's he coming back?" inquired the steward.

Mr. Smith shook his head. "Couldn't say," he returned. "He couldn't say 'imself. Between you an' me, I expect 'e's gone up to have a reg'lar fair spree."

"Why did you tell me last night he was up-stairs?" inquired the other.

"Cap'n's orders," repeated Mr. Smith, with relish. "Ask 'im, not me. As a matter o' fact, he spent the night at my place and went off this morning."

"An' wot about the five pounds?" inquired Mr. Wilks, spitefully. "You ain't earned it."

"I know I ain't," said Mr. Smith, mournfully. "That's wot's worrying me. It's like a gnawing pain in my side. D'you think it's conscience biting of me? I never felt it before. Or d'ye think it's sorrow to think that I've done the whole job too cheap You think it out and let me know later on. So long."

He waved his hand cheerily to the steward and departed. Mr. Wilks threw himself into a chair and, ignoring the cold and the general air of desolation of his best room, gave way to a fit of melancholy which would have made Mr. Edward Silk green with envy.

CHAPTER XIII

Days passed, but no word came from the missing captain, and only the determined opposition of Kate Nugent kept her aunt from advertising in the "Agony" columns of the London Press. Miss Nugent was quite as desirous of secrecy in the affair as her father, and it was a source of great annoyance to her when, in some mysterious manner, it leaked out. In a very short time the news was common property, and Mr. Wilks, appearing to his neighbours in an entirely new character, was besieged for information.

His own friends were the most tiresome, their open admiration of his lawlessness and their readiness to trace other mysterious disappearances to his agency being particularly galling to a man whose respectability formed his most cherished possession. Other people regarded the affair as a joke, and he sat gazing round-eyed one evening at the Two Schooners at the insensible figures of three men who had each had a modest half-pint at his expense. It was a pretty conceit and well played, but the steward, owing to the frenzied efforts of one of the sleeper whom he had awakened with a quart pot, did not stay to admire it. He finished up the evening at the Chequers, and after getting wet through on the way home fell asleep in his wet clothes before the dying fire.

He awoke with a bad cold and pains in the limbs. A headache was not unexpected, but the other symptoms were. With trembling hands he managed to light a fire and prepare a breakfast, which he left untouched. This last symptom was the most alarming of all, and going to the door he bribed a small boy with a penny to go for Dr. Murchison, and sat cowering over the fire until he came.

"Well, you've got a bad cold," said the doctor, after examining him." You'd better get to bed for the present. You'll be safe there."

"Is it dangerous?" faltered the steward.

"And keep yourself warm," said the doctor, who was not in the habit of taking his patients into his confidence. "I'll send round some medicine."

"I should like Miss Nugent to know I'm bad," said Mr. Wilks, in a weak voice.

"She knows that," replied Murchison. "She was telling me about you the other day."

He put his hand up to his neat black moustache to hide a smile, and met the steward's indignant gaze without flinching.

"I mean ill," said the latter, sharply.

"Oh, yes," said the other. "Well, you get to bed now. Good morning."

He took up his hat and stick and departed. Mr. Wilks sat for a little while over the fire, and then, rising, hobbled slowly upstairs to bed and forgot his troubles in sleep.

He slept until the afternoon, and then, raising himself in bed, listened to the sounds of stealthy sweeping in the room below. Chairs were being moved about, and the tinkle of ornaments on the mantelpiece announced that dusting operations were in progress. He lay down again with a satisfied smile; it was like a tale in a story-book: the faithful old servant and his master's daughter. He closed his eyes as he heard her coming upstairs.

"Ah, pore dear," said a voice.

Mr. Wilks opened his eyes sharply and beheld the meagre figure of Mrs. Silk. In one hand she held a medicine-bottle and a glass and in the other paper and firewood.

"I only 'eard of it half an hour ago," she said, reproachfully. "I saw the doctor's boy, and I left my work and came over at once. Why didn't you let me know?"

Mr. Wilks muttered that he didn't know, and lay crossly regarding his attentive neighbour as she knelt down and daintily lit the fire. This task finished, she proceeded to make the room tidy, and then set about making beef-tea in a little saucepan.

"You lay still and get well," she remarked, with tender playfulness. "That's all you've got to do. Me and Teddy'll look after you."

"I couldn't think of troubling you," said the steward, earnestly.

"It's no trouble," was the reply. "You don't think I'd leave you here alone helpless, do you?"

"I was going to send for old Mrs. Jackson if I didn't get well to-day," said Mr. Wilks.

Mrs. Silk shook her head at him, and, after punching up his pillow, took an easy chair by the fire and sat there musing. Mr. Edward Silk came in to tea, and, after remarking that Mr. Wilks was very flushed and had got a nasty look about the eyes and a cough which he didn't like, fell to discoursing on death-beds.

"Good nursing is the principal thing," said his mother. "I nursed my pore dear 'usband all through his last illness. He couldn't bear me to be out of the room. I nursed my mother right up to the last, and your pore Aunt Jane went off in my arms."

Mr. Wilks raised himself on his elbow and his eyes shone feverishly in the lamplight. "I think I'll get a 'ospital nurse to-morrow," he said, decidedly.

"Nonsense," said Mrs. Silk. "It's no trouble to me at all. I like nursing; always did."

Mr. Wilks lay back again and, closing his eyes, determined to ask the doctor to provide a duly qualified nurse on the morrow. To his disappointment, however, the doctor failed to come, and although he felt much better Mrs. Silk sternly negatived a desire on his part to get up.

"Not till the doctor's been," she said, firmly. "I couldn't think of it."

"I don't believe there's anything the matter with me now," he declared.

"'Ow odd—'ow very odd that you should say that!" said Mrs. Silk, clasping her hands.

"Odd!" repeated the steward, somewhat crustily. "How do you mean—odd?"

"They was the very last words my Uncle Benjamin ever uttered in this life," said Mrs. Silk, with dramatic impressiveness.

The steward was silent, then, with the ominous precedent of Uncle Benjamin before him, he began to talk until scores of words stood between himself and a similar ending.

"Teddy asked to be remembered to you as 'e went off this morning," said Mrs. Silk, pausing in her labours at the grate.

"I'm much obliged," muttered the invalid.

"He didn't 'ave time to come in," pursued the widow. "You can 'ardly believe what a lot 'e thinks of you, Mr. Wilks. The last words he said to me was, 'Let me know at once if there's any change.'"

Mr. Wilks distinctly felt a cold, clammy sensation down his spine and little quivering thrills ran up and down his legs. He glared indignantly at the back of the industrious Mrs. Silk.

"Teddy's very fond of you," continued the unconscious woman. "I s'pose it's not 'aving a father, but he seems to me to think more of you than any-body else in the wide, wide world. I get quite jealous sometimes. Only the other day I said to 'im, joking like, 'Well, you'd better go and live with 'im if you're so fond of 'im,' I said."

"Ha, ha!" laughed Mr. Wilks, uneasily.

"You'll never guess what 'e said then," said Mrs. Silk dropping her dustpan and brush and gazing at the hearth.

"Said 'e couldn't leave you, I s'pose," guessed the steward, gruffly.

"Well, now," exclaimed Mrs. Silk, clapping her hands, "if you 'aven't nearly guessed it. Well, there! I never did! I wouldn't 'ave told you for anything if you 'adn't said that. The exact words what 'e did say was, 'Not without you, mother.'"

Mr. Wilks closed his eyes with a snap and his heart turned to water. He held his breath and ran-sacked his brain in vain for a reply which should ignore the inner meaning of the fatal words. Something careless and jocular he wanted, combined with a voice which should be perfectly under control. Failing these things, he kept his eyes closed, and, very wide-awake indeed, feigned sleep. He slept straight away from eleven o'clock in the morning until Edward Silk came in at seven o'clock in the evening.

"I feel like a new man," he said, rubbing his eyes and yawning.

"I don't see no change in your appearance," said the comforting youth.

"'E's much better," declared his mother. "That's what comes o' good nursing; some nurses would 'ave woke 'im up to take food, but I just let 'im sleep on. People don't feel hunger while they're asleep."

She busied herself over the preparation of a basin of arrowroot, and the steward, despite his distaste for this dish, devoured it in a twinkling. Beef-tea and a glass of milk in addition failed to take more than the edge off his appetite.

"We shall pull 'im through," said Mrs. Silk, smiling, as she put down the empty glass. "In a fortnight he'll be on 'is feet."

It is a matter of history that Mr. Wilks was on 'is feet at five o'clock the next morning, and not only on his feet but dressed and ready for a journey after such a breakfast as he had not made for many a day. The discourtesy involved in the disregard of the doctor's instructions did not trouble him, and he smirked with some satisfaction as he noiselessly closed his door behind him and looked at the drawn blinds opposite. The stars were paling as he quitted the alley and made his way to the railway station. A note on his tumbled pillow, after thanking Mrs. Silk for her care of him, informed her that he was quite well and had gone to London in search of the missing captain.

Hardy, who had heard from Edward Silk of the steward's indisposition and had been intending to pay him a visit, learnt of his departure later on in the morning, and, being ignorant of the particulars, discoursed somewhat eloquently to his partner on the old man's devotion.

"H'm, may be," said Swann, taking off his glasses and looking at him. "But you don't think Captain Nugent is in London, do you?"

"Why not?" inquired Hardy, somewhat startled. "If what Wilks told you is true, Nathan Smith knows," said the other. "I'll ask him."

"You don't expect to get the truth out of him, do you?" inquired Hardy, superciliously.

"I do," said his partner, serenely; "and when I've got it I shall go and tell them at Equator Lodge. It will be doing those two poor ladies a service to let them know what has really happened to the captain."

"I'll walk round to Nathan Smith's with you," said Hardy. "I should like to hear what the fellow has to say."

"No, I'll go alone," said his partner; "Smith's a very shy man—painfully shy. I've run across him once or twice before. He's almost as bashful and retiring as you are."

Hardy grunted. "If the captain isn't in London, where is he?" he inquired.

The other shook his head. "I've got an idea," he replied, "but I want to make sure. Kybird and Smith are old friends, as Nugent might have known, only he was always too high and mighty to take any interest in his inferiors. There's something for you to go on."

He bent over his desk again and worked steadily until one o'clock—his hour for lunching. Then he put on his hat and coat, and after a comfortable meal sallied out in search of Mr. Smith.

The boarding-house, an old and dilapidated building, was in a bystreet convenient to the harbour. The front door stood open, and a couple of seamen lounging on the broken steps made way for him civilly as he entered and rapped on the bare boards with his stick. Mr. Smith, clattering down the stairs in response, had some difficulty in concealing his surprise at the visit, but entered genially into a conversation about the weather, a subject in which he was much interested. When the ship-broker began to discuss the object of his visit he led him to a small sitting-room at the back of the house and repeated the information he had given to Mr. Wilks.

"That's all there is to tell," he concluded, artlessly; "the cap'n was that ashamed of hisself, he's laying low for a bit. We all make mistakes sometimes; I do myself."

"I am much obliged to you," said Mr. Swann, gratefully.

"You're quite welcome, sir," said the boarding-master.

"And now," said the visitor, musingly—"now for the police."

"Police!" repeated Mr. Smith, almost hastily. "What for?"

"Why, to find the captain," said Mr. Swann, in a surprised voice.

Mr. Smith shook his head. "You'll offend the cap'n bitter if you go to the police about 'im, sir," he declared. "His last words to me was, 'Smith, 'ave this kept quiet.'"

"It'll be a little job for the police," urged the shipbroker. "They don't have much to do down here; they'll be as pleased as possible."

"They'll worry your life out of you, sir," said the other. "You don't know what they are."

"I like a little excitement," returned Mr. Swann. "I don't suppose they'll trouble me much, but they'll turn your place topsy-turvy, I expect. Still, that can't be helped. You know what fools the police are; they'll think you've murdered the captain and hidden his body under the boards. They'll have all the floors up. Ha, ha, ha!"

"'Aving floors up don't seem to me to be so amusing as wot it does to you," remarked Mr. Smith, coldly.

"They may find all sorts of treasure for you," continued his visitor. "It's a very old house, Smith, and there may be bags of guineas hidden away under the flooring. You may be able to retire."

"You're a gentleman as is fond of his joke, Mr. Swann," returned the boarding-master, lugubriously. "I wish I'd got that 'appy way of looking at things you 'ave."

"I'm not joking, Smith," said the other, quietly.

Mr. Smith pondered and, stealing a side-glance at him, stood scraping his foot along the floor.

"There ain't nothing much to tell," he grumbled, "and, mind, the worst favour you could do to the cap'n would be to put it about how he was done. He's gone for a little trip instead of 'is son, that's all."

"Little trip!" repeated the other; "you call a whaling cruise a little trip?"

"No, no, sir," said Mr. Smith, in a shocked voice, "I ain't so bad as that; I've got some 'art, I hope. He's just gone for a little trip with 'is old pal Hardy on the *Conqueror*. Kybird's idea it was."

"Don't you know it's punishable?" demanded the shipbroker, recovering.

Mr. Smith shook his head and became serious. "The cap'n fell into 'is own trap," he said, slowly. "There's no lor for 'im! He'd only get laughed at. The idea of trying to get me to put little Amelia Kybird's young man away. Why, I was 'er god-father."

Mr. Swann stared at him, and then with a friendly "good morning" departed. Half-way along the passage he stopped, and retracing his steps produced his cigar-case and offered the astonished boarding-master a cigar.

"I s'pose," said that gentleman as he watched the other's retreating figure and dubiously smelt the cigar; "I s'pose it's all right; but he's a larky sort, and I 'ave heard of 'em exploding. I'll give it to Kybird, in case."

To Mr. Smith's great surprise his visitor sat down suddenly and began to laugh. Tears of honest mirth suffused his eyes and dimmed his glasses. Mr. Smith, regarding him with an air of kindly interest, began to laugh to keep him company.

CHAPTER XIV

Captain Nugent awoke the morning after his attempt to crimp his son with a bad headache. Not an ordinary headache, to disappear with a little cold water and fresh air; but a splitting, racking affair, which made him feel all head and dulness. Weights pressed upon his eye-lids and the back of his head seemed glued to his pillow.

He groaned faintly and, raising himself upon his elbow, opened his eyes and sat up with a sharp exclamation. His bed was higher from the floor than usual and, moreover, the floor was different. In the dim light he distinctly saw a ship's forecastle, untidy bunks with frouzy bedclothes, and shiny oil-skins hanging from the bulkhead.

For a few moments he stared about in mystification; he was certainly ill, and no doubt the forecastle was an hallucination. It was a strange symptom, and the odd part of it was that everything was so distinct. Even the smell. He stared harder, in the hope that his surroundings would give place to the usual ones, and, leaning a little bit more on his elbow, nearly rolled out of the bunk. Resolved to probe this mystery to the bottom he lowered himself to the floor and felt distinctly the motion of a ship at sea.

There was no doubt about it. He staggered to the door and, holding by the side, looked on to the deck. The steamer was rolling in a fresh sea and a sweet strong wind blew refreshingly into his face. Funnels, bridge, and masts swung with a rhythmical motion; loose gear rattled, and every now and then a distant tinkle sounded faintly from the steward's pantry.

He stood bewildered, trying to piece together the events of the preceding night, and to try and understand by what miracle he was back on board his old ship the *Conqueror*. There was no doubt as to her identity. He knew every inch of her, and any further confirmation that might be required was fully supplied by the appearance of the long, lean figure of Captain Hardy on the bridge.

Captain Nugent took his breath sharply and began to realize the situation. He stepped to the side and looked over; the harbour was only a little way astern, and Sunwich itself, looking cold and cheerless beyond the dirty, tumbling seas, little more than a mile distant.

At the sight his spirits revived, and with a hoarse cry he ran shouting towards the bridge. Captain Hardy turned sharply at the noise, and recognizing the intruder stood peering down at him in undisguised amazement.

"Put back," cried Nugent, waving up at him. "Put back."

"What on earth are you doing on my ship?" inquired the astonished Hardy.

"Put me ashore," cried Nugent, imperiously; "don't waste time talking. D'ye hear? Put me ashore."

The amazement died out of Hardy's face and gave way to an expression of anger. For a time he regarded the red and threatening visage of Captain Nugent in silence, then he turned to the second officer.

"This man is not one of the crew, Mr. Prowle?" he said, in a puzzled voice.

"No, sir," said Mr. Prowle.

"How did he get aboard here?"

Captain Nugent answered the question himself. "I was crimped by you and your drunken bullies," he said, sternly.

"How did this man get aboard here? repeated Captain Hardy, ignoring him.

"He must have concealed 'imself somewhere, sir," said the mate; "this is the first I've seen of him."

"A stowaway?" said the captain, bending his brows. "He must have got some of the crew to hide him aboard. You'd better make a clean breast of it, my lad. Who are your confederates?"

Captain Nugent shook with fury. The second mate had turned away, with his hand over his mouth and a suspicious hunching of his shoulders, while the steward, who had been standing by, beat a hasty retreat and collapsed behind the chart-room.

"If you don't put me ashore," said Nugent, restraining his passion by a strong effort, "I'll take proceedings against you for crimping me, the moment I reach port. Get a boat out and put me aboard that smack."

He pointed as he spoke to a smack which was just on their beam, making slowly for the harbour.

"When you've done issuing orders," said the captain, in an indifferent voice, "perhaps you'll explain what you are doing aboard my crag."

Captain Nugent gazed at the stern of the fast-receding smack; Sunwich was getting dim in the distance and there was no other sail near. He began to realize that he was in for a long voyage.

"I awoke this morning and found myself in a bunk in vow fo'c's'le," he said, regarding Hardy steadily. "However I got there is probably best known to yourself. I hold you responsible for the affair."

"Look here my lad," said Captain Hardy, in patronizing tones, "I don't know how you got aboard my ship and I don't care. I am willing to believe that it was not intentional on your part, but either the outcome of a drunken freak or else a means of escaping from some scrape you have got into ashore. That being so, I shall take a merciful view of it, and if you behave yourself and make yourself useful you will not hear anything more of it. He has something the look of a seafaring man, Mr. Prowle. See what you can make of him."

"Come along with me, my lad," said the grinning Mr. Prowle, tapping him on the shoulder.

The captain turned with a snarl, and, clenching his huge, horny fist, let drive full in the other's face and knocked him off his feet.

"Take that man for'ard," cried Captain Hardy, sharply. "Take him for'ard."

Half-a-dozen willing men sprang forward. Captain Nugent's views concerning sailormen were well known in Sunwich, and two of the men present had served under him. He went forward, the centre of an attentive and rotating circle, and, sadly out of breath, was bestowed in the forecastle and urged to listen to reason.

For the remainder of the morning he made no sign. The land was almost out of sight, and he sat down quietly to consider his course of action for the next few weeks. Dinner-time found him still engrossed in thought, and the way in which he received an intimation from a good-natured seaman that his dinner was getting cold showed that his spirits were still unquelled.

By the time afternoon came he was faint with hunger, and, having determined upon his course of action, he sent a fairly polite message to Captain Hardy and asked for an interview.

The captain, who was resting from his labours in the chart-room, received him with the same air of cold severity which had so endeared Captain Nugent himself to his subordinates.

"You have come to explain your extraordinary behaviour of this morning, I suppose?" he said, curtly.

"I have come to secure a berth aft," said Captain Nugent. "I will pay a small deposit now, and you will, of course, have the balance as soon as we get back. This is without prejudice to any action I may bring against you later on."

"Oh, indeed," said the other, raising his eyebrows. "We don't take passengers."

"I am here against my will," said Captain Nu-gent, "and I demand the treatment due to my position."

"If I had treated you properly," said Captain Hardy, "I should have put you in irons for knocking down my second officer. I know nothing about you or your position. You're a stowaway, and you must do the best you can in the circumstances."

"Are you going to give me a cabin?" demanded the other, menacingly.

"Certainly not," said Captain Hardy. "I have been making inquiries, and I find that you have only yourself to thank for the position in which you find yourself. I am sorry to be harsh with you."

"Harsh?" repeated the other, hardly able to believe his ears. "You— harsh to me?"

"But it is for your own good," pursued Captain Hardy; "it is no pleasure to me to punish you. I shall keep an eye on you while you're aboard, and if I see that your conduct is improving you will find that I am not a hard man to get on with."

Captain Nugent stared at him with his lips parted. Three times he essayed to speak and failed; then he turned sharply and, gaining the open air, stood for some time trying to regain his composure before going forward again. The first mate, who was on the bridge, regarded him curiously, and then, with an insufferable air of authority, ordered him away.

The captain obeyed mechanically and, turning a deaf ear to the inquiries of the men, prepared to make the best of an intolerable situation, and began to cleanse his bunk. First of all he took out the bedding and shook it thoroughly, and then, pro-curing soap and a bucket of water, began to scrub with a will. Hostile comments followed the action.

"We ain't clean enough for 'im," said one voice.

"Partikler old party, ain't he, Bill?" said another.

"You leave 'im alone," said the man addressed, surveying the captain's efforts with a smile of approval. "You keep on, Nugent, don't you mind 'im. There's a little bit there you ain't done."

"Keep your head out of the way, unless you want it knocked off," said the incensed captain.

"Ho!" said the aggrieved Bill. "Ho, indeed! D'ye 'ear that, mates? A man musn't look at 'is own bunk now."

The captain turned as though he had been stung. "This is my bunk," he said, sharply.

"Ho, is it?" said Bill. "Beggin' of your pardon, an' apologizing for a-contradictin' of you, but it's mine. You haven't got no bunk."

"I slept in it last night," said the captain, conclusively.

"I know you did," said Bill, "but that was all my kind-'artedness."

"And 'arf a quid, Bill," a voice reminded him.

"And 'arf a quid," assented Bill, graciously, "and I'm very much obliged to you, mate, for the careful and tidy way in which you've cleaned up arter your-self."

The captain eyed him. Many years of command at sea had given him a fine manner, and force of habit was for a moment almost too much for Bill and his friends. But only for a moment.

"I'm going to keep this bunk," said the captain, deliberately.

"No, you ain't, mate," said Bill, shaking his head, "don't you believe it. You're nobody down here; not even a ordinary seaman. I'm afraid you'll 'ave to clean a place for yourself on the carpet. There's a nice corner over there."

"When I get back," said the furious captain, "some of you will go to gaol for last night's work."

"Don't be hard on us," said a mocking voice, "we did our best. It ain't our fault that you look so ridikerlously young, that we took you for your own son."

"And you was in that state that you couldn't contradict us," said another man.

"If it is your bunk," said the captain, sternly, "I suppose you have a right to it. But perhaps you'll sell it to me? How much?"

"Now you're talking bisness," said the highly gratified Bill, turning with a threatening gesture upon a speculator opposite. "Wot do you say to a couple o' pounds?"

The captain nodded.

"Couple o' pounds, money down," said Bill, holding out his hand.

The captain examined the contents of his pocket, and after considerable friction bought the bunk for a pound cash and an I O U for the balance.

A more humane man would have shown a little concern as to his benefactor's sleeping-place; but the captain never gave the matter a thought. In fact, it was not until three days later that he discovered there was a spare bunk in the forecastle, and that the unscrupulous seaman was occupying it.

It was only one of many annoyances, but the captain realizing his impotence made no sign. From certain remarks let fall in his hearing he had no difficulty in connecting Mr. Kybird with his discomfiture and, of his own desire, he freely included the unfortunate Mr. Wilks.

He passed his time in devising schemes of vengeance, and when Captain Hardy, relenting, offered him a cabin aft, he sent back such a message of refusal that the steward spent half an hour preparing a paraphrase. The offer was not repeated, and the captain, despite the strong representations of Bill and his friends, continued to eat the bread of idleness before the mast.

CHAPTER XV

Mr. Adolphus Swann spent a very agreeable afternoon after his interview with Nathan Smith in refusing to satisfy what he termed the idle curiosity of his partner. The secret of Captain Nugent's whereabouts, he declared, was not to be told to everybody, but was to be confided by a man of insinuating address and appearance—here he looked at himself in a hand-glass—to Miss Nugent. To be broken to her by a man with no ulterior motives for his visit; a man in the prime of life, but not too old for a little tender sympathy.

"I had hoped to have gone this afternoon," he said, with a glance at the clock; "but I'm afraid I can't get away. Have you got much to do, Hardy?"

"No," said his partner, briskly. "I've finished."

"Then perhaps you wouldn't mind doing my work for me, so that I can go?" said Mr. Swann, mildly.

Hardy played with his pen. The senior partner had been amusing himself at his expense for some time, and in the hope of a favour at his hands he had endured it with unusual patience.

"Four o'clock," murmured the senior partner; "hadn't you better see about making yourself presentable, Hardy?"

"Thanks," said the other, with alacrity, as he took off his coat and crossed over to the little washstand. In five minutes he had finished his toilet and, giving his partner a little friendly pat on the shoulder, locked up his desk.

"Well?" he said, at last.

"Well?" repeated Mr. Swann, with a little surprise.

"What am I to tell them?" inquired Hardy, struggling to keep his temper.

"Tell them?" repeated the innocent Swann. "Lor' bless my soul, how you do jump at conclusions, Hardy. I only asked you to tidy yourself for my sake. I have an artistic eye. I thought you had done it to please me."

"When you're tired of this nonsense," said the indignant Hardy, "I shall be glad."

Mr. Swann looked him over carefully and, coming to the conclusion that his patience was exhausted, told him the result of his inquiries. His immediate reward was the utter incredulity of Mr. Hardy, together with some pungent criticisms of his veracity. When the young man did realize at last that he was speaking the truth he fell to wondering blankly what was happening aboard the *Conqueror*.

"Never mind about that," said the older man. "For a few weeks you have got a clear field. It is quite a bond between you: both your fathers on the same ship. But whatever you do, don't remind her of the fate of the Kilkenny cats. Draw a fancy picture of the two fathers sitting with their arms about each other's waists and wondering whether their children——"

Hardy left hurriedly, in fear that his indignation at such frivolity should overcome his gratitude, and he regretted as he walked briskly along that the diffidence peculiar to young men in his circumstances had prevented him from acquainting his father with the state of his feelings towards Kate Nugent.

The idea of taking advantage of the captain's enforced absence had occurred to other people besides Mr. James Hardy. Dr. Murchison, who had found the captain, despite his bias in his favour, a particularly tiresome third, was taking the fullest advantage of it; and Mrs. Kybird had also judged it an admirable opportunity for paying a first call. Mr. Kybird, who had not taken her into his confidence in the affair, protested in vain; the lady was determined, and, moreover, had the warm support of her daughter.

"I know what I'm doing, Dan'l," she said to her husband.

Mr. Kybird doubted it, but held his peace; and the objections of Jack Nugent, who found to his dismay that he was to be of the party, were deemed too trivial to be worthy of serious consideration.

They started shortly after Jem Hardy had left his office, despite the fact that Mrs. Kybird, who was troubled with asthma, was suffering untold agonies in a black satin dress which had been originally made for a much smaller woman, and had come into her husband's hands in the way of business. It got into hers in what the defrauded Mr. Kybird considered an extremely unbusinesslike manner, and it was not without a certain amount of satisfaction that he regarded her discomfiture as the party sallied out.

Mr. Nugent was not happy. Mrs. Kybird in the snug seclusion of the back parlour was one thing; Mrs. Kybird in black satin at its utmost tension and a circular hat set with sable ostrich plumes nodding in the breeze was another. He felt that the public eye was upon them and that it twinkled. His gaze wandered from mother to daughter.

"What are you staring at?" demanded Miss Kybird, pertly.

"I was thinking how well you are looking," was the reply.

Miss Kybird smiled. She had hoisted some daring colours, but she was of a bold type and carried them fairly well.

"If I 'ad the woman what made this dress 'ere," gasped Mrs. Kybird, as she stopped with her hand on her side, "I'd give her a bit o' my mind."

"I never saw you look so well in anything before, ma," said her daughter.

Mrs. Kybird smiled faintly and continued her pilgrimage. Jem Hardy coming up rapidly behind composed his amused features and stepped into the road to pass.

"Halloa, Hardy," said Nugent. "Going home?"

"I am calling on your sister," said Hardy, bowing.

"By Jove, so are we," said Nugent, relieved to find this friend in need. "We'll go together. You know Mrs. Kybird and Miss Kybird? That is Mrs. Kybird."

Mrs. Kybird bade him "Go along, do," and acknowledged the introduction with as stately a bow as the black satin would permit, and before the dazed Jem quite knew how it all happened he was leading the way with Mrs. Kybird, while the young people, as she called them, followed behind.

"We ain't looking at you," she said, playfully, over her shoulder.

"And we're trying to shut our eyes to your goings on," retorted Nugent.

Mrs. Kybird stopped and, with a half-turn, play-fully reached for him with her umbrella. The exertion and the joke combined took the remnant of her breath away, and she stood still, panting.

"You had better take Hardy's arm, I think," said Nugent, with affected solicitude.

"It's my breath," explained Mrs. Kybird, turning to the fuming young man by her side. "I can 'ardly get along for it—I'm much obliged to you, I'm sure."

Mr. Hardy, with a vain attempt to catch Jack Nugent's eye, resigned himself to his fate, and with his fair burden on his arm walked with painful slowness towards Equator Lodge. A ribald voice from the other side of the road, addressing his companion as "Mother Kybird," told her not to hug the man, and a small boy whom they met loudly asseverated his firm intention of going straight off to tell Mr. Kybird.

By the time they reached the house Mr. Hardy entertained views on homicide which would have appeared impossible to him half an hour before. He flushed crimson as he saw the astonished face of Kate Nugent at the window, and, pausing at the gate to wait for the others, discovered that they had disappeared. A rooted dislike to scenes of any kind, together with a keen eye for the ludicrous, had prompted Jack Nugent to suggest a pleasant stroll to Amelia and put in an appearance later on.

"We won't wait for 'im," said Mrs. Kybird, with decision; "if I don't get a sit down soon I shall drop."

Still clinging to the reluctant Hardy she walked up the path; farther back in the darkness of the room the unfortunate young gentleman saw the faces of Dr. Murchison and Mrs. Kingdom.

"And 'ow are you, Bella?" inquired Mrs. Kybird with kindly condescension. "Is Mrs. Kingdom at 'ome?"

She pushed her way past the astonished Bella and, followed by Mr. Hardy, entered the room. Mrs. Kingdom, with a red spot on each cheek, rose to receive them.

"I ought to 'ave come before," said Mrs. Kybird, subsiding thankfully into a chair, "but I'm such a bad walker. I 'ope I see you well."

"We are very well, thank you," said Mrs. Kingdom, stiffly.

"That's right," said her visitor, cordially; "what a blessing 'ealth is. What should we do without it, I wonder?"

She leaned back in her chair and shook her head at the prospect. There was an awkward lull, and in the offended gaze of Miss Nugent Mr. Hardy saw only too plainly that he was held responsible for the appearance of the unwelcome visitor.

"I was coming to see you," he said, leaving his chair and taking one near her, "I met your brother coming along, and he introduced me to Mrs. Kybird and her daughter and suggested we should come together."

Miss Nugent received the information with a civil bow, and renewed her conversation with Dr. Murchison, whose face showed such a keen appreciation of the situation that Hardy had some difficulty in masking his feelings.

"They're a long time a-coming," said Mrs. Kybird, smiling archly; "but there, when young people are keeping company they forget everything and everybody. They didn't trouble about me; if it 'adn't been for Mr. 'Ardy giving me 'is arm I should never 'ave got here."

There was a prolonged silence. Dr. Murchison gave a whimsical glance at Miss Nugent, and meeting no response in that lady's indignant eyes, stroked his moustache and awaited events.

"It looks as though your brother is not coming," said Hardy to Miss Nugent.

"He'll turn up by-and-by," interposed Mrs. Kybird, looking somewhat morosely at the company. "They don't notice 'ow the time flies, that's all."

"Time does go," murmured Mrs. Kingdom, with a glance at the clock.

Mrs. Kybird started. "Ah, and we notice it too, ma'am, at our age," she said, sweetly, as she settled herself in her chair and clasped her hands in her lap "I can't 'elp looking at you, my dear," she continued, looking over at Miss Nugent. "There's such a wonderful likeness between Jack and you. Don't you think so, ma'am?"

Mrs. Kingdom in a freezing voice said that she had not noticed it.

"Of course," said Mrs. Kybird, glancing at her from the corner of her eye, "Jack has 'ad to rough it, pore feller, and that's left its mark on 'im. I'm sure, when we took 'im in, he was quite done up, so to speak. He'd only got what 'e stood up in, and the only pair of socks he'd got to his feet was in such a state of 'oles that they had to be throwed away. I throwed 'em away myself."

"Dear me," said Mrs. Kingdom.

"He don't look like the same feller now," continued the amiable Mrs. Kybird; "good living and good clothes 'ave worked wonders in 'im. I'm sure if he'd been my own son I couldn't 'ave done more for 'im, and, as for Kybird, he's like a father to him."

"Dear me," said Mrs. Kingdom, again.

Mrs. Kybird looked at her. It was on the tip of her tongue to call her a poll parrot. She was a free-spoken woman as a rule, and it was terrible to have to sit still and waste all the good things she could have said to her in favour of unsatisfying pin-pricks. She sat smouldering.

"I s'pose you miss the capt'in very much?" she said, at last.

"Very much," was the reply.

"And I should think 'e misses you," retorted Mrs. Kybird, unable to restrain herself; "'e must miss your conversation and what I might call your liveliness."

Mrs. Kingdom turned and regarded her, and the red stole back to her cheeks again. She smoothed down her dress and her hands trembled. Both ladies were now regarding each other in a fashion which caused serious apprehension to the rest of the company.

"I am not a great talker, but I am very careful whom I converse with," said Mrs. Kingdom, in her most stately manner.

"I knew a lady like that once," said Mrs. Kybird; "leastways, she wasn't a lady," she added, meditatively.

Mrs. Kingdom fidgeted, and looked over piteously at her niece; Mrs. Kybird, with a satisfied sniff, sat bolt upright and meditated further assaults. There were at least a score of things she could have said about her adversary's cap alone: plain, straightforward remarks which would have torn it to shreds. The cap fascinated her, and her fingers itched as she gazed at it. In more congenial surroundings she might have snatched at it, but, being a woman of strong character, she suppressed her natural instincts, and confined herself to more polite methods of attack.

"Your nephew don't seem to be in no hurry," she remarked, at length; "but, there, direckly 'e gets along o' my daughter 'e forgits everything and everybody."

"I really don't think he is coming," said Hardy, moved to speech by the glances of Miss Nugent.

"I shall give him a little longer," said Mrs. Kybird. "I only came 'ere to please 'im, and to get 'ome alone is more than I can do."

Miss Nugent looked at Mr. Hardy, and her eyes were soft and expressive. As plainly as eyes could speak they asked him to take Mrs. Kybird home, lest worse things should happen.

"Would it be far out of your way?" she asked, in a low voice.

"Quite the opposite direction," returned Mr. Hardy, firmly.

"How I got 'ere I don't know," said Mrs. Kybird, addressing the room in general; "it's a wonder to me. Well, once is enough in a lifetime."

"Mr. Hardy," said Kate Nugent, again, in a low voice, "I should be so much obliged if you would take Mrs. Kybird away. She seems bent on quarrelling with my aunt. It is very awkward."

It was difficult to resist the entreaty, but Mr. Hardy had a very fair idea of the duration of Miss Nugent's gratitude; and, besides that, Murchison was only too plainly enjoying his discomfiture.

"She can get home alone all right," he whispered.

Miss Nugent drew herself up disdainfully; Dr. Murchison, looking scandalized at his brusqueness, hastened to the rescue.

"As a medical man," he said, with a considerable appearance of gravity, "I don't think that Mrs. Kybird ought to go home alone."

"Think not?" inquired Hardy, grimly.

"Certain of it," breathed the doctor.

"Well, why don't you take her?" retorted Hardy; "it's all on your way. I have some news for Miss Nugent."

Miss Nugent looked from one to the other, and mischievous lights appeared in her eyes as she gazed at the carefully groomed and fastidious Murchison. From them she looked to the other side of the room, where Mrs. Kybird was stolidly eyeing Mrs. Kingdom, who was trying in vain to appear ignorant of the fact.

"Thank you very much," said Miss Nugent, turning to the doctor.

"I'm sorry," began Murchison, with an indignant glance at his rival.

"Oh, as you please," said the girl, coldly. "Pray forgive me for asking you."

"If you really wish it," said the doctor, rising. Miss Nugent smiled upon him, and Hardy also gave him a smile of kindly encouragement, but this he ignored. He crossed the room and bade Mrs. Kingdom good-bye; and then in a few disjointed words asked Mrs. Kybird whether he could be of any assistance in seeing her home.

"I'm sure I'm much obliged to you," said that lady, as she rose. "It don't seem much use for me waiting for my future son-in-law. I wish you good afternoon, ma'am. I can understand now why Jack didn't come."

With this parting shot she quitted the room and, leaning on the doctor's arm, sailed majestically down the path to the gate, every feather on her hat trembling in response to the excitement below.

"Good-natured of him," said Hardy, glancing from the window, with a triumphant smile.

"Very," said Miss Nugent, coldly, as she took a seat by her aunt. "What is the news to which you referred just now? Is it about my father?"

CHAPTER XVI

The two ladies received Mr. Hardy's information with something akin to consternation, the idea of the autocrat of Equator Lodge as a stowaway on board the ship of his ancient enemy proving too serious for ordinary comment. Mrs. Kingdom's usual expressions of surprise, "Well, I never did!" and "Good gracious alive!" died on her lips, and she sat gazing helpless and round-eyed at her niece.

"I wonder what he said," she gasped, at last.

Miss Nugent, who was trying to imagine her father in his new role aboard the Conqueror, paid no heed. It was not a pleasant idea, and her eyes flashed with temper as she thought of it. Sooner or later the whole affair would be public property.

"I had an idea all along that he wasn't in London," murmured Mrs. Kingdom. "Fancy that Nathan Smith standing in Sam's room telling us falsehoods like that! He never even blushed."

"But you said that you kept picturing father walking about the streets of London, wrestling with his pride and trying to make up his mind to come home again," said her niece, maliciously.

Mrs. Kingdom fidgeted, but before she could think of a satisfactory reply Bella came to the door and asked to speak to her for a moment. Profiting by her absence, Mr. Hardy leaned towards Miss Nugent, and in a low voice expressed his sorrow at the mishap to her father and his firm conviction that everything that could be thought of for that unfortunate mariner's comfort would be done. "Our fathers will probably come back good friends," he concluded. "There is nothing would give me more pleasure than that, and I think that we had better begin and set them a good example."

"It is no good setting an example to people who are hundreds of miles away," said the matter-of-fact Miss Nugent. "Besides, if they have made friends, they don't want an example set them."

"But in that case they have set us an example which we ought to follow," urged Hardy.

Miss Nugent raised her eyes to his. "Why do you wish to be on friendly terms?" she asked, with disconcerting composure.

"I should like to know your father," returned Hardy, with perfect gravity; "and Mrs. Kingdom—and you."

He eyed her steadily as he spoke, and Miss Nugent, despite her utmost efforts, realized with some indignation that a faint tinge of colour was creeping into her cheeks. She remembered his covert challenge at their last interview at Mr. Wilks's, and the necessity of reading this persistent young man a stern lesson came to her with all the force of a public duty.

"Why?" she inquired, softly, as she lowered her eyes and assumed a pensive expression.

"I admire him, for one thing, as a fine seaman," said Hardy.

"Yes," said Miss Nugent, "and—"

"And I've always had a great liking for Mrs. Kingdom," he continued; "she was very good-natured to me when I was a very small boy, I remember. She is very kind and amiable."

The baffled Miss Nugent stole a glance at him. "And—" she said again, very softly.

"And very motherly," said Hardy, without moving a muscle.

Miss Nugent pondered and stole another glance at him. The expression of his face was ingenuous, not to say simple. She resolved to risk it. So far he had always won in their brief encounters, and monotony was always distasteful to her, especially monotony of that kind.

"And what about me?" she said, with a friendly smile.

"You," said Hardy, with a gravity of voice belied by the amusement in his eye; "you are the daughter of the fine seaman and the niece of the good-natured and motherly Mrs. Kingdom."

Miss Nugent looked down again hastily, and all the shrew within her clamoured for vengeance. It was the same masterful Jem Hardy that had forced his way into their seat at church as a boy. If he went on in this way he would become unbearable; she resolved, at the cost of much personal inconvenience, to give him a much-needed fall. But she realized quite clearly that it would be a matter of time.

"Of course, you and Jack are already good friends?" she said, softly.

"Very," assented Hardy. "Such good friends that I have been devoting a lot of time lately to considering ways and means of getting him out of the snares of the Kybirds."

"I should have thought that that was his affair," said Miss Nugent, haughtily.

"Mine, too," said Hardy. "I don't want him to marry Miss Kybird."

For the first time since the engagement Miss Nugent almost approved of it. "Why not let him know your wishes?" she said, gently. "Surely that would be sufficient."

"But you don't want them to marry?" said Hardy, ignoring the remark.

"I don't want my brother to do anything shabby," replied the girl; "but I shouldn't be sorry, of course, if they did not."

"Very good," said Hardy. "Armed with your consent I shall leave no stone unturned. Nugent was let in for this, and I am going to get him out if I can. All's fair in love and war. You don't mind my doing anything shabby?"

"Not in the least," replied Miss Nugent, promptly.

The reappearance of Mrs. Kingdom at this moment saved Mr. Hardy the necessity of a reply.

Conversation reverted to the missing captain, and Hardy and Mrs. Kingdom together drew such a picture of the two captains fraternizing that Miss Nugent felt that the millennium itself could have no surprises for her.

"He has improved very much," said Mrs. Kingdom, after the door had closed behind their visitor; "so thoughtful."

"He's thoughtful enough," agreed her niece.

"He is what I call extremely considerate," pursued the elder lady, "but I'm afraid he is weak; anybody could turn him round their little finger."

"I believe they could," said Miss Nugent, gazing at her with admiration, "if he wanted to be turned."

The ice thus broken, Mr. Hardy spent the following day or two in devising plausible reasons for another visit. He found one in the person of Mr. Wilks, who, having been unsuccessful in finding his beloved master at a small tavern down by the London docks, had returned to Sunwich, by no means benefited by his change of air, to learn the terrible truth as to his disappearance from Hardy.

"I wish they'd Shanghaid me instead," he said to that sympathetic listener, "or Mrs. Silk."

"Eh?" said the other, staring.

"Wot'll be the end of it I don't know," said Mr. Wilks, laying a hand, which still trembled, on the other' knee. "It's got about that she saved my life by 'er careful nussing, and the way she shakes 'er 'ead at me for risking my valuable life, as she calls it, going up to London, gives me the shivers."

"Nonsense," said Hardy; "she can't marry you against your will. Just be distantly civil to her."

"'Ow can you be distantly civil when she lives just opposite?" inquired the steward, querulously. "She sent Teddy over at ten o'clock last night to rub my chest with a bottle o' liniment, and it's no good me saying I'm all right when she's been spending eighteen-pence o' good money over the stuff."

"She can't marry you unless you ask her," said the comforter.

Mr. Wilks shook his head. "People in the alley are beginning to talk," he said, dolefully. "Just as I came in this afternoon old George Lee screwed up one eye at two or three women wot was gossiping near, and when I asked 'im wot 'e'd got to wink about he said that a bit o' wedding-cake 'ad blowed in his eye as I passed. It sent them silly creeturs into fits a'most."

"They'll soon get tired of it," said Hardy.

Mr. Wilks, still gloomy, ventured to doubt it, but cheered up and became almost bright when his visitor announced his intention of trying to smooth over matters for him at Equator Lodge. He became quite voluble in his defence, and attached much importance to the fact that he had nursed Miss Nugent when she was in long clothes and had taught her to whistle like an angel at the age of five.

"I've felt being cut adrift by her more than anything," he said, brokenly. "Nine-an'-twenty years I sailed with the cap'n and served 'im faithful, and this is my reward."

Hardy pleaded his case next day. Miss Nugent was alone when he called, and, moved by the vivid picture he drew of the old man's loneliness, accorded her full forgiveness, and decided to pay him a visit at once. The fact that Hardy had not been in the house five minutes she appeared to have overlooked.

"I'll go upstairs and put my hat and jacket on and go now," she said, brightly.

"That's very kind of you," said Hardy. His voice expressed admiring gratitude; but he made no sign of leaving his seat.

"You don't mind?" said Miss Nugent, pausing in front of him and slightly extending her hand.

"Not in the least," was the reply; "but I want to see Wilks myself. Perhaps you'll let me walk down with you?"

The request was so unexpected that the girl had no refusal ready. She hesitated and was lost. Finally, she expressed a fear that she might keep him waiting too long while she got ready—a fear which he politely declined to consider.

"Well, we'll see," said the marvelling Miss Nugent to herself as she went slowly upstairs. "He's got impudence enough for forty."

She commenced her preparations for seeing Mr. Wilks by wrapping a shawl round her shoulders and reclining in an easy-chair with a novel. It was a good story, but the room was very cold, and even the pleasure of snubbing an intrusive young man did not make amends for the lack of warmth. She read and shivered for an hour, and then with chilled fingers lit the gas and proceeded to array herself for the journey.

Her temper was not improved by seeing Mr. Hardy sitting in the dark over a good fire when she got downstairs.

"I'm afraid I've kept you waiting," she said, crisply.

"Not at all," said Hardy. "I've been very comfortable."

Miss Nugent repressed a shiver and, crossing to the fire, thoughtlessly extended her fingers over the blaze.

"I'm afraid you're cold," said Hardy.

The girl looked round sharply. His face, or as much of it as she could see in the firelight, bore a look of honest concern somewhat at variance with the quality of his voice. If it had not been for the absurdity of altering her plans on his account she would have postponed her visit to the steward until another day.

The walk to Fullalove Alley was all too short for Jem Hardy. Miss Nugent stepped along with the air of a martyr anxious to get to the stake and have it over, and she answered in monosyllables when her companion pointed out the beauties of the night.

A bitter east wind blew up the road and set her yearning for the joys of Mr. Wilks's best room. "It's very cold," she said, shivering.

Hardy assented, and reluctantly quickened his pace to keep step with hers. Miss Nugent with her chin sunk in a fur boa looked neither to the right nor the left, and turning briskly into the alley, turned the handle of Mr. Wilks's door and walked in, leaving her companion to follow.

The steward, who was smoking a long pipe over the fire, looked round in alarm. Then his expression changed, and he rose and stammered out a welcome. Two minutes later Miss Nugent, enthroned in the best chair with her toes on the fender, gave her faithful subject a free pardon and full permission to make hot coffee.

"And don't you ever try and deceive me again, Sam," she said, as she sipped the comforting beverage.

"No, miss," said the steward, humbly. "I've 'ad a lesson. I'll never try and Shanghai anybody else agin as long as I live."

After this virtuous sentiment he sat and smoked placidly, with occasional curious glances divided between his two visitors. An idle and ridiculous idea, which occurred to him in connection with them, was dismissed at once as too preposterous for a sensible steward to entertain.

"Mrs. Kingdom well?" he inquired.

"Quite well," said the girl. "If you take me home, Sam, you shall see her, and be forgiven by her, too."

"Thankee, miss," said the gratified steward.

"And what about your foot, Wilks?" said Hardy, somewhat taken aback by this arrangement.

"Foot, sir?" said the unconscious Mr. Wilks; "wot foot?"

"Why, the bad one," said Hardy, with a significant glance.

"Ho, that one?" said Mr. Wilks, beating time and waiting further revelations.

"Do you think you ought to use it much?" inquired Hardy.

Mr. Wilks looked at it, or, to be more exact, looked at both of them, and smiled weakly. His previous idea recurred to him with renewed force now, and several things in the young man's behaviour, hitherto disregarded, became suddenly charged with significance. Miss Nugent looked on with an air of cynical interest.

"Better not run any risk," said Hardy, gravely. "I shall be very pleased to see Miss Nugent home, if she will allow me."

"What is the matter with it?" inquired Miss Nugent, looking him full in the face.

Hardy hesitated. Diplomacy, he told himself, was one thing; lying another. He passed the question on to the rather badly used Mr. Wilks.

"Matter with it?" repeated that gentleman, glaring at him reproachfully. "It's got shootin' pains right up it. I suppose it was walking miles and miles every day in London, looking for the cap'n, was too much for it."

"Is it too bad for you to take me home, Sam?" inquired Miss Nugent, softly.

The perturbed Mr. Wilks looked from one to the other. As a sportsman his sympathies were with Hardy, but his duty lay with the girl.

"I'll do my best, miss," he said; and got up and limped, very well indeed for a first attempt, round the room.

Then Miss Nugent did a thing which was a puzzle to herself for some time afterwards. Having won the victory she deliberately threw away the fruits of it, and declining to allow the steward to run any risks, accepted Hardy's escort home. Mr. Wilks watched them from the door, and with his head in a whirl caused by the night's proceedings mixed himself a stiff glass of grog to set it right, and drank to the health of both of them.

The wind had abated somewhat in violence as they walked home, and, moreover, they had their backs to it. The walk was slower and more enjoyable in many respects than the walk out. In an unusually soft mood she replied to his remarks and stole little critical glances up at him. When they reached the house she stood a little while at the gate gazing at the starry sky and listening to the crash of the sea on the beach.

"It is a fine night," she said, as she shook hands.

"The best I have ever known," said Hardy. "Good-bye."

CHAPTER XVII

The weeks passed all too quickly for James Hardy. He saw Kate Nugent at her own home; met her, thanks to the able and hearty assistance of Mr. Wilks, at Fullalove Alley, and on several occasions had the agreeable task of escorting her back home.

He cabled to his father for news of the illustrious stowaway immediately the *Conqueror* was notified as having reached Port Elizabeth. The reply—"Left ship"—confirmed his worst fears, but he cheerfully accepted Mrs. Kingdom's view that the captain, in order to relieve the natural anxiety of his family, had secured a passage on the first vessel homeward bound.

Captain Hardy was the first to reach home. In the early hours of a fine April morning the *Conqueror* steamed slowly into Sunwich Harbour, and in a very short time the town was revelling in a description of Captain Nugent's first voyage before the mast from lips which were never tired of repeating it. Down by the waterside Mr. Nathan Smith found that he had suddenly attained the rank of a popular hero, and his modesty took alarm at the publicity afforded to his action. It was extremely distasteful to a man who ran a quiet business on old-fashioned lines and disbelieved in advertisement. He lost three lodgers the same day.

Jem Hardy was one of the few people in Sunwich for whom the joke had no charms, and he betrayed such an utter lack of sympathy with his father's recital that the latter accused him at last of wanting a sense of humour.

"I don't see anything amusing in it," said his son, stiffly.

Captain Hardy recapitulated one or two choice points, and was even at some pains to explain them.

"I can't see any fun in it," repeated his son. "Your behaviour seems to me to have been deplorable."

"What?" shouted the captain, hardly able to believe his ears.

"Captain Nugent was your guest," pursued the other; "he got on your ship by accident, and he should have been treated decently as a saloon passenger."

"And been apologized to for coming on board, I suppose?" suggested the captain.

"It wouldn't have been amiss," was the reply.

The captain leaned back in his chair and regarded him thoughtfully. "I can't think what's the matter with you, Jem," he said.

"Ordinary decent ideas, that's all," said his son, scathingly.

"There's something more in it than that," said the other, positively. "I don't like to see this love-your-enemy business with you, Jem; it ain't natural to you. Has your health been all right while I've been away?"

"Of course it has," said his son, curtly. "If you didn't want Captain Nugent aboard with you why didn't you put him ashore? It wouldn't have delayed you long. Think of the worry and anxiety you've caused poor Mrs. Kingdom."

"A holiday for her," growled the captain.

"It has affected her health," continued his son; "and besides, think of his daughter. She's a high-spirited girl, and all Sunwich is laughing over her father's mishap."

"Nugent fell into his own trap," exclaimed the captain, impatiently. "And it won't do that girl of his any harm to be taken down a peg or two. Do her good. Knock some of the nonsense out of her."

"That's not the way to speak of a lady," said Jem, hotly.

The offended captain regarded him somewhat sourly; then his face changed, and he got up from his chair and stood before his son with consternation depicted on every feature.

"You don't mean to tell me," he said, slowly; "you don't mean to tell me that you're thinking anything of Kate Nugent?"

"Why not?" demanded the other, defiantly; "why shouldn't I?"

Captain Hardy, whistling softly, made no reply, but still stood eyeing him.

"I thought there was some other reason for your consideration besides 'ordinary decent ideas,'" he said, at last. "When did it come on? How long have you had it?"

Mr. Hardy, jun., in a studiously unfilial speech, intimated that these pleasantries were not to his taste.

"No, of course not," said the captain, resuming his seat. "Well, I'm sorry if it's serious, Jem, but I never dreamt you had any ideas in that quarter. If I had I'd have given old Nugent the best bunk on the ship and sung him to sleep myself. Has she given you any encouragement?"

"Don't know," said Jem, who found the conversation awkward.

"Extraordinary thing," said the captain, shaking his head, "extraordinary. Like a play."

"Play?" said his son, sharply.

"Play," repeated his father, firmly. "What is the name of it? I saw it once at Newcastle. The lovers take poison and die across each other's chests because their people won't let 'em marry. And that reminds me. I saw some phosphor-paste in the kitchen, Jem. Whose is it?"

"I'm glad to be the means of affording you amusement," said Jem, grinding his teeth.

Captain Hardy regarded him affectionately. "Go easy, my lad," he said, equably; "go easy. If I'd known it before, things would have been different; as I didn't, we must make the best of it. She's a pretty girl, and a good one, too, for all her airs, but I'm afraid she's too fond of her father to overlook this."

"That's where you've made such a mess of things," broke in his son. "Why on earth you two old men couldn't—"

"Easy," said the startled captain. "When you are in the early fifties, my lad, your ideas about age will be more accurate. Besides, Nugent is seven or eight years older than I am."

"What became of him?" inquired Jem.

"He was off the moment we berthed," said his father, suppressing a smile. "I don't mean that he bolted—he'd got enough starch left in him not to do that—but he didn't trespass on our hospitality a moment longer than was necessary. I heard that he got a passage home on the Columbus. He knew the master. She sailed some time before us for London. I thought he'd have been home by this."

It was not until two days later, however, that the gossip in Sunwich received a pleasant fillip by the arrival of the injured captain. He came down from London by the midday train, and, disdaining the privacy of a cab, prepared to run the gauntlet of his fellow-townsmen.

A weaker man would have made a detour, but he held a direct course, and with a curt nod to acquaintances who would have stopped him walked swiftly in the direction of home. Tradesmen ran to their shop-doors to see him, and smoking amphibians lounging at street corners broke out into sunny smiles as he passed. He met these annoyances with a set face and a cold eye, but his views concerning children were not improved by the crowd of small creatures which fluttered along the road ahead of him and, hopeful of developments, clustered round the gate as he passed in.

It is the pride and privilege of most returned wanderers to hold forth at great length concerning their adventures, but Captain Nugent was commendably brief. At first he could hardly be induced to speak of them at all, but the necessity of contradicting stories which Bella had gleaned for Mrs. Kingdom from friends in town proved too strong for him. He ground his teeth with suppressed fury as he listened to some of them. The truth was bad enough, and his daughter, sitting by his side with her hand in his, was trembling with indignation.

"Poor father," she said, tenderly; "what a time you must have had." "It won't bear thinking of," said Mrs. Kingdom, not to be outdone in sympathy.

"He met these annoyances with a set face."

"Well, don't think of it," said the captain, shortly.

Mrs. Kingdom sighed as though to indicate that her feelings were not to be suppressed in that simple fashion.

"The anxiety has been very great," she said, shaking her head, "but everybody's been very kind. I'm sure all our friends have been most sympathetic. I couldn't go outside the house without somebody stopping me and asking whether there was any news of you. I'd no idea you were so popular; even the milkman—"

"I'd like some tea," interrupted the captain, roughly; "that is, when you have finished your very interesting information."

Mrs. Kingdom pursed her lips together to suppress the words she was afraid to utter, and rang the bell.

"Your master would like some tea," she said, primly, as Bella appeared. "He has had a long journey." The captain started and eyed her fiercely; Mrs. Kingdom, her good temper quite restored by this little retort, folded her hands in her lap and gazed at him with renewed sympathy.

"We all missed you very much," said Kate, softly. "But we had no fears once we knew that you were at sea."

"And I suppose some of the sailors were kind to you?" suggested the unfortunate Mrs. Kingdom. "They are rough fellows, but I suppose some of them have got their hearts in the right place. I daresay they were sorry to see you in such a position."

The captain's reply was of a nature known to Mrs. Kingdom and her circle as "snapping one's head off." He drew his chair to the table as Bella brought in the tray and, accepting a cup of tea, began to discuss with his daughter the events which had transpired in his absence.

"There is no news," interposed Mrs. Kingdom, during an interval. Mr. Hall's aunt died the other day."

"Never heard of her," said the captain. "Neither had I, till then," said his sister. "What a lot of people there are one never hears of, John." The captain stared at her offensively and went on with his meal. A long silence ensued.

"I suppose you didn't get to hear of the cable that was sent?" said Mrs. Kingdom, making another effort to arouse interest.

"What cable?" inquired her brother.

"The one Mr. Hardy sent to his father about you," replied Mrs. Kingdom.

The captain pushed his chair back and stared her full in the face. "What do you mean?" he demanded.

His sister explained.

"Do you mean to tell me that you've been speaking to young Hardy?" exclaimed the captain.

"I could hardly help doing so, when he came here," returned his sister, with dignity. "He has been very anxious about you."

Captain Nugent rose and strode up and down the room. Then he stopped and glanced sharply at his daughter.

"Were you here when he called?" he demanded.

"Yes," was the reply.

"And you—you spoke to him?" roared the captain.

"I had to be civil," said Miss Nugent, calmly; "I'm not a sea-captain."

Her father walked up and down the room again. Mrs. Kingdom, terrified at the storm she had evoked, gazed helplessly at her niece.

"What did he come here for?" said the captain.

Miss Nugent glanced down at her plate. "I can't imagine," she said, demurely. "The first time he came to tell us what had become of you."

The captain stopped in his walk and eyed her sternly. "I am very fortunate in my children," he said, slowly. "One is engaged to marry the daughter of the shadiest rascal in Sunwich, and the other—"

"And the other?" said his daughter, proudly, as he paused.

"The other," said the captain, as he came round the table and put his hand on her shoulder, "is my dear and obedient daughter."

"Yes," said Miss Nugent; "but that isn't what you were going to say. You need not worry about me; I shall not do anything that would displease you."

CHAPTER XVIII

With a view to avoiding the awkwardness of a chance meeting with any member of the Nugent family Hardy took the sea road on his way to the office the morning after the captain's return. Common sense told him to leave matters for the present to the healing hand of Time, and to cultivate habits of self-effacement by no means agreeable to one of his temperament.

Despite himself his spirits rose as he walked. It was an ideal spring morning, cool and sunny. The short turf by the side of the road was fragrant under his heel, and a light wind stirred the blueness of the sea. On the beach below two grizzled men of restful habit were endeavouring to make an old boat waterproof with red and green paint.

A long figure approaching slowly from the opposite direction broke into a pleasant smile as he drew near and quickened his pace to meet him.

"You're out early," said Hardy, as the old man stopped and turned with him.

"'Ave to be, sir," said Mr. Wilks, darkly; "out early and 'ome late, and more often than not getting my dinner out. That's my life nowadays."

"Can't you let her see that her attentions are undesirable?" inquired Hardy, gravely.

"Can't you let her see that her attentions are undesirable?"

"I can't be rude to a woman," said the steward, with a melancholy smile; "if I could, my life would ha' been very different. She's always stepping across to ask my advice about Teddy, or something o' that sort. All last week she kept borrowing my frying-pan, so at last by way of letting 'er see I didn't like it I went out and bought 'er one for herself. What's the result? Instead o' being offended she went out and bought me a couple o' neck-ties. When I didn't wear 'em she pretended it was because I didn't like the colour, and she went and bought two more. I'm wearing one now."

He shook his head ruefully, and Hardy glanced at a tie which would have paled the glories of a rainbow. For some time they walked along in silence.

"I'm going to pay my respects to Cap'n Nugent this afternoon," said Mr. Wilks, suddenly.

"Ah," said the other.

"I knew what it 'ud be with them two on the same ship," continued Mr. Wilks. "I didn't say nothing when you was talking to Miss Kate, but I knew well enough."

"Ah," said Hardy again. There was no mistaking the significance of the steward's remarks, and he found them somewhat galling. It was all very well to make use of his humble friend, but he had no desire to discuss his matrimonial projects with him.

"It's a great pity," pursued the unconscious Mr. Wilks, "just as everything seemed to be going on smoothly; but while there's life there's 'ope."

"That's a smart barge over there," said Hardy, pointing it out.

Mr. Wilks nodded. "I shall keep my eyes open this afternoon," he said reassuringly. "And if I get a chance of putting in a word it'll be put in. Twenty-nine years I sailed with the cap'n, and if there's anybody knows his weak spots it's me."

He stopped as they reached the town and said "good-bye." He pressed the young man's hand sympathetically, and a wink of intense artfulness gave point to his last remark.

"There's always Sam Wilks's cottage," he said, in a husky whisper; "and if two of 'is friends *should* 'appen to meet there, who'd be the wiser?"

He gazed benevolently after the young man's retreating figure and continued his stroll, his own troubles partly forgotten in the desire to assist his friends. It would be a notable feat for the humble steward to be the means of bringing the young people together and thereby bringing to an end the feud of a dozen years. He pictured himself eventually as the trusted friend and adviser of both families, and in one daring flight of fancy saw himself hobnobbing with the two captains over pipes and whisky.

Neatly dressed and carrying a small offering of wallflowers, he set out that afternoon to call on his old master, giving, as he walked, the last touches to a little speech of welcome which he had prepared during dinner. It was a happy effort, albeit a trifle laboured, but Captain Nugent's speech, the inspiration of the moment, gave it no chance.

He started the moment the bowing Mr. Wilks entered the room, his voice rising gradually from low, bitter tones to a hurricane note which Bella. could hear in the kitchen without even leaving her chair. Mr. Wilks stood dazed and speechless before him, holding the wallflowers in one hand and his cap in the other. In this attitude he listened to a description of his character drawn with the loving skill of an artist whose whole heart was in his work, and who seemed never tired of filling in details.

"If you ever have the hardihood to come to my house again," he concluded, "I'll break every bone in your misshapen body. Get!"

Mr. Wilks turned and groped his way to the door. Then he went a little way back with some idea of defending himself, but the door of the room was slammed in his face. He walked slowly down the path to the road and stood there for some time in helpless bewilderment. In all his sixty years of life his feelings had never been so outraged. His cap was still in his hand, and, with a helpless gesture, he put it on and scattered his floral offering in the road. Then he made a bee-line for the Two Schooners.

Though convivial by nature and ever free with his money, he sat there drinking alone in silent misery. Men came and went, but he still sat there noting with mournful pride the attention caused by his unusual bearing. To casual inquiries he shook his head; to more direct ones he only sighed heavily and applied himself to his liquor. Curiosity increased with numbers as the day wore on, and the steward, determined to be miserable, fought manfully against an ever-increasing cheerfulness due to the warming properties of the ale within.

"I 'ope you ain't lost nobody, Sam?" said a discomfited inquirer at last.

Mr. Wilks shook his head.

"You look as though you'd lost a shilling and found a ha'penny," pursued the other.

"Found a what?" inquired Mr. Wilks, wrinkling his forehead.

"A ha'penny," said his friend.

"Who did?" said Mr. Wilks.

The other attempted to explain and was ably assisted by two friends, but without avail; the impression left on Mr. Wilks's mind being that somebody had got a shilling of his. He waxed exceeding bitter, and said that he had been missing shillings for a long time.

"You're labourin' under a mistake, Sam," said the first speaker.

Mr. Wilks laughed scornfully and essayed a sneer, while his friends, regarding his contortions with some anxiety, expressed a fear that he was not quite himself. To this suggestion the steward deigned no reply, and turning to the landlord bade him replenish his mug.

"You've 'ad enough, Mr. Wilks," said that gentleman, who had been watching him for some time.

Mr. Wilks, gazing at him mistily, did not at first understand the full purport of this remark; but when he did, his wrath was so majestic and his remarks about the quality of the brew so libellous that the landlord lost all patience.

"You get off home," he said, sharply.

"Listen t' me," said Mr. Wilks, impressively.

"I don't want no words with you," said the land-lord. "You get off home while you can."

"That's right, Sam," said one of the company, putting his hand on the steward's arm. "You take his advice."

Mr. Wilks shook the hand off and eyed his adviser ferociously. Then he took a glass from the counter and smashed it on the floor. The next moment the bar was in a ferment, and the landlord, gripping Mr. Wilks round the middle, skilfully piloted him to the door and thrust him into the road.

The strong air blowing from the sea disordered the steward's faculties still further. His treatment inside was forgotten, and, leaning against the front of the tavern, he stood open-mouthed, gazing at marvels. Ships in the harbour suddenly quitted their native element and were drawn up into the firmament; nobody passed but twins.

"Evening, Mr. Wilks," said a voice.

The steward peered down at the voice. At first he thought it was another case of twins, but looking close he saw that it was Mr. Edward Silk alone. He saluted him graciously, and then, with a wave of his hand toward the sky, sought to attract his attention to the ships there.

"Yes," said the unconscious Mr. Silk, sign of a fine day to-morrow. "Are you going my way?"

Mr. Wilks smiled, and detaching himself from the tavern with some difficulty just saved Mr. Silk from a terrible fall by clutching him forcibly round the neck. The ingratitude of Mr. Silk was a rebuff to a nature which was at that moment overflowing with good will. For a moment the steward was half inclined to let him go home alone, but the reflection that he would never get there softened him.

"Pull yourself t'gether," he said, gravely, "Now, 'old on me."

The road, as they walked, rose up in imitation of the shipping, but Mr. Wilks knew now the explanation:

Teddy Silk was intoxicated. Very gently he leaned towards the erring youth and wagged his head at him.

"Are you going to hold up or aren't you?" demanded Mr. Silk, shortly.

The steward waived the question; he knew from experience the futility of arguing with men in drink. The great thing was to get Teddy Silk home, not to argue with him. He smiled good-temperedly to himself, and with a sudden movement pinned him up against the wall in time to arrest another` fall.

With frequent halts by the way, during which the shortness of Mr. Silk's temper furnished Mr. Wilks with the texts of several sermons, none of which he finished, they at last reached Fullalove Alley, and the steward, with a brief exhortation to his charge to hold his head up, bore down on Mrs. Silk, who was sitting in her doorway.

"I've brought 'im 'ome," he said, steadying himself against the doorpost; "brought 'im 'ome."

"Brought 'im 'ome?" said the bewildered Mrs. Silk.

"Don' say anything to 'im," entreated Mr. Wilks, "my sake. Thing might 'appen anybody."

"He's been like that all the way," said Mr. Silk, regarding the steward with much disfavour. "I don't know why I troubled about him, I'm sure."

"Crowd roun 'im," pursued the imaginative Mr. Wilks. "'Old up, Teddy."

"I'm sure it's very kind of you, Mr. Wilks," said the widow, as she glanced at a little knot of neighbours standing near. "Will you come inside for a minute or two?"

She moved the chair to let him pass, and Mr. Wilks, still keeping the restraining hand of age on the shoulder of intemperate youth, passed in and stood, smiling amiably, while Mrs. Silk lit the lamp and placed it in the centre of the table, which was laid for supper. The light shone on a knuckle of boiled pork, a home-made loaf, and a fresh-cut wedge of cheese.

"I suppose you won't stay and pick a bit o' sup-per with us?" said Mrs. Silk.

"Why not?" inquired Mr. Wilks.

"I'm sure, if I had known," said Mrs. Silk, as she piloted him to a seat, "I'd 'ave 'ad something nice. There, now! If I 'aven't been and forgot the beer."

She left the table and went into the kitchen, and Mr. Wilks's eyes glistened as she returned with a large brown jug full of foaming ale and filled his glass.

"Teddy mustn't 'ave any," he said, sharply, as she prepared to fill that gentleman's glass.

"Just 'alf a glass," she said, winsomely.

"Not a drop," said Mr. Wilks, firmly.

Mrs. Silk hesitated, and screwing up her forehead glanced significantly at her son. "'Ave some by-and-by," she whispered.

"Give me the jug," said Mr. Silk, indignantly. "What are you listening to 'im for? Can't you see what's the matter with 'im?"

"Not to 'ave it," said Mr. Wilks; "put it 'ere."

He thumped the table emphatically with his hand, and before her indignant son could interfere Mrs. Silk had obeyed. It was the last straw. Mr. Edward Silk rose to his feet with tremendous effect and, first thrusting his plate violently away from him, went out into the night, slamming the door behind him with such violence that the startled Mr. Wilks was nearly blown out of his chair.

"He don't mean nothing," said Mrs. Silk, turning a rather scared face to the steward. "'E's a bit jealous of you, I s'pose."

Mr. Wilks shook his head. Truth to tell, he was rather at a loss to know exactly what had happened.

"And then there's 'is love affair," sighed Mrs. Silk. "He'll never get over the loss of Amelia Kybird. I always know when 'e 'as seen her, he's that miserable there's no getting a word out of 'im."

Mr. Wilks smiled vaguely and went on with his supper, and, the meal finished, allowed himself to be installed in an easy-chair, while his hostess cleared the table. He sat and smoked in high good humour with himself, the occasional remarks he made being received with an enthusiasm which they seldom provoked elsewhere.

"I should like t' sit 'ere all night," he said, at last.

"I don't believe it," said Mrs. Silk, playfully.

"Like t' sit 'ere all night," repeated Mr. Wilks, somewhat sternly. "All nex' day, all day after, day after that, day—"

Mrs. Silk eyed him softly. "Why would you like to sit here all that time?" she inquired, in a low voice.

"B'cause," said Mr. Wilks, simply, "b'cause I don't feel's if I can stand. Goo'-night."

He closed his eyes on the indignant Mrs. Silk and fell fast asleep. It was a sound sleep and dreamless, and only troubled by the occasional ineffectual attempts of his hostess to arouse him. She gave up the attempt at last, and taking up a pair of socks sat working thoughtfully the other side of the fire-place.

The steward awoke an hour or two later, and after what seemed a terrible struggle found himself standing at the open door with the cold night air blowing in his face, and a voice which by an effort of memory he identified as that of Edward Silk inviting him "to go home and lose no time about it." Then the door slammed behind him and he stood balancing himself with some difficulty on the step, wondering what had happened. By the time he had walked up and down the deserted alley three or four times light was vouchsafed to him and, shivering slightly, he found his own door and went to bed.

CHAPTER XIX

Any hopes which Hardy might have entertained as to the attitude of Miss Nugent were dispelled the first time he saw her, that dutiful daughter of a strong-willed sire favouring him with a bow which was exactly half an inch in depth and then promptly bestowing her gaze elsewhere. He passed Captain Nugent next day, and for a week afterwards he had only to close his eyes to see in all its appalling virulence the glare with which that gentleman had acknowledged his attempt at recognition.

He fared no better in Fullalove Alley, a visit to Mr. Wilks eliciting the fact that that delectable thoroughfare had been put out of bounds for Miss Nugent. Moreover, Mr. Wilks was full of his own troubles and anxious for any comfort and advice that could be given to him. All the alley knew that Mrs. Silk had quarrelled with her son over the steward, and, without knowing the facts, spoke their mind with painful freedom concerning them.

"She and Teddy don't speak to each other now," said Mr. Wilks, gloomily, "and to 'ear people talk you'd think it was my fault."

Hardy gave him what comfort he could. He even went the length of saying that Mrs. Silk was a fine woman.

"She acts like a suffering martyr," exclaimed Mr. Wilks. "She comes over 'ere dropping hints that people are talking about us, and that they ask 'er awkward questions. Pretending to misunderstand 'er every time is enough to send me crazy; and she's so sudden in what she says there's no being up to 'er. On'y this morning she asked me if I should be sorry if she died."

"What did you say?" inquired his listener.

"I said 'yes,'" admitted Mr. Wilks, reluctantly. "I couldn't say anything else; but I said that she wasn't to let my feelings interfere with 'er in any way."

Hardy's father sailed a day or two later, and after that nothing happened. Equator Lodge was an impregnable fortress, and the only member of the garrison he saw in a fortnight was Bella.

His depression did not escape the notice of his partner, who, after first advising love-philtres and then a visit to a well-known specialist for diseases of the heart, finally recommended more work, and put a generous portion of his own on to the young man's desk. Hardy, who was in an evil temper, pitched it on to the floor and, with a few incisive remarks on levity unbecoming to age, pursued his duties in gloomy silence.

A short time afterwards, however, he had to grapple with his partner's work in real earnest. For the first time in his life the genial shipbroker was laid up with a rather serious illness. A chill caught while bathing was going the round of certain unsuspected weak spots, and the patient, who was of an inquiring turn of mind, was taking a greater interest in medical works than his doctor deemed advisable.

"Most interesting study," he said, faintly, to Hardy, as the latter sat by his bedside one evening and tried to cheer him in the usual way by telling him that there was nothing the matter with him. "There are dozens of different forms of liver complaint alone, and I've got 'em all."

"Liver isn't much," said his visitor, with the confidence of youth.

"Mine is," retorted the invalid; "it's twice its proper size and still growing. Base of the left lung is solidifying, or I'm much mistaken; the heart, instead of waltzing as is suitable to my time of life, is doing a galop, and everything else is as wrong as it can be."

"When are you coming back?" inquired the other.

"Back?" repeated Swann. "Back? You haven't been listening. I'm a wreck. All through violating man's primeval instinct by messing about in cold water. What is the news?"

Hardy pondered and shook his head. "Nugent is going to be married in July," he said, at last.

"He'd better have had that trip on the whaler," commented Mr. Swann; "but that is not news. Nathan Smith told it me this morning."

"Nathan Smith?" repeated the other, in surprise.

"I've done him a little service," said the invalid. "Got him out of a mess with Garth and Co. He's been here two or three times, and I must confess I find him a most alluring rascal."

"Birds of a feather—" began Hardy, superciliously.

"Don't flatter me," said Swann, putting his hand out of the bed-clothes with a deprecatory gesture.

"I am not worthy to sit at his feet. He is the most amusing knave on the coast. He is like a sunbeam in a sick room when you can once get him to talk of his experiences. Have you seen young Nugent lately? Does he seem cheerful?"

"Yes, but he is not," was the reply.

"Well, it's natural for the young to marry," said the other, gravely. "Murchison will be the next to go, I expect."

"Possibly," returned Hardy, with affected calmness.

"Blaikie was saying something about it this morning," resumed Swann, regarding him from half-closed lids, "but he was punching and tapping me all about the ribs while he was talking, and I didn't catch all he said, but I think it's all arranged. Murchison is there nearly every day, I understand; I suppose you meet him there?"

Mr. Hardy, whistling softly, rose and walked round the room, uncorking medicine bottles and sniffing at their contents. A smile of unaffected pleasure lit up his features as he removed the stopper from one particularly pungent mixture.

"Two tablespoonfuls three times a day," he read, slowly. "When did you have the last, Swann? Shall I ring for the nurse?"

The invalid shook his head impatiently. "You're an ungrateful dog," he muttered, "or you would tell me how your affair is going. Have you got any chance?"

"You're getting light-headed now," said Hardy, calmly. "I'd better go."

"All right, go then," responded the invalid; "but if you lose that girl just for the want of a little skilled advice from an expert, you'll never forgive yourself—I'm serious."

"Well, you must be ill then," said the younger man, with anxiety.

"Twice," said Mr. Swann, lying on his back and apparently addressing the ceiling, "twice I have given this young man invaluable assistance, and each time he has bungled."

Hardy laughed and, the nurse returning to the room, bade him "good-bye" and departed. After the close atmosphere of the sick room the air was delicious, and he walked along slowly, deep in thought. From Nathan Smith his thoughts wandered to Jack Nugent and his unfortunate engagement, and from that to Kate Nugent. For months he had been revolving impossible schemes in his mind to earn her gratitude, and possibly that of the captain, by extricating Jack. In the latter connection he was also reminded of that unhappy victim of unrequited affection, Edward Silk.

It was early to go indoors, and the house was dull. He turned and retraced his steps, and, his thoughts reverting to his sick partner, smiled as he remembered remarks which that irresponsible person had made at various times concerning the making of his last will and testament. Then he came to a sudden standstill as a wild, forlorn-hope kind of idea suddenly occurred to him. He stood for some time thinking, then walked a little way, and then stopped again as various difficulties presented themselves for solution. Finally, despite the lateness of the hour, he walked back in some excitement to the house he had quitted over half an hour before with the intention of speaking to the invalid concerning a duty peculiarly incumbent upon elderly men of means.

The nurse, who came out of the sick room, gently closing the door after her, demurred a little to this second visit, but, receiving a promise from the visitor not to excite the invalid, left them together. The odour of the abominable physic was upon the air.

"Well?" said the invalid.

"I have been thinking that I was rather uncivil a little while ago," said Hardy.

"Ah!" said the other. "What do you want?"

"A little of that skilled assistance you were speaking of."

Mr. Swann made an alarming noise in his throat. Hardy sprang forward in alarm, but he motioned him back.

"I was only laughing," he explained.

Hardy repressed his annoyance by an effort, and endeavoured, but with scant success, to return the other's smile.

"Go on," said the shipbroker, presently.

"I have thought of a scheme for upsetting Nugent's marriage," said Hardy, slowly.

"It is just a forlorn hope which depends for its success on you and Nathan Smith."

"He's a friend of Kybird's," said the other, drily.

"That is the most important thing of all," rejoined Hardy. "That is, next to your shrewdness and tact; everything depends upon you, really, and whether you can fool Smith. It is a great thing in our favour that you have been taking him up lately."

"Are you coming to the point or are you not?" demanded the shipbroker.

Hardy looked cautiously round the room, and then, drawing his chair close to the bed, leaned over the prostrate man and spoke rapidly into his ear.

"What?" cried the astounded Mr. Swann, suddenly sitting up in his bed. "You—you scoundrel!"

"It's to be done," said Hardy.

"You ghoul!" said the invalid, glaring at him. "Is that the way to talk to a sick man? You unscrupulous rascal!"

"It'll be amusement for you," pleaded the other, "and if we are successful it will be the best thing in the end for everybody. Think of the good you'll do."

"Where you get such rascally ideas from, I can't think," mused the invalid. "Your father is a straightforward, honest man, and your partner's uprightness is the talk of Sunwich."

"It doesn't take much to make Sunwich talk," retorted Hardy.

"A preposterous suggestion to make to a man of my standing," said the shipbroker, ignoring the remark. "If the affair ever leaked out I should never hear the end of it."

"It can't leak out," said Hardy, "and if it does there is no direct evidence. They will never really know until you die; they can only suspect."

"Very well," said the shipbroker, with a half-indulgent, half-humorous glance. "Anything to get rid of you. It's a crack-brained scheme, and could only originate with a young man whose affections have weakened his head—I consent."

"Bravo!" said Hardy and patted him on the back; Mr. Swann referred to the base of his left lung, and he apologized.

"I'll have to fix it up with Blaikie," said the invalid, lying down again. "Murchison got two of his best patients last week, so that it ought to be easy. And besides, he is fond of innocent amusement."

"I'm awfully obliged to you," said Hardy.

"It might be as well if we pretended to quarrel," said the invalid, reflectively, "especially as you are known to be a friend of Nugent's. We'll have a few words—before my housekeeper if possible, to insure publicity—and then you had better not come again. Send Silk instead with messages."

Hardy thanked him and whispered a caution as a footstep was heard on the landing. The door opened and the nurse, followed by the housekeeper bearing a tray, entered the room.

"And I can't be worried about these things," said Swann, in an acrimonious voice, as they entered. "If you are not capable of settling a simple question like that yourself, ask the office-boy to instruct you."

"It's your work," retorted Hardy, "and a nice mess it's in."

"H'sh!" said the nurse, coming forward hastily. "You must leave the room, sir. I can't have you exciting my patient."

Hardy bestowed an indignant glance at the invalid.

"Get out!" said that gentleman, with extraordinary fierceness for one in his weak condition. "In future, nurse, I won't have this person admitted to my room."

"Yes, yes; certainly," said the nurse. "You must go, sir; at once, please."

"I'm going," said Hardy, almost losing his gravity at the piteous spectacle afforded by the house-keeper as she stood, still holding the tray and staring open-mouthed at the combatants. "When you're tired of skulking in bed, perhaps you'll come and do your share of the work."

Mr. Swann rose to a sitting position, and his demeanour was so alarming that the nurse, hastening over to him, entreated him to lie down, and waved Hardy peremptorily from the room.

"Puppy!" said the invalid, with great relish. "Blockhead!"

He gazed fixedly at the young man as he departed and then, catching sight in his turn of the housekeeper's perplexity, laid himself down and buried his face in the bed-clothes. The nurse crossed over to her assistant and, taking the tray from her, told her in a sharp whisper that if she ever admitted Mr. Hardy again she would not be answerable for the consequences.

CHAPTER XX

Charmed at the ease with which he had demolished the objections of Mr. Adolphus Swann and won that suffering gentleman over to his plans, Hardy began to cast longing glances at Equator Lodge. He reminded himself that the labourer was worthy of his hire, and it seemed moreover an extremely desirable thing that Captain Nugent should know that he was labouring in his vineyard with the full expectation of a bounteous harvest. He resolved to call.

Kate Nugent, who heard the gate swing behind him as he entered the front garden, looked up and stood spellbound at his audacity. As a fairly courageous young person she was naturally an admirer of boldness in others, but this seemed sheer recklessness. Moreover, it was recklessness in which, if she stayed where she was, she would have to bear a part or be guilty of rudeness, of which she felt incapable. She took a third course, and, raising her eyebrows at the unnecessarily loud knocking with which the young man announced his arrival, retreated in good order into the garden, where her father, in a somewhat heated condition, was laboriously planting geraniums. She had barely reached him when Bella, in a state of fearsome glee, came down the garden to tell the captain of his visitor.

"Who?" said the latter, sharply, as he straightened his aching back.

"Young Mr. Hardy," said Bella, impressively. "I showed 'im in; I didn't ask 'im to take a chair, but he took one."

"Young Hardy to see me!" said the captain to his daughter, after Bella had returned to the house. "How dare he come to my house? Infernal impudence! I won't see him."

"Shall I go in and see him for you?" inquired Kate, with affected artlessness.

"You stay where you are, miss," said her father. "I won't have him speak to you; I won't have him look at you. I'll—"

He beat his dirty hands together and strode off towards the house. Jem Hardy rose from his chair as the captain entered the room and, ignoring a look of black inquiry, bade him "Good afternoon."

"What do you want?" asked the captain, gruffly, as he stared him straight in the eye.

"I came to see you about your son's marriage," said the other. "Are you still desirous of preventing it?"

"I'm sorry you've had the trouble," said the captain, in a voice of suppressed anger; "and now may I ask you to get out of my house?"

Hardy bowed. "I am sorry I have troubled you," he said, calmly, "but I have a plan which I think would get your son out of this affair, and, as a business man, I wanted to make something out of it."

The captain eyed him scornfully, but he was glad to see this well-looking, successful son of his old enemy tainted with such sordid views. Instead of turning him out he spoke to him almost fairly.

"How much do you want?" he inquired.

"All things considered, I am asking a good deal," was the reply.

"How much?" repeated the captain, impatiently.

Hardy hesitated. "In exchange for the service I want permission to visit here when I choose," he said, at length; "say twice a week."

Words failed the captain; none with which he was acquainted seemed forcible enough for the occasion. He faced his visitor stuttering with rage, and pointed to the door.

"Get out of my house," he roared.

"I'm sorry to have intruded," said Hardy, as he crossed the room and paused at the door; "it is none of my business, of course. I thought that I saw an opportunity of doing your son a good turn—he is a friend of mine—and at the same time paying off old scores against Kybird and Nathan Smith. I thought that on that account it might suit you. Good afternoon."

He walked out into the hall, and reaching the front door fumbled clumsily with the catch. The captain watching his efforts in grim silence began to experience the twin promptings of curiosity and temptation.

"What is this wonderful plan of yours?" he demanded, with a sneer.

"Just at present that must remain a secret," said the other. He came from the door and, unbidden, followed the captain into the room again.

"What do you want to visit at my house for?" inquired the latter, in a forbidding voice.

"To see your daughter," said Hardy.

The captain had a relapse. He had not expected a truthful answer, and, when it came, in the most matter-of-fact tone, it found him quite unprepared. His first idea was to sacrifice his dignity and forcibly eject his visitor, but more sensible thoughts prevailed.

"You are quite sure, I suppose, that your visits would be agreeable to my daughter?" he said, contemptuously.

Hardy shook his head. "I should come ostensibly to see you," he said, cheerfully; "to smoke a pipe with you."

"Smoke!" stuttered the captain, explosively; "smoke a pipe with ME?"

"Why not?" said the other. "I am offering you my services, and anything that is worth having is worth paying for. I suppose we could both smoke pipes under pleasanter conditions. What have you got against me? It isn't my fault that you and my father have quarrelled."

"I don't want anything more to say to you," said the captain, sternly. "I've shown you the door once. Am I to take forcible measures?"

Hardy shrugged his broad shoulders. "I am sorry," he said, moving to the door again.

"So am I," said the other.

"It's a pity," said Hardy, regretfully. "It's the chance of a lifetime. I had set my heart on fooling Kybird and Smith, and now all my trouble is wasted. Nathan Smith would be all the better for a fall."

The captain hesitated. His visitor seemed to be confident, and he would have given a great deal to prevent his son's marriage and a great deal to repay some portion of his debt to the ingenious Mr. Smith. Moreover, there seemed to be an excellent opportunity of punishing the presumption of his visitor by taking him at his word.

"I don't think you'd enjoy your smoking here much," he said, curtly.

"I'll take my chance of that," said the other. "It will only be a matter of a few weeks, and then, if I am unsuccessful, my visits cease."

"And if you're successful, am I to have the pleasure of your company for the rest of my life?" demanded the captain.

"That will be for you to decide," was the reply. "Is it a bargain?"

The captain looked at him and deliberated. "All right. Mondays and Thursdays," he said, laconically.

Hardy saw through the ruse, and countered.

"Now Swann is ill I can't always get away when I wish," he said, easily. "I'll just drop in when I can. Good day."

He opened the door and, fearful lest the other should alter his mind at the last moment, walked briskly down the path to the gate. The captain stood for some time after his departure deep in thought, and then returned to the garden to be skilfully catechized by Miss Nugent.

"And when my young friend comes with his pipe you'll be in another room," he concluded, warningly.

Miss Nugent looked up and patted his cheek tenderly. "What a talent for organization you have," she remarked, softly. "A place for everything and everything in its place. The idea of his taking such a fancy to you!"

The captain coughed and eyed her suspiciously. He had been careful not to tell her Hardy's reasons for coming, but he had a shrewd idea that his caution was wasted.

"Today is Thursday," said Kate, slowly; "he will be here to-morrow and Saturday. What shall I wear?"

The captain resumed his gardening operations by no means perturbed at the prophecy. Much as he disliked the young man he gave him credit for a certain amount of decency, and his indignation was proportionately great the following evening when Bella announced Mr. Hardy. He made a genial remark about Shylock and a pound of flesh, but finding that it was only an excellent conversational opening, the subject of Shakespeare's plays lapsed into silence.

It was an absurd situation, but he was host and Hardy allowed him to see pretty plainly that he was a guest. He answered the latter's remarks with a very ill grace, and took covert stock of him as one of a species he had not encountered before. One result of his stock-taking was that he was spared any feeling of surprise when his visitor came the following evening.

"It's the thin end of the wedge," said Miss Nugent, who came into the room after Hardy had departed; "you don't know him as well as I do."

"Eh?" said her father, sharply.

"I mean that you are not such a judge of character as I am," said Kate; "and besides, I have made a special study of young men. The only thing that puzzles me is why you should have such an extraordinary fascination for him."

"You talk too much, miss," said the captain, drawing the tobacco jar towards him and slowly filling his pipe.

Miss Nugent sighed, and after striking a match for him took a seat on the arm of his chair and placed her hand on his shoulder. "I can quite understand him liking you," she said, slowly.

The captain grunted.

"And if he is like other sensible people," continued Miss Nugent, in a coaxing voice, "the more he sees of you the more he'll like you. I do hope he has not come to take you away from me."

The indignant captain edged her off the side of his chair; Miss Nugent, quite undisturbed, got on again and sat tapping the floor with her foot. Her arm stole round his neck and she laid her cheek against his head and smiled wickedly.

"Nice-looking, isn't he?" she said, in a careless voice.

"I don't know anything about his looks," growled her father.

Miss Nugent gave a little exclamation of surprise. "First thing I noticed," she said, with commendable gravity. "He's very good-looking and very determined. What are you going to give him if he gets poor Jack out of this miserable business?"

"Give him?" said her father, staring.

"I met Jack yesterday," said Kate, "and I can see that he is as wretched as he can be. He wouldn't say so, of course. If Mr. Hardy is successful you ought to recognize it. I should suggest one of your new photos in an eighteenpenny frame."

She slipped off the chair and quitted the room before her father could think of a suitable retort, and he sat smoking silently until the entrance of Mrs. Kingdom a few minutes later gave him an opportunity of working off a little accumulated gall.

While the junior partner was thus trying to obtain a footing at Equator Lodge the gravest rumours of the senior partner's health were prevalent in the town. Nathan Smith, who had been to see him again, ostensibly to thank him for his efforts on his behalf, was of opinion that he was breaking up, and in conversation with Mr. Kybird shook his head over the idea that there would soon be one open-handed gentleman the less in a world which was none too full of them.

"We've all got to go some day," observed Mr. Kybird, philosophically. "'Ow's that cough o' yours getting on, Nat?"

Mr. Smith met the pleasantry coldly; the ailment referred to was one of some standing and had been a continual source of expense in the way of balsams and other remedies.

"He's worried about 'is money," he said, referring to Mr. Swann.

"Ah, we sha'n't 'ave that worry," said Mr. Kybird.

"Nobody to leave it to," continued Mr. Smith. "Seems a bit 'ard, don't it?"

"P'r'aps if 'e 'ad 'ad somebody to leave it to 'e wouldn't 'ave 'ad so much to leave," observed Mr. Kybird, sagely; "it's a rum world."

He shook his head over it and went on with the uncongenial task of marking down wares which had suffered by being exposed outside too long. Mr. Smith, who always took an interest in the welfare of his friends, made suggestions.

"I shouldn't put a ticket marked 'Look at this!' on that coat," he said, severely. "It oughtn't to be looked at."

"It's the best out o' three all 'anging together," said Mr. Kybird, evenly.

"And look 'ere," said Mr. Smith. "Look what an out-o'-the-way place you've put this ticket. Why not put it higher up on the coat?"

"Becos the moth-hole ain't there," said Mr. Kybird.

Mr. Smith apologized and watched his friend without further criticism.

"Gettin' ready for the wedding, I s'pose?" he said, presently.

Mr. Kybird assented, and his brow darkened as he spoke of surreptitious raids on his stores made by Mrs. Kybird and daughter.

"Their idea of a wedding," he said, bitterly, "is to dress up and make a show; my idea is a few real good old pals and plenty of licker."

"You'll 'ave to 'ave both," observed Nathan Smith, whose knowledge of the sex was pretty accurate.

Mr. Kybird nodded gloomily. "'Melia and Jack don't seem to 'ave been 'itting it off partikler well lately," he said, slowly. "He's getting more uppish than wot 'e was when 'e come here first. But I got 'im to promise that he'd settle any money that 'e might ever get left him on 'Melia."

Mr. Smith's inscrutable eyes glistened into something as nearly approaching a twinkle as they were capable. "That'll settle the five 'undred," he said, warmly. "Are you goin' to send Cap'n Nugent an invite for the wedding?"

"They'll 'ave to be asked, o' course," said Mr. Kybird, with an attempt at dignity, rendered necessary by a certain lightness in his friend's manner. "The old woman don't like the Nugent lot, but she'll do the proper thing."

"O' course she will," said Mr. Smith, soothingly. "Come over and 'ave a drink with me, Dan'l it's your turn to stand."

CHAPTER XXI

Gossip from one or two quarters, which reached Captain Nugent's ears through the medium of his sister, concerning the preparations for his son's marriage, prevented him from altering his mind with regard to the visits of Jem Hardy and showing that painstaking young man the door. Indeed, the nearness of the approaching nuptials bade fair to eclipse, for the time being, all other grievances, and when Hardy paid his third visit he made a determined but ineffectual attempt to obtain from him some information as to the methods by which he hoped to attain his ends. His failure made him suspicious, and he hinted pretty plainly that he had no guarantee that his visitor was not obtaining admittance under false pretences.

"Well, I'm not getting much out of it," returned Hardy, frankly.

"I wonder you come," said his hospitable host.

"I want you to get used to me," said the other.

The captain started and eyed him uneasily; the remark seemed fraught with hidden meaning. "And then?" he inquired, raising his bushy eyebrows.

"Then perhaps I can come oftener."

The captain gave him up. He sank back in his chair and crossing his legs smoked, with his eyes fixed on the ceiling. It was difficult to know what to do with a young man who was apparently destitute of any feelings of shame or embarrassment. He bestowed a puzzled glance in his direction and saw that he was lolling in the chair with an appearance of the greatest ease and enjoyment. Following the direction of his eyes, he saw that he was gazing with much satisfaction at a photograph of Miss Nugent which graced the mantelpiece. With an odd sensation the captain suddenly identified it as one which usually stood on the chest of drawers in his bedroom, and he wondered darkly whether charity or mischief was responsible for its appearance there.

In any case, it disappeared before the occasion of Hardy's next visit, and the visitor sat with his eyes unoccupied, endeavouring to make conversation with a host who was if anything more discourteous than usual. It was uphill work, but he persevered, and in fifteen minutes had ranged unchecked from North Pole explorations to poultry farming. It was a relief to both of them when the door opened and

Bella ushered in Dr. Murchison.

The captain received the new arrival with marked cordiality, and giving him a chair near his own observed with some interest the curt greeting of the young men. The doctor's manner indicated polite surprise at seeing the other there, then he turned to the captain and began to talk to him.

For some time they chatted without interruption, and the captain's replies, when Hardy at last made an attempt to make the conversation general, enabled the doctor to see, without much difficulty, that the latter was an unwelcome guest. Charmed with the discovery he followed his host's lead, and, with a languid air, replied to his rival in monosyllables. The captain watched with quiet satisfaction, and at each rebuff his opinion of Murchison improved. It was gratifying to find that the interloper had met his match.

Hardy sat patient. "I am glad to have met you to-night," he said, after a long pause, during which the other two were discussing a former surgical experience of the captain's on one of his crew.

"Yes?" said Murchison.

"You are just the man I wanted to see."

"Yes?" said the doctor, again.

"Yes," said the other, nodding. "I've been very busy of late owing to my partner's illness, and you are attending several people I want to hear about."

"Indeed," said Murchison, with a half-turn towards him.

"How is Mrs. Paul?" inquired Hardy.

"Dead!" replied the other, briefly.

"Dead!" repeated Mr. Hardy. "Good Heavens! I didn't know that there was much the matter with her."

"There was no hope for her from the first," said Murchison, somewhat sharply. It was merely a question of prolonging her life a little while. She lived longer than I deemed possible. She surprised everybody by her vitality."

"Poor thing," said Hardy. "How is Joe Banks?"

"Dead," said Murchison again, biting his lip and eyeing him furiously.

"Dear me," said Hardy, shaking his head; "I met him not a month ago. He was on his way to see you then."

"The poor fellow had been an invalid nearly all his life," said Murchison, to the captain, casually. "Aye, I remember him," was the reply.

"I am almost afraid to ask you," continued Hardy, "but shut up all day I hear so little. How is old Miss

Ritherdon?"

Murchison reddened with helpless rage; Captain Nugent, gazing at the questioner with something almost approaching respect, waited breathlessly for the invariable answer.

"She died three weeks ago; I'm surprised that you have not heard of it," said the doctor, pointedly.

"Of course she was old," said Hardy, with the air of one advancing extenuating circumstances.

"Very old," replied the doctor, who knew that the other was now at the end of his obituary list.

"Are there any other of my patients you are anxious to hear about?"

"No, thank you," returned Hardy, with some haste.

The doctor turned to his host again, but the charm was broken. His talk was disconnected, owing probably to the fact that he was racking his brain for facts relative to the seamy side of shipbroking. And Hardy, without any encouragement whatever, was interrupting with puerile anecdotes concerning the late lamented Joe Banks. The captain came to the rescue.

"The ladies are in the garden," he said to the doctor; "perhaps you'd like to join them."

He looked coldly over at Hardy as he spoke to see the effect of his words. Their eyes met, and the young man was on his feet as soon as his rival.

"Thanks," he said, coolly; "it is a trifle close indoors."

Before the dismayed captain could think of any dignified pretext to stay him he was out of the room. The doctor followed and the perturbed captain, left alone, stared blankly at the door and thought of his daughter's words concerning the thin end of the wedge.

He was a proud man and loth to show discomfiture, so that it was not until a quarter of an hour later that he followed his guests to the garden. The four people were in couples, the paths favouring that formation, although the doctor, to the detriment of the border, had made two or three determined attempts to march in fours. With a feeling akin to scorn the captain saw that he was walking with Mrs. Kingdom, while some distance in the rear Jem Hardy followed with Kate.

He stood at the back door for a little while watching; Hardy, upright and elate, was listening with profound attention to Miss Nugent; the doctor, sauntering along beside Mrs. Kingdom, was listening with a languid air to an account of her celebrated escape from measles some forty-three years before. As a professional man he would have died rather than have owed his life to the specific she advocated.

Kate Nugent, catching sight of her father, turned, and as he came slowly towards them, linked her arm, in his. Her face was slightly flushed and her eyes sparkled.

"I was just coming in to fetch you," she observed; "it is so pleasant out here now."

"Delightful," said Hardy.

"We had to drop behind a little," said Miss Nugent, raising her voice. "Aunt and Dr. Murchison *will* talk about their complaints to each other! They have been exchanging prescriptions."

The captain grunted and eyed her keenly.

"I want you to come in and give us a little music," he said, shortly.

Kate nodded. "What is your favourite music, Mr. Hardy?" she inquired, with a smile.

"Unfortunately, Mr. Hardy can't stay," said the captain, in a voice which there was no mistaking.

Hardy pulled out his watch. "No; I must be off," he said, with a well-affected start. "Thank you for reminding me, Captain Nugent."

"I am glad to have been of service," said the other, looking his grimmest.

He acknowledged the young man's farewell with a short nod and, forgetting his sudden desire for music, continued to pace up and down with his daughter.

"What have you been saying to that—that fellow?" he demanded, turning to her, suddenly.

Miss Nugent reflected. "I said it was a fine evening," she replied, at last.

"No doubt," said her father. "What else?"

"I think I asked him whether he was fond of gardening," said Miss Nugent, slowly. "Yes, I'm sure I did."

"You had no business to speak to him at all," said the fuming captain.

"I don't quite see how I could help doing so," said his daughter. "You surely don't expect me to be rude to your visitors? Besides, I feel rather sorry for him."

"Sorry?" repeated the captain, sharply. "What for?"

"Because he hasn't got a nice, kind, soft-spoken father," said Miss Nugent, squeezing his arm affectionately.

The appearance of the other couple at the head of the path saved the captain the necessity of a retort. They stood in a little knot talking, but Miss Nugent, contrary to her usual habit, said but little. She was holding her father's arm and gazing absently at the dim fields stretching away beyond the garden.

At the same time Mr. James Hardy, feeling, despite his bold front, somewhat badly snubbed, was sitting on the beach thinking over the situation. After a quarter of an hour in the company of Kate Nugent all else seemed sordid and prosaic; his own conduct in his attempt to save her brother from the consequences of his folly most sordid of all. He wondered, gloomily, what she would think when she heard of it.

He rose at last and in the pale light of the new moon walked slowly along towards the town. In his present state of mind he wanted to talk about Kate Nugent, and the only person who could be depended upon for doing that was Samson Wilks. It was a never-tiring subject of the steward's, and since his discovery of the state of Hardy's feelings in that quarter the slightest allusion was sufficient to let loose a flood of reminiscences.

It was dark by the time Hardy reached the alley, and in most of the houses the lamps were lit behind drawn blinds. The steward's house, however, was in darkness and there was no response when he tapped. He turned the handle of the door and looked in. A dim figure rose with a start from a chair.

"I hope you were not asleep?" said Hardy.

"No, sir," said the steward, in a relieved voice. "I thought it was somebody else."

He placed a chair for his visitor and, having lit the lamp, slowly lowered the blind and took a seat opposite.

"I've been sitting in the dark to make a certain party think I was out," he said, slowly. "She keeps making a excuse about Teddy to come over and see me. Last night 'e talked about making a 'ole in the water to celebrate 'Melia Kybird's wedding, and she came over and sat in that chair and cried as if 'er 'art would break. After she'd gone Teddy comes over, fierce as a eagle, and wants to know wot I've been saying to 'is mother to make 'er cry. Between the two of 'em I 'ave a nice life of it."

"He is still faithful to Miss Kybird, then?" said Hardy, with a sudden sense of relief.

"Faithful?" said Mr. Wilks. "Faithful ain't no word for it. He's a sticker, that's wot 'e is, and it's my misfortune that 'is mother takes after 'im. I 'ave to go out afore breakfast and stay out till late at night, and even then like as not she catches me on the doorstep."

"Well, perhaps she will make a hole in the water," suggested Hardy.

Mr. Wilks smiled, but almost instantly became grave again. "She's not that sort," he said, bitterly, and went into the kitchen to draw some beer.

He drank his in a manner which betokened that the occupation afforded him no enjoyment, and, full of his own troubles, was in no mood to discuss anything else. He gave a short biography of Mrs. Silk which would have furnished abundant material for half-a-dozen libel actions, and alluding to the demise of the late Mr. Silk, spoke of it as though it were the supreme act of artfulness in a somewhat adventurous career.

Hardy walked home with a mind more at ease than it had been at any time since his overtures to Mr. Swann. The only scruple that had troubled him was now removed, and in place of it he felt that he was acting the part of a guardian angel to Mr. Edward Silk.

CHAPTER XXII

Mr. Nathan Smith, usually one of the most matter-of-fact men in the world, came out of Mr. Swann's house in a semi-dazed condition, and for some time after the front door had closed behind him stood gaping on the narrow pavement.

He looked up and down the quiet little street and shook his head sadly. It was a street of staid and substantial old houses; houses which had mellowed and blackened with age, but whose quaint windows and chance-opened doors afforded glimpses of comfort attesting to the prosperity of those within. In the usual way Mr. Nathan Smith was of too philosophical a temperament to experience the pangs of envy, but to-day these things affected him, and he experienced a strange feeling of discontent with his lot in life.

"Some people 'ave all the luck," he muttered, and walked slowly down the road.

He continued his reflections as he walked through the somewhat squalid streets of his own quarter. The afternoon was wet and the houses looked dingier than usual; dirty, inconvenient little places most of them, with a few cheap gimcracks making a brave show as near the window as possible. Mr. Smith observed them with newly opened eyes, and, for perhaps the first time in his life, thought of the draw-backs and struggles of the poor.

In his own untidy little den at the back of the house he sat for some time deep in thought over the events of the afternoon. He had been permitted a peep at wealth; at wealth, too, which was changing hands, but was not coming his way. He lit his pipe and, producing a bottle of rum from a cupboard, helped himself liberally. The potent fluid softened him somewhat, and a half-formed intention to keep the news from Mr. Kybird melted away beneath its benign influence.

"After all, we've been pals for pretty near thirty years," said Mr. Smith to himself.

He took another draught. "Thirty years is a long time," he mused.

He finished the glass. "And if 'e don't give me something out of it I'll do 'im as much 'arm as I can," he continued; and, buttoning up his coat, he rose and set out in the direction of the High Street.

The rain had ceased and the sun was making faint efforts to break through watery clouds. Things seemed brighter, and Mr. Smith's heart beat in response. He was going to play the part of a benefactor to Mr. Kybird; to offer him access, at any rate, to such wealth as he had never dreamed of. He paused at the shop window, and, observing through a gap in the merchandise that Mr. Kybird was be-hind the counter, walked in and saluted him.

"I've got news for you," he said, slowly; "big news."

"Oh," said Mr. Kybird, with indifference.

"Big news," repeated Mr. Smith, sinking thoughtlessly into the broken cane-chair and slowly extricating himself. "Something that'll make your eyes start out of your 'ed."

The small black eyes in question were turned shrewdly in his direction. "I've 'ad news of you afore, Nat," remarked Mr. Kybird, with simple severity.

The philanthropist was chilled; he fixed his eyes in a stony stare on the opposite wall. Mr. Kybird, who had ever a wholesome dread of falling a victim to his friend's cuteness, regarded him with some uncertainty, and reminded him of one or two pieces of information which had seriously depleted his till.

"Banns up yet for the wedding?" inquired Mr. Smith, still gazing in front of him with fathomless eyes.

"They'll be put up next week," said Mr. Kybird.

"Ah!" said his friend, with great emphasis. "Well, well!"

"Wot d'ye mean by 'well, well'?" demanded the other, with some heat.

"I was on'y thinking," replied Mr. Smith, mildly. "P'r'aps it's all for the best, and I'd better 'old my tongue. True love is better than money. After all it ain't my bisness, and I shouldn't get much out of it."

"Out of wot, Nat?" inquired Mr. Kybird, uneasily.

Mr. Smith, still gazing musingly before him, appeared not to hear the question. "Nice after the rain, ain't it?" he said, slowly.

"It's all right," said the other, shortly.

"Everything smells so fresh and sweet," continued his nature-loving friend; "all the little dickey-birds was a-singing as if their little 'arts would break as I come along."

"I don't wonder at it," said the offended Mr. Kybird.

"And the banns go up next week," murmured the boarding-master to himself. "Well, well."

"'Ave you got anything to say agin it?" demanded Mr. Kybird.

"Cert'nly not," replied the other. "On'y don't blame me when it's too late; that's all."

Mr. Kybird, staring at him wrathfully, turned this dark saying over in his mind. "Too late for wot?" he inquired.

"Ah!" said Nathan Smith, slowly. "Nice and fresh after the rain, ain't it? As I come along all the little dickey-birds—"

"Drat the little dickey-birds," interrupted Mr. Kybird, with sudden violence. "If you've got anything to say, why don't you say it like a man?"

The parlour door opened suddenly before the other could reply, and revealed the face of Mrs. Kybird. "Wot are you two a-quarrelling about?" she demanded. "Why don't you come inside and sit down for a bit?"

Mr. Smith accepted the invitation, and following her into the room found Miss Kybird busy stitching in the midst of a bewildering assortment of brown paper patterns and pieces of cloth. Mrs. Kybird gave him a chair, and, having overheard a portion of his conversation with her husband, made one or two casual inquiries.

"I've been spending a hour or two at Mr. Swann's," said Mr. Smith.

"And 'ow is 'e?" inquired his hostess, with an appearance of amiable interest.

The boarding-master shook his head. "'E's slipping 'is cable," he said, slowly. "'E's been making 'is will, and I was one o' the witnesses."

Something in Mr. Smith's manner as he uttered this simple statement made his listeners anxious to hear more. Mr. Kybird, who had just entered the room and was standing with his back to the door holding the handle, regarded him expectantly.

"It's been worrying 'im some time," pursued Mr. Smith. "'E 'asn't got nobody belonging to 'im, and for a long time 'e couldn't think 'ow to leave it. Wot with 'ouse property and other things it's a matter of over ten thousand pounds."

"Good 'eavens!" said Mr. Kybird, who felt that he was expected to say something.

"Dr. Blaikie was the other witness," continued Mr. Smith, disregarding the interruption; "and Mr. Swann made us both promise to keep it a dead secret till 'e's gone, but out o' friendship to you I thought I'd step round and let you know."

The emphasis on the words was unmistakable; Mrs. Kybird dropped her work and sat staring at him, while her husband wriggled with excitement.

"'E ain't left it to me, I s'pose?" he said, with a feeble attempt at jocularity.

"Not a brass farden," replied his friend, cheerfully. "Not to none of you. Why should 'e?

"He ain't left it to Jack, I s'pose?" said Miss Kybird, who had suspended her work to listen.

"No, my dear," replied the boarding-master. "'E's made 'is will all ship-shape and proper, and 'e's left everything—all that 'ouse property and other things, amounting to over ten thousand pounds—to a young man becos 'e was jilt—crossed in love a few months ago, and becos 'e's been a good and faithful servant to 'im for years."

"Don't tell me," said Mr. Kybird, desperately; "don't tell me that 'e's been and left all that money to young Teddy Silk."

"Well, I won't if you don't want me to," said the accommodating Mr. Smith, "but, mind, it's a dead secret."

Mr. Kybird wiped his brow, and red patches, due to excitement, lent a little variety to an otherwise commonplace face; Mrs. Kybird's dazed inquiry. "Wot are we a-coming to?" fell on deaf ears; while Miss Kybird, leaning forward with lips parted, fixed her eyes intently on Mr. Smith's face.

"It's a pity 'e didn't leave it to young Nugent," said that gentleman, noting with much pleasure the effect of his announcement, "but 'e can't stand 'in: at no price; 'e told me so 'imself. I s'pose young Teddy'll be quite the gentleman now, and 'e'll be able to marry who 'e likes."

Mr. Kybird thrust his handkerchief into his tail-pocket, and all the father awoke within him. "Ho, will 'e?" he said, with fierce sarcasm. "Ho, indeed! And wot about my daughter? I 'ave 'eard of such things as breach o' promise. Before Mr. Teddy gets married 'e's got to 'ave a few words with me."

"'E's behaved very bad," said Mrs. Kybird, nodding.

"'E come 'ere night after night," said Mr. Kybird, working himself up into a fury; "'e walked out with my gal for months and months, and then 'e takes 'imself off as if we wasn't good enough for 'im."

"The suppers 'e's 'ad 'ere you wouldn't believe," said Mrs. Kybird, addressing the visitor.

"Takes 'imself off," repeated her husband; "takes 'imself off as if we was dirt beneath 'is feet, and never been back to give a explanation from that day to this."

"I'm not easy surprised," said Mrs. Kybird, "I never was from a gal, but I must say Teddy's been a surprise to me. If anybody 'ad told me 'e'd ha' behaved like that I wouldn't ha' believed it; I couldn't. I've never said much about it, becos my pride wouldn't let me. We all 'ave our faults, and mine is pride."

"I shall bring a breach o' promise action agin 'im for five thousand pounds," said Mr. Kybird, with decision.

"Talk sense," said Nathan Smith, shortly.

"Sense!" cried Mr. Kybird. "Is my gal to be played fast and loose with like that? Is my gal to be pitched over when 'e likes? Is my gal—"

"Wot's the good o' talking like that to me?" said the indignant Mr. Smith. "The best thing you can do is to get 'er married to Teddy at once, afore 'e knows of 'is luck."

"And when'll that be?" inquired his friend, in a calmer voice.

"Any time," said the boarding-master, shrugging his shoulders. "The old gentleman might go out to-night, or again 'e might live on for a week or more. 'E was so weak 'e couldn't 'ardly sign 'is name."

"I 'ope 'e 'as signed it all right," said Mr. Kybird, starting.

"Safe as 'ouses," said his friend.

"Well, why not wait till Teddy 'as got the money?" suggested Mrs. Kybird, with a knowing shake of her head.

"Becos," said Mr. Smith, in a grating voice, "be-cos for one thing 'e'd be a rich man then and could 'ave 'is pick. Teddy Silk on a pound or thereabouts a week and Teddy Silk with ten thousand pounds 'ud be two different people. Besides that 'e'd think she was marrying 'im for 'is money."

"If 'e thought that," said Mrs. Kybird, firmly, "I'd never forgive 'im."

"My advice to you," said Nathan Smith, shaking his forefinger impressively, "is to get 'em married on the quiet and as soon as possible. Once they're tied up Teddy can't 'elp 'imself."

"Why on the quiet?" demanded Mr. Kybird, sharply.

The boarding-master uttered an impatient exclamation. "Becos if Mr. Swann got to 'ear of it he'd guess I'd been blabbing, for one thing," he said, sharply, "and for another, 'e left it to 'im partly to make up for 'is disappointment—he'd been disappointed 'imself in 'is younger days, so 'e told me."

"Suppose 'e managed to get enough strength to alter 'is will?"

Mr. Kybird shivered. "It takes time to get married, though," he objected.

"Yes," said Mr. Smith, ironically, "it does. Get round young Teddy, and then put the banns up. Take your time about it, and be sure and let Mr. Swann know. D'ye think 'e wouldn't understand wot it meant, and spoil it, to say nothing of Teddy seeing through it?

"Well, wot's to be done, then?" inquired the staring Mr. Kybird.

"Send 'em up to London and 'ave 'em married by special license," said Mr. Smith, speaking rapidly—"to-morrow, if possible; if not, the day after. Go and pitch a tale to Teddy to-night, and make 'im understand it's to be done on the strict q.t."

"Special licenses cost money," said Mr. Kybird. "I 'ave 'eard it's a matter o' thirty pounds or thereabouts."

Mr. Nathan Smith rose, and his eyes were almost expressive. He nodded good-night to the ladies and crossed to the door. Mrs. Kybird suddenly seized him by the coat and held him.

"Don't be in a 'urry, Nat," she pleaded. "We ain't all as clever as you are."

"Talk about looking a gift-'orse in the mouth—" began the indignant Mr. Smith.

"Sit down," urged Mr. Kybird. "You can't expect us to be as quick in seeing things as wot you are."

He pushed his partly mollified friend into his chair again, and taking a seat next him began to view the affair with enthusiasm. "'Melia shall turn young Nugent off to-night," he said, firmly.

"That's right," said the other; "go and do a few more silly things like that and we shall be 'appy. If you'd got a 'ead instead of wot you 'ave got, you wouldn't talk of giving the show away like that. Nobody must know or guess about anything until young Teddy is married to 'Melia and got the money."

"It seems something like deceitfulness," said Miss Kybird, who had been listening to the plans for her future with admirable composure.

"It's for Teddy's own sake," said Nathan Smith. "Everybody knows 'e's half crazy after you."

"I don't know that I don't like 'im best, even without the money," said Miss Kybird, calmly. "Nobody could 'ave been more attentive than 'im. I believe that 'e'd marry me if 'e 'ad a hundred thousand, but it looks better your way."

"Better all round," said Nathan Smith, with at approving nod. "Now, Dan'l, 'op round to Teddy and whistle 'im back, and mind 'e's to keep it a dead secret on account o' trouble with young Nugent. D'ye twig?"

The admiring Mr. Kybird said that he was a wonder, and, in the discussion on ways and means which followed, sat listening with growing respect to the managing abilities both of his friend and his wife. Difficulties were only mentioned for the purpose of being satisfactorily solved, and he noticed with keen appreciation that the prospect of a ten thousand pound son-in-law was already adding to that lady's dignity. She sniffed haughtily as she spoke of "that Nugent lot"; and the manner in which she promised Mr. Smith that he should not lose by his services would have graced a duchess.

"I didn't expect to lose by it," said the boarding-master, pointedly. "Come over and 'ave a glass at the Chequers, Dan, and then you can go along and see Teddy."

CHAPTER XXIII

The summer evening was well advanced when Mr. Kybird and his old friend parted. The former gentleman was in almost a sentimental mood, and the boarding-master, satisfied that his pupil was in a particularly appropriate frame of mind for the object of his visit, renewed his instructions about binding Mr. Silk to secrecy, and departed on business of his own.

Mr. Kybird walked slowly towards Fullalove Alley with his head sunk in meditation. He was anxious to find Mr. Silk alone, as otherwise the difficulty of his errand would be considerably increased, Mrs. Silk's intelligence being by no means obscured by any ungovernable affection for the Kybird family. If she was at home she would have to invent some pretext for luring Teddy into the privacy of the open air.

The lamp was lit in the front room by the time he reached the house, and the shadows of geraniums which had won through several winters formed a straggling pattern on the holland blind. Mr. Kybird, first making an unsuccessful attempt to peep round the edges of this decoration, tapped gently on the door, and in response to a command to "Come in," turned the handle and looked into the room. To his relief, he saw that Mr. Silk was alone.

"Good evening, Teddy," he said, with a genial smile, as he entered slowly and closed the door behind him. "I 'ope I see you well?"

"I'm quite well," returned Mr. Silk, gazing at him with unconcealed surprise.

"I'm glad to 'ear it," said Mr. Kybird, in a somewhat reproachful voice, "for your sake; for every-body's sake, though, p'r'aps, I did expect to find you looking a little bit down. Ah! it's the wimmen that 'ave the 'arts after all."

Mr. Silk coughed. "What d'ye mean?" he inquired, somewhat puzzled.

"I came to see you, Teddy, on a very delikit business," said Mr. Kybird, taking a seat and gazing diffidently at his hat as he swung it between his hands; "though, as man to man, I'm on'y doing of my dooty. But if you don't want to 'ear wot I've got to say, say so, and Dan'l Kybird'll darken your door no more."

"How can I know whether I want to 'ear it or not when I don't know wot it is?" said Mr. Silk, judiciously.

Mr. Kybird sat biting his thumb-nail, then he looked up suddenly. "'Melia," he said, with an outburst of desperate frankness, "'Melia is crying 'er eyes out."

Mr. Silk, with a smothered exclamation, started up from his chair and regarded him eagerly.

"If she knew I'd been 'ere," pursued Mr. Kybird, "she'd I don't know wot she wouldn't do. That's 'er pride; but I've got my pride too; the pride of a father's 'art."

"What—what's she crying about?" inquired Mr. Silk, in an unsteady voice.

"She's been looking poorly for some time," continued the veracious Mr. Kybird, "and crying. When I tell you that part o' the wedding-dress wot she was making 'ad to be taken away from 'er because o' the tears she dropped on it, you may 'ave some idea of wot things are like. She's never forgot you, Teddy, and it was on'y your quick temper that day that made 'er take on with young Nugent. She's got a temper, too, but she give 'er love once, and, being my daughter, she couldn't give it agin."

He stole a glance at his listener. Mr. Silk, very pale and upright, was standing on the hearthrug, shaking all over with nervous excitement. Twice he tried to speak and failed.

"That's 'ow it is, Teddy," sighed Mr. Kybird, rising as though to depart. "I've done my dooty. It was a 'ard thing to do, but I've done it."

"Do you mean," said Mr. Silk, recovering his voice at last, "do you mean that Amelia would marry me after all?"

"Do I mean?" repeated Mr. Kybird, naturally indignant that his very plain speaking should be deemed capable of any misconstruction. "Am I speaking to a stock or a stone, Teddy?"

Mr. Silk took a deep breath, and buttoned up his coat, as though preparing to meet Mr. Nugent there and then in deadly encounter for the person of Miss Kybird. The colour was back in his cheeks by this time, and his eyes were unusually bright. He took a step towards Mr. Kybird and, pressing his hand warmly, pushed him back into his seat again.

"There's 'er pride to consider, Teddy," said the latter gentleman, with the whisper of a conspirator.

"She can't stand being talked about all over the town and pointed at."

"Let me see anybody a-pointing at 'er," said the truculent Mr. Silk; "let me see 'em, that's all."

"That's the way to talk, Teddy," said Mr. Kybird, gazing at him with admiration.

"Talk!" said the heroic Mr. Silk. "I'll do more than talk." He clenched his fists and paced boldly up and down the hearthrug.

"You leave things to me," said Mr. Kybird, with a confidential wink. "I'll see that it's all right. All I ask of you is to keep it a dead secret; even your mother mustn't know."

"I'll be as secret as the grave," said the overjoyed Mr. Silk.

"There's lots o' things to be taken into consideration," said Mr. Kybird, truthfully; "it might be as well for you to be married immediate."

"Immediate?" said the astonished Mr. Silk.

"She 'asn't got the nerve to send young Nugent about 'is business," explained Mr. Kybird; "she feels sorry for 'im, pore fellow; but 'e's got a loving and affectionate 'art, and she can't bear 'im making love to 'er. You can understand what it is, can't you?"

"I can imagine it," said Mr. Silk, gloomily, and he flushed crimson as the possibilities suggested by the remark occurred to him.

"I've been thinking it over for some time," resumed Mr. Kybird; "twisting it and turning it all ways, and the only thing I can see for it is for you to be married on the strict q.t. Of course, if you don't like—"

"Like!" repeated the transported Mr. Silk.

"I'll go and be married now, if you like."

Mr. Kybird shook his head at such haste, and then softening a little observed that it did him credit. He proceeded to improve the occasion by anecdotes of his own courting some thirty years before, and was in the middle of a thrilling account of the manner in which he had bearded the whose of his future wife's family, when a quick step outside, which paused at the door, brought him to a sudden halt.

"Mother," announced Mr. Silk, in a whisper.

Mr. Kybird nodded, and the heroic appearance of visage which had accompanied his tale gave way to an expression of some uneasiness. He coughed behind his hand, and sat gazing before him as Mrs. Silk entered the room and gave vent to an exclamation of astonishment as she saw the visitor. She gazed sharply from him to her son. Mr. Kybird's expression was now normal, but despite his utmost efforts Mr. Silk could not entirely banish the smile which trembled on his lips.

"Me and Teddy," said Mr. Kybird, turning to her with a little bob, which served him for a bow, "'ave just been having a little talk about old times."

"He was just passing," said Mr. Silk.

"Just passing, and thought I'd look in," said Mr. Kybird, with a careless little laugh; "the door was open a bit."

"Wide open," corroborated Mr. Silk.

"So I just came in to say ''Ow d'ye do?'" said Mr. Kybird.

Mrs. Silk's sharp, white face turned from one to the other. "Ave you said it?" she inquired, blandly.

"I 'ave," said Mr. Kybird, restraining Mr. Silk's evident intention of hot speech by a warning glance; "and now I'll just toddle off 'ome."

"I'll go a bit o' the way with you," said Edward Silk. "I feel as if a bit of a walk would do me good."

Left alone, the astonished Mrs. Silk took the visitor's vacated chair and, with wrinkled brow, sat putting two and two together until the sum got beyond her powers of calculation. Mr. Kybird's affability and Teddy's cheerfulness were alike incomprehensible. She mended a hole in her pocket and darned a pair of socks, and at last, anxious for advice, or at least a confidant, resolved to see Mr. Wilks.

She opened the door and looked across the alley, and saw with some satisfaction that his blind was illuminated. She closed the door behind her sharply, and then stood gasping on the doorstep. So simultaneous were the two happenings that it actually appeared as though the closing of the door had blown Mr. Wilks's lamp out. It was a night of surprises, but after a moment's hesitation she stepped over and tried his door. It was fast, and there was no answer to her knuckling. She knocked louder and listened. A door slammed violently at the back of the house, a distant clatter of what sounded like saucepans came from beyond, and above it all a tremulous but harsh voice bellowed industriously through an interminable chant. By the time the third verse was reached Mr. Wilks's neighbours on both sides were beating madly upon their walls and blood-curdling threats strained through the plaster.

She stayed no longer, but regaining her own door sat down again to await the return of her son. Mr. Silk was long in coming, and she tried in vain to occupy herself with various small jobs as she speculated in vain on the meaning of the events of the night. She got up and stood by the open door, and as she waited the clock in the church-tower, which rose over the roofs hard by, slowly boomed out the hour of eleven. As the echoes of the last stroke died away the figure of Mr. Silk turned into the alley.

"You must 'ave 'ad quite a nice walk," said his mother, as she drew back into the room and noted the brightness of his eye.

"Yes," was the reply.

"I s'pose 'e's been and asked you to the wedding?" said the sarcastic Mrs. Silk.

Her son started and, turning his back on her, wound up the clock. "Yes, 'e has," he said, with a, sly grin.

Mrs. Silk's eyes snapped. "Well, of all the impudence," she said, breathlessly.

"Well, 'e has," said her son, hugging himself over the joke. "And, what's more, I'm going."

He composed his face sufficiently to bid her "good-night," and, turning a deaf ear to her remonstrances and inquiries, took up a candle and were off whistling.

CHAPTER XXIV

The idea in the mind of Mr. James Hardy when he concocted his infamous plot was that Jack Nugent would be summarily dismissed on some pretext by Miss Kybird, and that steps would at once be taken by her family to publish her banns together with those of Mr. Silk. In thinking thus he had made no allowance for the workings and fears of such a capable mind as Nathan Smith's, and as days passed and nothing happened he became a prey to despair.

He watched Mr. Silk keenly, but that gentleman went about his work in his usual quiet and gloomy fashion, and, after a day's leave for the purpose of arranging the affairs of a sick aunt in Camberwell, came back only a little less gloomy than before. It was also clear that Mr. Swann's complaisance was nearly at an end, and a letter, couched in vigorous, not to say regrettable, terms for a moribund man, expressed such a desire for fresh air and exercise that Hardy was prepared to see him at any moment.

It was the more unfortunate as he thought that he had of late detected a slight softening in Captain Nugent's manner towards him. On two occasions the captain, who was out when he called, had made no comment to find upon his return that the visitor was being entertained by his daughter, going so far, indeed, as to permit the conversation to gain vastly in interest by that young person remaining in the room. In face of this improvement he thought with dismay of having to confess failure in a scheme which apart from success was inexcusable.

The captain had also unbent in another direction, and Mr. Wilks, to his great satisfaction, was allowed to renew his visits to Equator Lodge and assist his old master in the garden. Here at least the steward was safe from the designs of Mrs. Silk and the innuendoes of Fullalove Alley.

It was at this time, too, that the widow stood in most need of his advice, the behaviour of Edward Silk being of a nature to cause misgivings in any mother's heart. A strange restlessness possessed him, varied with occasional outbursts of hilarity and good nature. Dark hints emanated from him at these times concerning a surprise in store for her at no distant date, hints which were at once explained away in a most unsatisfactory manner when she became too pressing in her inquiries. He haunted the High Street, and when the suspicious Mrs. Silk spoke of Amelia he only laughed and waxed humorous over such unlikely subjects as broken hearts and broken vows.

It was a week after Mr. Kybird's visit to the alley that he went, as usual, for a stroll up and down the High Street. The evening was deepening, and some of the shops had already lit up, as Mr. Silk, with his face against the window-pane, tried in vain to penetrate the obscurity of Mr. Kybird's shop. He could just make out a dim figure behind the counter, which he believed to be Amelia, when a match was struck and a gas jet threw a sudden light in the shop and revealed Mr. Jack Nugent standing behind the counter with his hand on the lady's shoulder.

One glance was sufficient. The next moment there was a sharp cry from Miss Kybird and a bewildered stare from Nugent as something, only comparable to a human cracker, bounced into the shop and commenced to explode before them.

"Take your 'and off," raved Mr. Silk. "Leave 'er alone. 'Ow dare you? D'ye hear me? 'Melia, I won't 'ave it! I won't 'ave it!"

"Don't be silly, Teddy," remonstrated Mr. Nugent, following up Miss Kybird, as she edged away from him.

"Leave 'er alone, d'ye 'ear?" yelled Mr. Silk, thumping the counter with his small fist. "She's my *wife!*"

"Teddy's mad," said Mr. Nugent, calmly, "stark, staring, raving mad. Poor Teddy."

He shook his head sadly, and had just begun to recommend a few remedies when the parlour door opened and the figure of Mr. Kybird, with his wife standing close behind him, appeared in the doorway.

"Who's making all this noise?" demanded the former, looking from one to the other.

"I am," said Mr. Silk, fiercely. "It's no use your winking at me; I'm not going to 'ave any more of this nonsense. 'Melia, you go and get your 'at on and come straight off 'ome with me."

Mr. Kybird gave a warning cough. "Go easy, Teddy," he murmured.

"And don't you cough at me," said the irritated Mr. Silk, "because it won't do no good."

Mr. Kybird subsided. He was not going to quarrel with a son-in-law who might at any moment be worth ten thousand pounds.

"Isn't he mad?" inquired the amazed Mr. Nugent.

"Cert'nly not," replied Mr. Kybird, moving aside to let his daughter pass; "no madder than you are. Wot d'ye mean, mad?"

Mr. Nugent looked round in perplexity. "Do you mean to tell me that Teddy and Amelia are married?" he said, in a voice trembling with eagerness.

"I do," said Mr. Kybird. "It seems they've been fond of one another all along, and they went up all unbeknown last Friday and got a license and got married."

"And if I see you putting your 'and on 'er shoulder ag'in" said Mr. Silk, with alarming vagueness.

"But suppose she asks me to?" said the delighted Mr. Nugent, with much gravity.

"Look 'ere, we don't want none o' your non-sense," broke in the irate Mrs. Kybird, pushing her way past her husband and confronting the speaker.

"I've been deceived," said Mr. Nugent in a thrilling voice; "you've all been deceiving me. Kybird, I blush for you (that will save you a lot of trouble). Teddy, I wouldn't have believed it of you. I can't stay here; my heart is broken."

"Well we don't want you to," retorted the aggressive Mrs. Kybird. "You can take yourself off as soon as ever you like. You can't be too quick to please me."

Mr. Nugent bowed and walked past the counter. "And not even a bit of wedding-cake for me," he said, shaking a reproachful head at the heated Mr. Silk. "Why, I'd put you down first on my list."

He paused at the door, and after a brief intimation that he would send for his effects on the following day, provided that his broken heart had not proved fatal in the meantime, waved his hand to the company and departed. Mr. Kybird followed him to the door as though to see him off the premises, and gazing after the receding figure swelled with indignation as he noticed that he favoured a mode of progression which was something between a walk and a hornpipe.

Mr. Nugent had not been in such spirits since his return to Sunwich, and, hardly able to believe in his good fortune, he walked on in a state of growing excitement until he was clear of the town. Then he stopped to consider his next move, and after a little deliberation resolved to pay a visit to Jem Hardy and acquaint him with the joyful tidings.

That gentleman, however, was out, and Mr. Nugent, somewhat irritated at such thoughtlessness, stood in the road wondering where to go next. It was absolutely impossible for him to sleep that night without telling the good news to somebody, and after some thought he selected Mr. Wilks. It was true that relations had been somewhat strained between them since the latter's attempt at crimping him, but he was never one to bear malice, and to-night he was full of the kindliest thoughts to all mankind.

He burst into Mr. Wilks's front room suddenly and then pulled up short. The steward, with a pitiable look of anxiety on his pallid features, was leaning awkwardly against the mantelpiece, and opposite him Mrs. Silk sat in an easy-chair, dissolved in tears.

"Busy, Sam?" inquired Mr. Nugent, who had heard of the steward's difficulties from Hardy.

"No, sir," said Mr. Wilks, hastily; "sit down, sir."

He pushed forward a chair and, almost pulling his visitor into it, stood over him attentively and took his hat.

"Are you quite sure I'm not interrupting you?" inquired the thoughtful Mr. Nugent.

"Certain sure, sir," said Mr. Wilks, eagerly. "I was just 'aving a bit of a chat with my neighbour, Mrs. Silk, 'ere, that's all."

The lady in question removed her handkerchief from her eyes and gazed at him with reproachful tenderness. Mr. Wilks plunged hastily into conversation.

"She came over 'ere to tell me a bit o' news," he said, eyeing the young man doubtfully. "It seems that Teddy——"

Mr. Nugent fetched a mighty sigh and shook his head; Mrs. Silk gazed at him earnestly.

"Life is full of surprises, sir," she remarked.

"And sadness," added Mr. Nugent. "I hope that they will be happy."

"It struck me all of a 'eap," said Mrs. Silk, rolling her handkerchief into a ball and placing it in her lap. "I was doing a bit of ironing when in walks Teddy with Amelia Kybird, and says they was married last Friday. I was that shaken I didn't know what I did or what I said. Then I came over as soon as I could, because I thought Mr. Wilks ought to know about it."

Mr. Wilks cleared his throat and turned an agonized eye on Mr. Nugent. He would have liked to have asked why Mrs. Silk should think it necessary to inform him, but the fear of precipitating a crisis stayed his tongue.

"What I'm to do, I don't know," continued Mrs. Silk, feebly. You can't 'ave two queens in one 'ouse, so to speak."

"But she was walking out with Teddy long ago," urged Mr. Wilks. "It's no worse now than then."

"But I wouldn't be married by license," said Mrs. Silk, deftly ignoring the remark. "If I can't be asked in church in the proper way I won't be married at all."

"Quite right," said Mr. Nugent; "there's something so sudden about a license," he added, with feeling.

"Me and Mr. Wilks was talking about marriage only the other day," pursued Mrs. Silk, with a bashfulness which set every nerve in the steward's body quivering, "and we both agreed that banns was the proper way.

"You was talking about it," corrected Mr. Wilks, in a hoarse voice. "You brought up the subject and I agreed with you—not that it matters to me 'ow people get married. That's their affair. Banns or license, it's all one to me."

"I won't be married by license," said Mrs. Silk, with sudden petulance; "leastways, I'd rather not be," she added, softening.

Mr. Wilks took his handkerchief from his pocket and blew his nose violently. Mrs. Silk's methods of attack left him little opportunity for the plain speaking which was necessary to dispel illusions. He turned a watery, appealing eye on to Mr. Nugent, and saw to his surprise that that gentleman was winking at him with great significance and persistence. It would have needed a heart of stone to have been unaffected by such misery, and to-night Mr. Nugent, thankful for his own escape, was in a singularly merciful mood.

"All this sounds as though you are going to be married," he said, turning to Mrs. Silk with a polite smile.

The widow simpered and looked down, thereby affording Mr. Nugent an opportunity of another signal to the perturbed steward, who sat with such a look of anxiety on his face lest he should miss his cue that the young man's composure was tried to the utmost.

"It's been a understood thing for a long time," she said, slowly, "but I couldn't leave my son while 'e was single and nobody to look after 'im. A good mother makes a good wife, so they say. A woman can't always 'ave 'er own way in everything, and if it's not to be by banns, then by license it must be, I suppose."

"Well, he'll be a fortunate man, whoever he is," said Mr. Nugent, with another warning glance at Mr. Wilks; "and I only hope that he'll make a better husband than you do, Sam," he added, in a low but severe voice.

Mrs. Silk gave a violent start. "Better husband than 'e does?" she cried, sharply. "Mr. Wilks ain't married."

Mr. Nugent's baseless charge took the steward all aback. He stiffened in his chair, a picture of consternation, and guilt appeared stamped on every feature; but he had the presence of mind to look to Mr. Nugent's eye for guidance and sufficient strength of character to accept this last bid for liberty.

"That's my business, sir," he quavered, in offended tones.

"But you ain't *married?*" screamed Mrs. Silk.

"Never mind," said Nugent, pacifically. "Perhaps I ought not to have mentioned it; it's a sore subject with Sam. And I daresay there were faults on both sides. Weren't there, Sam?"

"Yes, sir," said Mr. Wilks, in a voice which he strove hard to make distinct; "especially 'ers."

"You—you never told me you were married," said Mrs. Silk, breathlessly.

"I never said I wasn't," retorted the culprit, defiantly. "If people liked to think I was a single man, I don't care; it's got nothing to do with them. Besides, she lives at Stepney, and I don't 'ear from 'er once in six months; she don't interfere with me and I don't interfere with her."

Mrs. Silk got up from her chair and stood confronting him with her hand grasping the back of it. Her cold eyes gleamed and her face worked with spite as she tried in vain to catch his eye. Of Mr. Nugent and his ingenuous surprise at her behaviour she took no notice at all.

"You're a deceiver," she gasped; "you've been behaving like a single man and everybody thought you was a single man."

"I hope you haven't been paying attentions to anybody, Sam," said Mr. Nugent in a shocked voice.

"A-ah," said Mrs. Silk, shivering with anger. "Ask 'im; the deceiving villain. Ask anybody, and see what they'll tell you. Oh, you wicked man, I wonder you can look me in the face!"

Truth to tell, Mr. Wilks was looking in any direction but hers. His eyes met Nugent's, but there was a look of such stern disdain on that gentleman's face that he was fain to look away again.

"Was it a friend of yours?" inquired the artless Mr. Nugent.

"Never mind," said Mrs. Silk, recovering herself. "Never mind who it was. You wait till I go and tell Teddy," she continued, turning to the trembling Mr. Wilks. "If 'e's got the 'art of a man in 'im you'll see."

With this dire threat, and turning occasionally to bestow another fierce glance upon the steward, she walked to the door and, opening it to its full extent, closed it behind her with a crash and darted across the alley to her own house. The two men gazed at each other without speaking, and then Mr. Wilks, stepping over to the door, turned the key in the lock.

"You're not afraid of Teddy?" said the staring Nugent.

"Teddy!" said Mr. Wilks, snapping his huge fingers. "I'm not afraid o' fifty Teddies; but she might come back with 'im. If it 'adn't ha' been for you, sir, I don't know wot wouldn't 'ave happened."

"Go and draw some beer and get me a clean pipe," said Nugent, dropping into a chair. "We've both been mercifully preserved, Sam, and the best thing we can do is to drink to our noble selves and be more careful for the future."

Mr. Wilks obeyed, and again thanking him warmly for his invaluable services sat down to compile a few facts about his newly acquired wife, warranted to stand the severest cross-examination which might be brought to bear upon them, a task interspersed with malicious reminiscences of Mrs. Silk's attacks on his liberty. He also insisted on giving up his bed to Nugent for the night.

"I suppose," he said later on, as Mr. Nugent, after a faint objection or two, took his candle—"I suppose this yarn about my being married will get about?"

"I suppose so," said Nugent, yawning, as he paused with his foot on the stair. "What about it?"

"Nothing," said Mr. Wilks, in a somewhat dissatisfied voice. "Nothing."

"What about it?" repeated Mr. Nugent, sternly.

"Nothing, sir," said Mr. Wilks, with an insufferable simper. "Nothing, only it'll make things a little hit slow for me, that's all."

Mr. Nugent eyed him for a space in speechless amazement, and then, with a few strong remarks on ingratitude and senile vanity, mounted the winding little stairs and went to bed.

CHAPTER XXV

The day after Mr. Silk's sudden and unexpected assertion of his marital rights Mr. Kybird stood in the doorway of his shop, basking in the sun. The High Street was in a state of post-prandial repose, and there was no likelihood of a customer to interfere with his confidential chat with Mr. Nathan Smith, who was listening with an aspect of great severity to his explanations.

"It ought not to 'ave happened," he said, sharply. "It was Teddy done it," said Mr. Kybird, humbly.

Mr. Smith shrugged his shoulders. "It wouldn't 'ave happened if I'd been there," he observed, arrogantly.

"I don't see 'ow" began Mr. Kybird.

"No, o' course you don't," said his friend. "Still, it's no use making a fuss now. The thing is done. One thing is, I don't suppose it'll make any diff—"

"Difference," suggested Mr. Kybird, after waiting for him to finish.

"Difference," said Mr. Smith, with an obvious effort. His face had lost its scornful expression and given way to one almost sheepish in its mildness. Mr. Kybird, staring at him in some surprise, even thought that he detected a faint shade of pink.

"We ain't all as clever as wot you are, Nat," he said, somewhat taken aback at this phenomenon. "It wouldn't do."

Mr. Smith made a strange noise in his throat and turned on him sharply. Mr. Kybird, still staring in surprise at his unwonted behaviour, drew back a little, and then his lips parted and his eyes grew round as he saw the cause of his friend's concern. An elderly gentleman with a neatly trimmed white beard and a yellow rose in his button-hole was just passing on the other side of the road. His tread was elastic, his figure as upright as a boy's, and he swung a light cane in his hand as he walked. As Mr. Kybird gazed he bestowed a brisk nod upon the bewildered Mr. Smith, and crossed the road with the evident intention of speaking to him.

"How do, Smith?" he said, in a kindly voice.

The boarding-master leaned against the shop-window and regarded him dumbly. There was a twinkle in the shipbroker's eyes which irritated him almost beyond endurance, and in the doorway Mr. Kybird—his face mottled with the intensity of his emotions—stood an unwelcome and frantic witness of his shame.

"You're not well, Smith?" said Mr. Swann, shaking his head at him gently. "You look like a man who has been doing too much brain-work lately. You've been getting the better of some-body, I know."

Mr. Smith gasped and, eyeing him wickedly, strove hard to recover his self-possession.

"I'm all right, sir," he said, in a thin voice. "I'm glad to see you're looking a trifle better, sir."

"Oh, I'm quite right, now," said the other, with a genial smile at the fermenting Mr. Kybird. "I'm as well as ever I was. Illness is a serious thing, Smith, but it is not without its little amusements."

Mr. Smith, scratching his smooth-shaven chin and staring blankly in front of him, said that he was glad to hear it.

"I've had a long bout of it," continued the ship-broker, "longer than I intended at first. By the way, Smith, you've never spoken to anybody of that business, of course?"

"Of course not, sir," said the boarding-master, grinding his teeth.

"One has fancies when one is ill," said Mr. Swann, in low tones, as his eye dwelt with pleasure on the strained features of Mr. Kybird. "I burnt the document five minutes after you had gone."

"Did you, reely?" said Mr. Smith, mechanically.

"I'm glad it was only you and the doctor that saw my foolishness," continued the other, still in a low voice. "Other people might have talked, but I knew that you were a reliable man, Smith. And you won't talk about it in the future, I'm quite certain of that. Good afternoon."

Mr. Smith managed to say, "Good afternoon," and stood watching the receding figure as though it belonged to a species hitherto unknown to him. Then he turned, in obedience to a passionate tug at his coat sleeve from Mr. Kybird.

"Wot 'ave you got to say for yourself?" demanded that injured person, in tones of suppressed passion. "Wot do you mean by it? You've made a pretty mess of it with your cleverness."

"Wonderful old gentleman, ain't he?" said the discomfited Mr. Smith. "Fancy 'im getting the better o' me. Fancy me being 'ad. I took it all in as innercent as you please."

"Ah, you're a clever fellow, you are," said Mr. Kybird, bitterly. "'Ere's Amelia lost young Nugent and 'is five 'undred all through you. It's a got-up thing between old Swann and the Nugent lot, that's wot it is."

"Looks like it," admitted Mr. Smith; "but fancy 'is picking me out for 'is games. That's wot gets over me."

"Wot about all that money I paid for the license?" demanded Mr. Kybird, in a threatening manner. "Wot are you going to do about it?"

"You shall 'ave it," said the boarding-master, with sudden blandness, "and 'Melia shall 'ave 'er five 'undred."

"'Ow?" inquired the other, staring.

"It's as easy as easy," said Mr. Smith, who had been greatly galled by his friend's manner. "I'll leave it in my will. That's the cheapest way o' giving money I know of. And while I'm about it I'll leave you a decent pair o' trousers and a shirt with your own name on it."

While an ancient friendship was thus being dissolved, Mr. Adolphus Swann was on the way to his office. He could never remember such a pleasant air from the water and such a vivid enjoyment in the sight of the workaday world. He gazed with delight at the crowd of miscellaneous shipping in the harbour and the bustling figures on the quay, only pausing occasionally to answer anxious inquiries concerning his health from seafaring men in tarry trousers, who had waylaid him with great pains from a distance.

He reached his office at last, and, having acknowledged the respectful greetings of Mr. Silk, passed into the private room, and celebrated his return to work by at once arranging with his partner for a substantial rise in the wages of that useful individual.

"My conscience is troubling me," he declared, as he hung up his hat and gazed round the room with much relish.

"Silk is happy enough," said Hardy. "It is the best thing that could have happened to him."

"I should like to raise everybody's wages," said the benevolent Mr. Swann, as he seated himself at his desk. "Everything is like a holiday to me after being cooped up in that bedroom; but the rest has done me a lot of good, so Blaikie says. And now what is going to happen to you?"

Hardy shook his head.

"Strike while the iron is hot," said the ship-broker. "Go and see Captain Nugent before he has got used to the situation. And you can give him to understand, if you like (only be careful how you do it), that I have got something in view which may suit his son. If you fail in this affair after all I've done for you, I'll enter the lists myself."

The advice was good, but unnecessary, Mr. Hardy having already fixed on that evening as a suitable opportunity to disclose to the captain the nature of the efforts he had been making on his behalf. The success which had attended them had put him into a highly optimistic mood, and he set off for Equator Lodge with the confident feeling that he had, to say the least of it, improved his footing there.

Captain Nugent, called away from his labours in the garden, greeted his visitor in his customary short manner as he entered the room. "If you've come to tell me about this marriage, I've heard of it," he said, bluntly. "Murchison told me this afternoon."

"He didn't tell you how it was brought about, I suppose?" said Hardy.

The captain shook his head. "I didn't ask him," he said, with affected indifference, and sat gazing out at the window as Hardy began his narration. Two or three times he thought he saw signs of appreciation in his listener's face, but the mouth under the heavy moustache was firm and the eyes steady. Only when he related Swann's interview with Nathan Smith and Kybird did the captain's features relax. He gave a chuckling cough and, feeling for his handkerchief, blew his nose violently. Then, with a strange gleam in his eye, he turned to the young man opposite.

"Very smart," he said, shortly.

"It was successful," said the other, modestly.

"Very," said the captain, as he rose and confronted him. "I am much obliged, of course, for the trouble you have taken in the affairs of my family. And now I will remind you of our agreement."

"Agreement?" repeated the other.

The captain nodded. "Your visits to me were to cease when this marriage happened, if I wished it," he said, slowly.

"That was the arrangement," said the dumb-founded Hardy, "but I had hoped——. Besides, it has all taken place much sooner than I had anticipated."

"That was the bargain," said the captain, stiffly. "And now I'll bid you good-day."

"I am sorry that my presence should be so distasteful to you," said the mortified Hardy.

"Distasteful, sir?" said the captain, sternly. "You have forced yourself on me for twice a week for some time past. You have insisted upon talking on every subject under the sun, whether I liked it or not. You have taken every opportunity of evading my wishes that you should not see my daughter, and you wonder that I object to you. For absolute brazenness you beat anything I have ever encountered."

"I am sorry," said Hardy, again.

"Good evening," said the captain

"Good evening."

Crestfallen and angry Hardy moved to the door, pausing with his hand on it as the captain spoke again.

"One word more," said the older man, gazing at him oddly as he stroked his grey beard; "if ever you try to come bothering me with your talk again I'll forbid you the house."

"Forbid me the house?" repeated the astonished Hardy.

"That's what I said," replied the other; "that's plain English, isn't it?"

Hardy looked at him in bewilderment; then, as the captain's meaning dawned upon him, he stepped forward impulsively and, seizing his hand, began to stammer out incoherent thanks.

"You'd better clear before I alter my mind," said Captain Nugent, roughly. "I've had more than enough of you. Try the garden, if you like."

He took up a paper from the table and resumed his seat, not without a grim smile at the promptitude with which the other obeyed his instructions.

Miss Nugent, reclining in a deck-chair at the bottom of the garden, looked up as she heard Hardy's footstep on the gravel. It was a surprising thing to see him walking down the garden; it was still more surprising to observe the brightness of his eye and the easy confidence of his bearing. It was evident that he was highly pleased with himself, and she was not satisfied until she had ascertained the reason. Then she sat silent, reflecting bitterly on the clumsy frankness of the male sex in general and fathers in particular. A recent conversation with the captain, in which she had put in a casual word or two in Hardy's favour, was suddenly invested with a new significance.

"I shall never be able to repay your father for his kindness," said Hardy, meaningly, as he took a chair near her.

"I expect he was pleased at this marriage," said Miss Nugent, coldly. "How did it happen?"

Mr. Hardy shifted uneasily in his chair. "There isn't much to tell," he said, reluctantly; "and you—you might not approve of the means by which the end was gained."

"Still, I want to hear about it," said Miss Nugent.

For the second time that evening Hardy told his story. It seemed more discreditable each time he told it, and he scanned the girl's face anxiously as he proceeded, but, like her father, she sat still and made no comment until he had finished. Then she expressed a strong feeling of gratitude that the Nugent family had not been mixed up in it.

"Why?" inquired Hardy, bluntly.

"I don't think it was a very nice thing to do," said Miss Nugent, with a superior air.

"It wouldn't have been a very nice thing for you if your brother had married Miss Kybird," said the indignant Jem. "And you said, if you remember, that you didn't mind what I did."

"I don't," said Miss Nugent, noticing with pleasure that the confident air of a few minutes ago had quite disappeared.

"You think I have been behaving badly?" pursued Hardy.

"I would rather not say what I think," replied Miss Nugent, loftily. "I have no doubt you meant well, and I should be sorry to hurt your feelings."

"Thank you," said Hardy, and sat gloomily gazing about him. For some time neither of them spoke.

"Where is Jack now?" inquired the girl, at last. "He is staying with me for a few days," said Hardy. "I sincerely hope that the association will not be injurious to him."

"Are you trying to be rude to me?" inquired Miss Nugent, raising her clear eyes to his.

"I am sorry," said Hardy, hastily. "You are quite right, of course. It was not a nice thing to do, but I would do a thousand times worse to please you."

Miss Nugent thanked him warmly; he seemed to understand her so well, she said.

"I mean," said Hardy, leaning forward and speaking with a vehemence which made the girl instinctively avert her head—"I mean that to please you would be the greatest happiness I could know. I love you."

Miss Nugent sat silent, and a strong sense of the monstrous unfairness of such a sudden attack possessed her. Such a declaration she felt ought to have been led up to by numerous delicate gradations of speech, each a little more daring than the last, but none so daring that they could not have been checked at any time by the exercise of a little firmness.

"If you would do anything to please me," she said at length in a low voice, and without turning her head, "would you promise never to try and see me or speak to me again if I asked you?"

"No," said Hardy, promptly.

Miss Nugent sat silent again. She knew that a good woman should be sorry for a man in such extremity, and should endeavour to spare his feelings by softening her refusal as much as possible, little as he might deserve such consideration. But man is impatient and jumps at conclusions. Before she was half-way through the first sentence he leaned forward and took her hand.

"Oh, good-bye," she said, turning to him, with a pleasant smile.

"I am not going," said Hardy, quietly; "I am never going," he added, as he took her other hand.

Captain Nugent, anxious for his supper, found them there still debating the point some two hours later. Kate Nugent, relieved at the appearance of her natural protector, clung to him with unusual warmth. Then, in a kindly, hospitable fashion, she placed her other arm in that of Hardy, and they walked in grave silence to the house.

W.W. Jacobs – A Short Biography

William Wymark Jacobs was born on September 8, 1863 in the Wapping district of London, England. An author, humorist and dramatist, Jacobs is best remembered for the enduring classic tale of horror - "The Monkey's Paw".

As a youth, Jacobs grew up near the Wapping docks in London, where his father was a wharf manager. The family's first home was home was a house on a River Thames wharf.

The docklands setting would show up frequently in his later literary output. Jacobs, the wharf rat, and his three siblings lost their mother when they were all still young children. Their father, William Gage Jacobs, remarried and fathered a further seven children with his erstwhile housekeeper Ellen Florey. Although he grew up surrounded by poverty, Jacobs himself received a formal education in London, first at a private prep school and later at the Birkbeck Literary and Scientific Institute (now part of the University of London and known as Birkbeck College).

Jacobs' adult working life began with a clerical position at the Post Office Savings Bank. The job was not a stimulating one but Jacobs put his imagination to good use and started to write short stories, sketches and articles, many of which appeared in the Post Office house publication "Blackfriars Magazine."

Although Jacobs did receive his fair share of rejection slips at the beginning of his career, many works written during this period of clerical employment appeared in the "Idler" and "Today" magazines, both of which were edited by noted humorist Jerome K. Jerome, who had taken a liking to Jacobs' stories.

From 1898, Jacobs also published stories in "The Strand", a popular, monthly fiction and general interest magazine. The arrangement stayed in place for most of his life and many of the works in Jacobs' subsequent collections – including the nautical serialization A Master of Craft (1899-1900) - appeared there first.

Jacobs' first volume of collected works was published in 1896. *Many Cargoes*, a selection of sea-faring yarns, established Jacobs as a popular writer and humorist with a penchant for authentic dialogue and trick endings (critics of the day referred to him as the "O. Henry of the Waterfront").

A year later he published a novelette, *The Skipper's Wooing*, and in 1898 and another collection of short stories titled **Sea Urchins**. These works painted vivid, if imaginatively stretched, pictures of dockland and seafaring London with colourful characters (such as "The Night Watchman", Ginger Dick) that now seem archetypal.

Many of Jacobs' periodical publications and first editions were illustrated with woodcuts and ink drawings, as was still the custom at the turn of the 20th century. The author worked regularly with artists such as E.W. Kemble, who had illustrated Mark Twain's Adventures of Huckleberry Finn and Harriet Beecher Stowe's Uncle Tom's Cabin, and his good friend Will Owen, who eventually became a household name on the strength of his iconic Bisto Kids, Bovril and Lux Soap advertising posters.

By 1899, Jacobs was able to quit the post office and finally begin a career making a living as a full-time writer.

He married the noted suffragist Agnes Eleanor Williams (who had been jailed for her protest activities) in 1900. They set up a household in Loughton, Essex as well as living part of the year in central London. The couple went on to have five children together though their marriage was considered an unhappy one.

The publication of two short novels: **At Sunwich Port** (a romantic tale of rival sea captains in the fictional seaside community of Sunwich standing in for the actual East England community of Sandwich, Kent) and **Dialstone Lane** (another small town romance involving intrigue and buried treasure), in 1902 and 1904 respectively, cemented Jacobs' reputation as one of the leading British authors of the new century.

On the foundations of a continuing ability to write for his audience he was readily published though he never strayed too far from what was becoming his familiar, dependable style. There followed a string of further successful publications, including **Captain's All** (1905), **Night Watches** (1914), **The Castaways** (1916), and **Sea Whispers** (1926). Jacobs published eighteen books in all during his lifetime; thirteen collections and five novels.

As a storyteller, Jacobs is perhaps better remembered for a handful of brief tales of the supernatural than for his popular nautical-themed works. The most famous of these, The Monkey's Paw, originally appeared as part of the 1902 short story collection **The Lady of the Barge**. It is an economically written story about a shriveled talisman, a monkey's paw that brings grief and horror in the wake of all too literal wish granting. The story has been adapted for other media repeatedly, starting with a one-act play performed at London's Haymarket Theatre in 1903. There have been multiple film adaptations of the story in the modern era; some of us are familiar with its appearance in an episode of the popular animated series, The Simpsons.

Another macabre gem, The Toll-House, was published as part of the collection Sailor's Knots in 1909. Jacob's once again employs a sparse style to tell the story of a group of men who spend the night in a famously haunted house on a dare (a noticeably similar narrative concept was put to use in the much earlier play **The Ghost of Jerry Bundler**, which had launched Jacobs' parallel career as a dramatist back in 1899 when it was produced at the St. James Theatre in London). Innovative at the time of writing, these sparingly written, atmospheric ghost stories are now familiar classics of the supernatural genre.

Though prolific in his younger years, Jacobs' productivity dropped dramatically after the start of World War I. Yet even in self-imposed semi-retirement Jacobs was still recognized as a leading humorist, ranked alongside such writers as P. G. Wodehouse and George Birmingham. He enjoyed continuing influence and elevated status among his fellow writers as evidenced by these comments attributed to his colleague Henry James:

"Mr. Jacobs, I envy you. You are popular! Your admirable work is appreciated by a wide circle of readers; it has achieved popularity. Mine never goes into a second edition."

James' literary fortunes would, of course, change, but his back-handedly complimentary admiration is compelling evidence of Jacobs' reputation as a writer and humourist both for his audience and his perhaps more admired literary colleagues.

Though Jacobs would create little in the way of new work after 1911, he was still writing. In these later years, seemingly burnt out creatively, Jacobs concentrated more on writing dramatizations and adaptations of his existing stories, including Beauty and the Barge (a film version starring Margaret Rutherford was also released in 1937) and In the Dark (a one act play that is often performed pr published with The Monkey's Paw adaptation).

Though admired by loyal readers throughout his lifetime, Jacobs has been almost completely forgotten since. Critics are at a loss to name a single reason why - Jacobs is universally considered to be a fine and imaginative literary craftsman. But, as critic John Wain suggested in a 1960 essay, perhaps Jacobs' humour may have been too gentle to persist into the cruel and sarcastic modern era, his dry pokes at proletariat hardship no longer suiting the times.

Nonetheless, Jacobs' legacy remains solid: he continued Dickens' (a writer with whom he is also often compared) tradition for sharing working class stories in authentic vernacular. And polished narratives such as The Monkey's Paw set a standard for the clever use of horror in fiction and popular culture that endures to this day. Indeed recently his works have begun to show an increased demand and appreciation in a world that is constantly looking over its shoulder.

William Wymark Jacobs died in a North London nursing home in Hornsey Lane, Islington on September 1st, 1943, just a week before his 80th birthday.

W.W. Jacobs – A Concise Bibliography

NOVELS AND SHORT STORY COLLECTIONS
MANY CARGOES (SHORT STORIES) (1896)
THE SKIPPER'S WOOING (1897)
SEA URCHINS (SHORT STORIES) (1898) aka MORE CARGOES
A MASTER OF CRAFT (1900)
LIGHT FREIGHTS (SHORT STORIES) (1901)
THE LADY OF THE BARGE (SHORT STORIES) (1902)
AT SUNWICH PORT (1902)
DIALSTONE LANE (1902)
SALTHAVEN (1908)
CAPTAINS ALL (SHORT STORIES) (1911)
NIGHT WATCHERS (SHORT STORIES) (1914)
DEEP WATERS (SHORT STORIES) (1919)

SHORT STORIES (INCLUDING THOSE USED IN THE COLLECTIONS ABOVE)
A BENEFIT PERFORMANCE
A BLACK AFFAIR
A CASE OF DESERTION
A CHANGE OF TREATMENT
A CIRCULAR TOUR
A DISCIPLINARIAN
A DISTANT RELATIVE
A GARDEN PLOT
A GOLDEN VENTURE
A HARBOUR OF REFUGE
A LOVE KNOT
A LOVE PASSAGE
A MARKED MAN
A MIXED PROPOSAL
A RASH EXPERIMENT
A SAFETY MATCH
A SPIRIT OF AVARICE
A TIGER'S SKIN
ADMIRAL PETERS
AFTER THE INQUEST
ALF'S DREAM
AN ADULTERATION ACT
AN ELABORATE ELOPEMENT
AN INTERVENTION
AN ODD FREAK
ANGELS' VISITS
BACK TO BACK
BEDRIDDEN
THE WINTER OFFENSIVE
THE BEQUEST
BILL'S LAPSE
BILL'S PAPER CHASE
BLUNDELL'S IMPROVEMENT
THE BOATSWAIN'S WATCH
THE BOATSWAIN'S MATE
BOB'S REDEMPTION
BREAKING A SPELL
BREVET RANK
BROTHER HUTCHINS
THE BULLY OF THE "CAVENDISH"
THE CABIN PASSENGER
CAPTAIN ROGERS
THE CAPTAIN'S EXPLOIT
CAPTAINS ALL
THE CASTAWAY

"MATRIMONIAL OPENINGS"
MIXED RELATIONS
MONEY CHANGERS
THE MONEY-BOX
THE MONKEY'S PAW
MRS. BUNKER'S CHAPERON
THE NEST EGG
ODD MAN OUT
THE OLD MAN OF THE SEA
OUTSAILED
OVER THE SIDE
PAYING OFF
THE PERSECUTION OF BOB PRETTY
PETER'S PENCE
PICKLED HERRING
PRIVATE CLOTHES
PRIZE MONEY
THE RESURRECTION OF MR. WIGGETT
THE RIVAL BEAUTIES
RULE OF THREE
SAM'S BOY
SAM'S GHOST
SELF-HELP
SENTENCE DEFERRED
SHAREHOLDERS
SKILLED ASSISTANCE
THE SKIPPER OF THE "OSPREY"
SMOKED SKIPPER
STEPPING BACKWARDS
STRIKING HARD
THE SUBSTITUTE
THE TEMPTATION OF SAMUEL BURGE
THE TEST
THE THREE SISTERS
TO HAVE AND TO HOLD
"THE TOLL-HOUSE"
TWIN SPIRITS
TWO OF A TRADE
THE UNDERSTUDY
THE UNKNOWN
THE VIGIL
WATCH-DOGS
THE WEAKER VESSEL
THE WELL
THE WHITE CAT

STAGE

THE GHOST OF JERRY BUNDLER (1899) (In London)